18TH
ABDUCTION

Meet The Women's Murder Club

EXCLUSIVE PROFILES by Our Crime Desk

LINDSAY BOXER

A homicide detective in the San Francisco Police Department, juggling the worst murder cases with the challenges of being a first-time mother. Her loving husband Joe, daughter Julie and loyal border-collie Martha give her a reason to protect the city. She didn't have the easiest start to life, with an absent father and an ill mother, but she didn't shy away from a difficult and demanding career. With the help of her friends, Lindsay makes it her mission to solve the toughest cases.

CLAIRE WASHBURN

Chief Medical Examiner for San Francisco and one of Lindsay's oldest friends. Wise, confident and viciously funny, she can be relied on to help whatever the problem. She virtually runs the Office of the Coroner for her overbearing, credit-stealing boss, but rarely complains. Happily married with children, her personal life is relatively calm in comparison to her professional life.

CINDY THOMAS

An up-and-coming journalist who's always looking for the next big story. She'll go the extra mile, risking life and limb to get her scoop. Sometimes she prefers to grill her friends over cocktails for a juicy secret, but, luckily for them, she's totally trustworthy (most of the time...). She somehow found the time to publish a book between solving cases, writing articles for the *San Francisco Chronicle* and keeping together her relationship with Lindsay's partner, Rich Conklin.

"When your job is murder, you need **friends you can count on** "

YUKI CASTELLANO

One of the best lawyers in the city, she's desperate to make her mark. Ambitious, intelligent and passionate, she'll fight for what's right, always defending the underdog even if it means standing in the way of those she loves. Often this includes her husband – who is also Lindsay's boss – Lt. Jackson Brady.

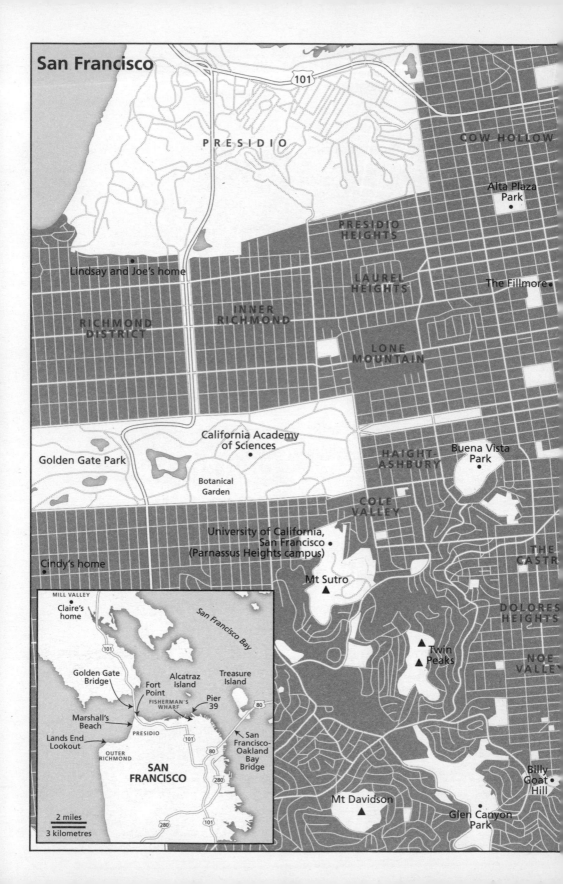

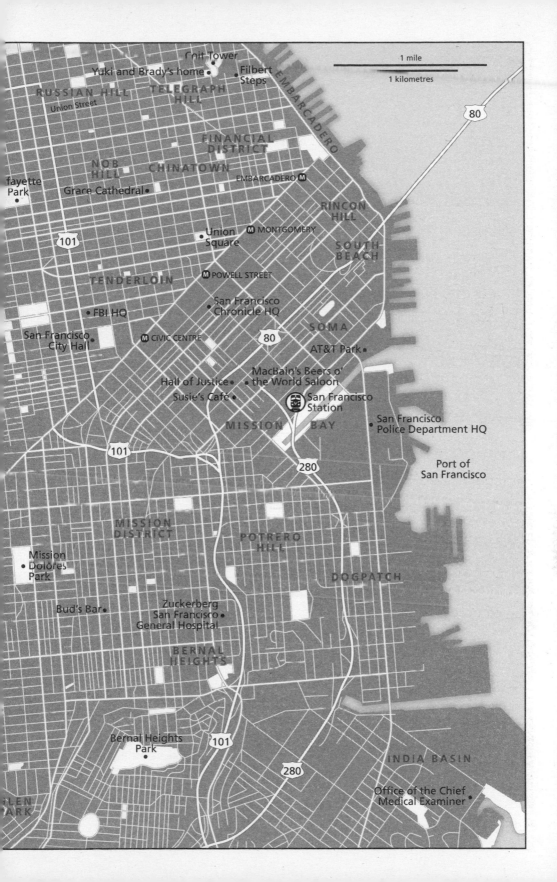

JAMES PATTERSON
& MAXINE PAETRO

18TH
ABDUCTION

CENTURY

1 3 5 7 9 10 8 6 4 2

Century
20 Vauxhall Bridge Road
London SW1V 2SA

Century is part of the Penguin Random House group of companies
whose addresses can be found at global.penguinrandomhouse.com

Penguin
Random House
UK

First published by Century in 2019

www.penguin.co.uk

A CIP catalogue record for this book is available from the British Library.

ISBN 9781780899329
ISBN 9781780899336 (trade paperback edition)

Printed and bound in Great Britain by Clays Ltd, Elcograf S.p.A.

Penguin Random House is committed to a sustainable future
for our business, our readers and our planet. This book is made
from Forest Stewardship Council® paper.

MIX
Paper from
responsible sources
FSC® C018179

In memory of
Alexander Campbell Paetro

PROLOGUE

ONE

JOE AND I were in the back seat of a black sedan, cruising along a motorway from Amsterdam Airport Schiphol to the International Criminal Court in The Hague.

The sky was gray, but shafts of light pierced the clouds, lighting up brilliant swaths of tulips in fields along A44. I had never been to the Netherlands, but I couldn't just open myself up to its charm. We were not on vacation, and this was no holiday.

I'm a homicide cop with the San Francisco PD. I own five pairs of blue trousers, matching blazers, and a rack of oxford cloth button-front shirts. I favor flat-heeled work shoes and customarily pull my blond hair into a ponytail.

Today I was wearing a severe black skirt suit with pearls, heels, and a fresh haircut—the full court press.

My husband, Joe, a former federal law enforcement officer and counterterrorism operative, is now one of the top risk assessment consultants in the field and works from home. In deference to the occasion, he'd swapped out his khakis and pullovers for a formal gray suit with an understated blue striped tie.

Formality was required.

A case had brought us here, and not just any case but one of monumental, even global significance. We both felt deeply invested in the outcome. My emotions veered between anxiety and anticipation, excitement and dread.

In less than an hour we would be seated in the ICC, an intergovernmental organization with the jurisdiction to prosecute individuals for the international offenses of genocide, crimes against humanity, and war crimes.

How would the court rule on Slobodan Petrović?

By the end of the day, we would know.

TWO

AS JOE AND I entered The Hague's International Zone, we saw demonstrators crowding the roadside with signs and banners, chanting. I gathered that they were rallying for human rights and justice for war crimes.

The skies darkened and a fine mist came down, wafting across Oude Waalsdorperweg, the road leading to the International Criminal Court.

Jan, our driver, slowed to avoid pedestrians. The sedan behind us did the same.

Joe was staring out the window, but it seemed to me that he was looking inward, remembering how this had started. He caught my reflection in the glass, turned, and gave me a tight-lipped smile.

"Ready, Lindsay?"

I nodded and squeezed Joe's hand.

"Are you?"

"I've been looking forward to this. Feels like forever."

The car swept up to the curb, beside a plaza with steps

leading to the compound of square glass-and-stone build-ings. Jan got out, unfurled a large umbrella, and opened our door.

The sedan behind us stopped, and the two prominent attorneys from San Francisco got out, put up their umbrellas, and helped Anna Sotovina, a woman of forty-five and our friend, out onto the pavement. The five of us walked quickly up the stairs and across the plaza toward the entrance.

I was surprised to see that a mob of people had gathered beneath an overhang of the main building. They saw us, too, and unfurling their umbrellas, they ran through the rain and swarmed three-deep around us.

I recognized the names of European press outlets on their jackets. Clearly, they recognized us, too, from the media coverage back home, which had been followed closely in Europe.

"Sergeant Boxer, I'm Marie Lavalle with Agence France-Presse," an unsmiling young woman said to me. Water rolled off the brim of her rain hat. "Will you give me a comment, please? What do you expect to happen in the court today?"

I backed away but she persisted. "A few words," she said. "A quote for our readers."

"I'm sorry," I said. "This just isn't a sound-bite kind of thing."

Lavalle was edged aside by a florid man holding a tape recorder.

"Madame, Hans Schultz. *Der Spiegel*. It is said that you are here today for a personal reason. Is that correct?"

Before I could answer, another reporter backed into me and shoved a microphone in front of Joe's face.

"Nigel Warwick, sir. BBC. I've followed your career, Mr. Molinari. FBI, Homeland Security, CIA. Are you representing government interests today?"

Cameramen moved in.

"My wife and I are here as private citizens," Joe snapped, turning his back, putting his arm around me, and sheltering me from the rain.

We pressed on toward the entrance and had almost reached it when I felt a hand on my sleeve. I turned, prepared to shake off a reporter, but it was Anna. Her face was shadowed by the hood of her coat, but I could see that her eyes were swollen from crying.

My eyes watered, too.

I reached out to her, and she hugged me very hard, then hugged Joe.

When they separated, I said, "Trust me. This is the right thing to do."

She said, "I do trust you, Lindsay, and I trust Joe. But I know the system. Even in this courtroom, justice will not be done. This has been my experience. Americans put faith in justice. We do not."

The mob of press, along with dozens of other interested parties, closed in and pushed us forward. Joe gripped my hand.

I said to my husband, "If this goes wrong, it's going to break my heart."

FIVE YEARS EARLIER

CHAPTER 1

ANNA ZIPPED UP a lightweight jacket over her sweater and slacks, wrapped a scarf over her hair, and tied it under her chin to hide the hand-size burn scar on the left side of her face.

She had to shop for dinner before it got dark, and if she went by bike, she could slip through the rush-hour traffic. She slung her backpack across her shoulders, locked the door behind her, then bumped her bike down two flights of stairs from her studio apartment and out the front door into a mild sixty degrees. She carried the bike across the stoop to the street, where she mounted it and pushed off.

As she always did, she took in the beauty of the vast greensward of Alamo Square Park across from her apartment on Fulton Street and felt truly lucky to be alive and here in America.

It never got old.

She passed the lovely old Victorian houses, San Francisco's Painted Ladies, and turned right onto Fell Street, the straightaway that would take her to the grocery store. She rode several blocks before pulling up at an intersection. Waiting for the light to turn green, Anna saw something that she knew just couldn't be.

A large, florid man smoking a cigar was coming down the steps of one of the Victorian homes. The sight of him was like a body blow, as if she'd been struck by a car.

Everything went black. Anna's knees buckled, but even as the blood left her head, she dug deep, gripped the handlebars, and steadied herself.

When she looked again, he was still there, pausing on the steps to relight his cigar, giving her seconds to make sure that she wasn't hallucinating or having a psychotic break with reality. She could be mistaken.

Anna fixed her gaze on the devil puffing on his cigar. His hair was gray now. But his face hadn't changed at all: same full lips, broad unlined brow, thick neck. And she would never forget the shape of his body, the way he walked—stiff and deliberate, like a bear on its hind legs.

It *was* Slobodan Petrović, a man seen in her night terrors and, before that, in real life.

Anna's brain was on fire. Flickering images came into her mind: Petrović standing on the rubble of what had been an apartment house. He bent to hug a little girl, wrapped his arms around her before raising his beaming face to the crowd and the cameras. His voice was enthusiastic and kind.

"If you put down your weapons, we will protect you. I promise this to you."

This speech was accompanied by the ongoing *racketa-rack-rack* sound of gunfire, the screams of babies, the air-shattering explosion of bombs. She remembered another promise Petrović had made: "We will shell you to the edge of madness."

In that, he had kept his word.

Anna locked in on the present; Petrović, walking down steps on Fell Street in his fine American clothing, smoking a cigar, alive and well in San Francisco.

Not seeing her at all.

A horn blew impatiently behind her, breaking her concentration. The light had turned green. Petrović opened the door to his Jaguar and got inside.

He didn't wait for the slow stream of traffic to pass. He wrenched the wheel, gunned the engine, and cut off the car just behind him.

Horns blew furiously, and Anna watched the Jaguar gathering speed. She gripped the handlebars of her bike and shoved off, following Petrović, trying to shut out the overlapping memories of his brutality—but she could not.

Those images still lived inside of her.

Petrović wouldn't get away with what he had done.

Not this time. Not again.

CHAPTER 2

ANNA KNEW CARS.

Her father and brother had been mechanics before the war, and from them she had picked up a lot of knowledge about engines. That Jaguar, she knew, could go from zero to sixty in about six seconds, but not without a clear lane on a straightaway.

Petrović's car was immediately mired in the evening rush hour, traffic moving at a stop-and-go speed averaging about twenty miles per hour.

Advantage Anna.

Petrović wouldn't notice a cyclist two cars back. She would follow him for as long as she could.

Traffic unlocked and Anna slipped behind an SUV on the Jag's tail, where she was hidden from Petrović's rear view. The pedaling was easy on the downhill, but the inevitable incline made it a struggle to keep up.

She put her whole self into the climb, stood up on the pedals, and forced the bike forward.

How long could she keep up? Petrović was driving a well-tuned sports car, while she worked her spent muscles on a twelve-year-old bike. A car honked and then passed her, too close, the compressed air shaking her bike, almost costing Anna her balance.

But she steadied her wheels and pressed on, fixing her gaze on Petrović's car just ahead of her, now coming to an intersection. The light was yellow, but as it turned red, the Jag shot through the cross street and continued on the one-way street leading toward Golden Gate Park.

Anna followed him, ignoring the shouts of pedestrians on the crosswalk, flying through to the other side of the intersection, and pedaling full bore like a madwoman.

She *was* a madwoman.

As drivers leaned on their horns, Anna kept her eyes on the Jaguar, but an ironic thought intruded.

After all these years she could still get killed by Petrović.

Quickly she murdered the thought. If there was any righteousness in the world, she would hunt him and put him down.

Anna was tailing a silver SUV, now four cars behind the Jaguar and losing ground, when the SUV slowed and, without signaling, peeled off onto Cole Street. Up ahead, cars filled in the gap between her and the Jag as Petrović pulled even farther away from her.

Anna had memorized his license plate number, but she no longer remembered it. Her chest hurt. Her legs burned. Tears slipped out of the corners of her eyes and streamed across her cheeks. Sweat rolled down her sides. And the terrible slide show of cruelty and death flashed behind her eyes, keeping time with the *racketa-rack-rack* of artillery.

She refused to quit, pedaling slower but still moving forward, and finally, as the road veered at the end of the Panhandle, leading to JFK Drive, she picked up speed. She could do this. She was winning.

She would find out where Petrović was going and she would make a plan. He wouldn't get away again.

Anna was coasting at a good speed, approaching the inter- section where the traffic from Fell and Oak merged, when a car honked behind her and then zoomed ahead and cut her off. She swiveled the handlebars toward the curb, lost her balance, tipped, and crashed.

Traffic sped on, leaving Anna Sotovina in the gutter.

She screamed at the sky. No one heard her.

CHAPTER 3

ON A CHILLY Wednesday morning my partner, Rich Conklin, parked our squad car on the downhill slope of Jackson Street in the shadow of Pacific View Preparatory School.

PVP was possibly the best high school in California, with a cutting-edge curriculum, five statewide team sports championships last year, a record number of top college acceptances, and a cadre of first-class teachers.

We were both entirely focused on a disturbing case involving the disappearance of three of those teachers. It was day two of our investigation, and it wasn't looking good.

On Monday evening Carly Myers, Adele Saran, and Susan Jones had apparently walked from Pacific View Prep to a local bar called the Bridge, had a good time at dinner, and after leaving the restaurant, vanished without a trace. The teachers were all single women in their late twenties to early thirties. A bartender knew what each of the women had had to drink. Their waitress and a customer had watched the

17

three women leave the Bridge together at around nine that night. Reportedly, all were in good spirits.

When the teachers didn't show up for work the next morning, their cars were discovered in the school's parking lot with the doors locked, their book bags and computer cases in the front passenger seats.

We'd spent yesterday checking out their homes and habits. They hadn't slept in their beds, called anyone to say they'd be out, or used cash machines or their credit cards. It appeared that they had simply vanished.

Director of CSI Charles Clapper had called in his best techs and investigators from all shifts.

They were going at it hard.

There were no surveillance cameras focused on faculty parking, but Forensics was reviewing the video taken inside the Bridge, frame by frame, dusting the women's cars inside and out, and examining everything on their computers.

So far our lab had found nothing suspicious and hadn't turned up a single clue.

Bottom line: thirty-six hours had passed since anyone had seen or heard from them.

By the time we'd finished checking their homes, Lieutenant Warren Jacobi had already contacted the women's parents. Understandably, as good at his job as he was, Jacobi's questions had sent the parents into a panic.

Carly Myers's family lived in town. Conklin and I had visited them last night after Jacobi's call to see if a stone had been left unturned. It had gone about as well as expected. Sheer terror, anger, unanswerable questions, demands for promises that their daughter would be all right.

Their fear and pain and denial had stuck with me and reverberated still.

I slugged down the last of my coffee, crumpled the empty container, and stuffed it into the plastic bag we kept in the car for trash. My partner did the same.

Rich Conklin is a sunny-side-up kind of guy, but you wouldn't have known that today. He sighed long and hard, not just frustrated over this puzzle box full of blank pieces. He was reasonably worried. He had wanted to be in Homicide for years, and now he was living the dark side of the dream. I knew what he was thinking, because I was thinking it, too.

Where were the teachers?

Were they alive?

How much time did they have left?

As I texted Joe, my new husband, my partner sang the refrain of an old Steve Miller song, "Time keeps on slippin', slippin', slippin' into the future."

I checked in with dispatch, then said to my partner, "Okay, Rich. Let's go."

CHAPTER 4

CONKLIN AND I got out of the car and headed up the stone stairway from the street to the school.

At the top of the stairway was a manicured lawn with a high 180-degree view of the ocean that was opaque with a foggy marine layer this morning. Ahead of us stood Pacific View Prep, a compound made up of three five-story buildings at right angles, forming a horseshoe around an open courtyard.

We approached the main entrance dead ahead in the central building and badged the armed security guard, whose name tag read K. STROOP.

I made the introductions.

"Sergeant Boxer," I said. "Homicide. My partner, Inspector Conklin."

"Homicide?" Stroop said. "Hey, *no.* You found their bodies?"

"No, no," Conklin said. "We're treating this missing persons as top priority. All units, all hands are on deck."

Stroop looked relieved. I asked him, "Did you see Myers, Jones, and Saran leave the school Monday night?"

He shook his head. "I go off duty at four."

"But you know them, right?"

"Sure, casually. I see them in the hallways, say, 'Morning,' 'Have a great weekend.' Like that."

I asked, "Would you know if any of them have enemies? Maybe a jealous boyfriend? Or a disgruntled student who didn't get the grade he or she wanted? Anyone showing inappropriate interest in any of them?"

He shook his head no again.

"They're all nice ladies. Our students are good kids."

I nodded. "I do have some routine questions for you."

He said, "Go ahead."

I asked where he had been the last couple of nights. He'd spent Monday home all night with the wife and son; last night he and his wife had gone to a birthday dinner at a restaurant with friends.

He pulled out his phone and produced time-stamped selfies at the dinner table, which he forwarded to me with his phone number and that of the birthday boy.

He said, "I wish I knew something. I want to help. I can't stop thinking about them."

Conklin handed his card to Stroop. "Call anytime if a thought strikes." Then we entered the main building and started down the wide hallway.

Two days ago Carly Myers, Adele Saran, and Susan Jones had walked this same hallway on their way to and from class. As Stroop had confirmed, Monday had been an ordinary workday. He hadn't seen any red flags that had caused alarm.

So what had happened to the three schoolteachers?

My sense was that they'd had no clue their lives were about to veer off from ordinary workday to an extraordinarily bad place. That they'd be abducted on Monday night within minutes of leaving the Bridge.

Every passing hour made it more likely that they were dead.

CHAPTER 5

CONKLIN AND I checked the names on the doors as we made our way down the broad, locker-lined hallway to the office of assistant dean Karin Slaughter.

In a conversation with the dean, we'd learned that Slaughter was thirty-two, had a master's degree in education, had been with Pacific View Prep for five years, and, importantly, was friends with the three missing women.

Even if she didn't know it yet, she might have a clue to their disappearance.

We found Slaughter's office, and Conklin knocked on her open door. Slaughter stood up from her desk and stepped forward to shake our hands. She was a conservative dresser, wearing a midcalf-length black jersey dress, low-heeled shoes, and a look of genuine concern.

I heard myself say, "You have the same name as one of my favorite writers."

"I hear that a lot," she said with a smile. "We're Google-gangers," she said.

"Googlegangers? Let me guess; people with the same name?"

"That's it. Google *Karin Slaughter* and we both come up. I'm a big fan of hers, too."

I liked her immediately. She indicated a row of Slaughter's bestsellers on her bookshelf, but as she returned to her desk, her welcoming expression drooped with worry.

My partner and I took the two chairs across from Slaughter's desk, and she blurted out, "I'm so frightened. I cannot sleep or think about anything but them. Did you know that I was supposed to go out with them Monday night? I couldn't go. I had too much work. I had to beg off."

Conklin and I had the missing women's photos, home addresses, and work schedules but knew little about their personalities, habits, and relationships. Karin Slaughter was eager to fill us in.

"Carly Myers is a born leader," she said. "She's the one to organize a party or a field trip. She teaches history and loves sports. Baseball, football, whatever. I'd say she's outgoing and adventuresome. In a good way."

Then Slaughter described Jones, who taught music, was divorced, watched late-night TV every night, and had lost thirty-five pounds in the last year. "She's fun and a gifted pianist, and she's looking for love," Slaughter said. She'd bought skinny jeans and become a blonde.

We asked about Saran next, and Slaughter told us that she was new to the school. "She came here about a year ago from a public school in Monterey. Teaches English lit, reads a lot, and works out at our gym every day at lunch. She's thoughtful. Serious. She'd been coming out of her shell lately. We're good for her, I'd say. Although now…"

Conklin and I had questions: Had any of the women had any recent problems at the school with students or faculty? Had any of them received threats? Did they have addictions, any trouble with relatives or suitors? Any sign of depression?

No, no, no, no.

According to Slaughter, the three young women had perfect attendance records, were well liked, and, except for Adele, were dating a bit.

"This is hell," she told us. "I feel very bad to say this, but really, I could be missing right now. You could be looking for me. Please tell me that they could still be…safe."

I couldn't tell her what she wanted to know, so I deflected.

"Every cop in the city is looking for them. Our forensics lab is going over their cars and apartments and electronics. We're in contact with their parents. We *will* find your friends."

I was reassuring Slaughter and convincing myself that we'd have a solid lead on this crime by day's end. There had to be a video, a witness, a tip, that would lead to the missing schoolteachers. Right? Even a ransom call would be welcome.

We thanked Karin Slaughter for her help, urged her to call if something useful occurred to her, and headed to our next appointment.

By the end of the school day, my partner and I had spoken to two dozen people at the school and had gotten a few thin, go-nowhere leads. We stopped off at the forensics lab around five that evening.

Clapper was putting on his jacket when we walked in.

"Their cars are dirty," he told us. "Like regular dirty. A lot of fingerprints, dirt on the floor mats, water bottles. We're running the prints off all of that. Nothing jumps out from their personal or office computers, but we're still working on those and their cell phone histories."

"So…nothing to tell us, right?"

"Boxer, we're dancing as fast as we can," said Clapper.

The three of us walked out to the parking lot together.

Even small talk eluded us.

Where were those women? With who? What had happened to them?

CHAPTER 6

JOE MOLINARI LEFT his office at the San Francisco branch of the FBI at around seven and walked to where he'd parked his car, on Golden Gate Avenue near Larkin.

This district, between Civic Center and the Tenderloin, was a maze of dark streets populated by rent-by-the-hour hotels and was the go-to neighborhood for drug pushers and their clientele, criminals (some of them violent), and the terminally out of luck.

Joe's keys were in hand and his car was under a streetlight, apparently untouched. He was thinking about home and dinner when he saw a woman sitting on the curb near his car with her head in her hands. She was sobbing.

As he came closer, Joe saw that she was wearing only one shoe and that her jacket sleeve was ripped at the shoulder. But otherwise, the quality of her clothing was good. Joe didn't think she was homeless.

Maybe she'd been mugged.

"Hey there," he said.

The woman looked up. The streetlight revealed a disfiguring burn scar on the left side of her face from the outer corner of her eye to her upper lip. She pulled at her scarf to cover it.

"Are you okay?" Joe asked.

"Fantastic," she said.

Then her expression crumpled and she lowered her head into her hands again.

Joe sat down on the curb next to her.

"What's your name?"

She dried her face with her sleeve and eventually said, "Anna."

"I'm Joe. Are you hurt, Anna?"

"Big picture or little picture?" she said.

He smiled at her. He gauged her age as late thirties. She had an accent. Eastern European.

"Immediate picture first. Are you injured?"

She shrugged. "I don't think so. I fell off my bike."

She pointed to the bike leaning against a building a little way down the block. The frame was bent and the chain was broken. It looked like it had some mileage on it before the accident.

"Do you need a lift?"

She looked very unsure. Vulnerable. He really didn't feel right leaving her in this neighborhood sitting on the sidewalk with her backpack.

"It's okay," he said. He opened the flap of his jacket and showed her his badge.

"Can I see that badge again?"

He showed it to her again, and she leaned in so she could

read the inscription around the crest: *Federal Bureau of Investigation*. She pulled back and said, "A lift would be great."

Joe asked Anna where she lived and helped her into his car. He got the bike, folded it into the trunk, and called Lindsay from the street.

"Blondie, I'm going to be a little late. A half hour, tops."

After they hung up, he got behind the wheel of his Benz. Anna was hugging the passenger-side door. She said, "Thank you."

"Happy to help out."

He started the car and headed east on Golden Gate, making a number of turns until they'd cleared the Tenderloin. He said, "Anna, tell me if you can. Why were you sitting by yourself on a corner in the worst neighborhood in the city?"

"I went to the FBI to tell them. I guess I look disreputable, because no one would listen to me. You won't believe me, either."

"I'm a good listener," he said. "Give me a try."

CHAPTER 7

JOE STRAINED TO hear Anna over the street sounds on McAllister.

Her voice cracked and then splintered as she worked to tell him what had brought her to the FBI. In the few words he clearly understood, he recognized the name of a war criminal who had been responsible for the death of thousands many years before.

"You're from Bosnia?"

She dipped her head. Yes.

"Srebrenica?"

"No. Djoba."

Djoba had been the warm-up act for the massacre at Srebrenica.

Joe knew a lot about the wars in Bosnia: How the six people's republics that had formed Yugoslavia had torn the country apart. Serbs living in both Bosnia and Croatia had sought to unite with their brothers in Serbia. Fighting between the Orthodox Christian Serbs and Muslim Bosnians had been particularly savage, a continuation of the wars set off by the Ottoman invasions centuries before.

But this was genocide—the slaughter of thousands of men and boys, the rapes of thousands of women, and the brutal murders of children.

Anna tried to stifle her tears, and then she broke down. Joe reached across to the glove box and handed her a packet of tissues, regretting that he hadn't asked her to come up to his office. She should be talking to the duty agent, who would decide if a case should be opened.

Meanwhile, she deserved his full attention and he had to watch the road. Joe buzzed up the windows and shut off the heat so he could better understand what Anna was saying.

"Do you understand? I saw him *here*, two hours ago. *Slobodan Petrović*."

"Yes. I know who he is. You can talk to me. I understand what you're saying, where you come from."

Anna blew her nose, unknotted her scarf, and began telling Joe about a hot summer day in the village of Djoba.

"I was washing my baby in the kitchen sink when soldiers entered the village by the main road," she said, staring through the windshield into the horrors from her past.

"They came on foot. Then the tanks and officers in jeeps.

"My little boy, Bakir, started to cry. My husband came into the room and said, 'Stay here.' And then he ran outside. Zerin wasn't yet thirty," Anna said. "So strong and vital. That was the last time I saw him alive."

Joe murmured, "I'm so sorry. So very sorry, Anna."

She was looking out into the darkened streets, projecting her terrible story onto this blank screen. She spoke of how her town had been declared a safe zone by the United Nations and how hundreds of refugees had fled there. How they had grouped together in the sweltering heat without enough food or water. And how most of those stranded in that so-called safe zone had been women, children, and the elderly.

Anna told him how the Serb soldiers had mingled among the refugees and executed the men at random, not stopping there but hunting down the ones who had hidden in the outlying fields and farmhouses. She described how the Serb soldiers had burned down the houses and barns and then turned their attention to the women and children left trapped in the town.

"I hid with Bakir in my house," Anna told him, her voice hollow with shock, "but they found me. They took my child away, my beautiful boy. Then they held me down and…you can imagine what they did. Four of them. Laughing. Trying to hurt me as much as possible. Anyway, I passed out. The next morning they were gone. I found my baby boy on the side of the road with his throat slit."

Anna groaned and then sobbed uncontrollably into her hands as she relived the unspeakable death of her child.

Joe pulled the car over to the curb and put his hand on Anna's shoulder. She shook him off and leaned against the window, crying in ragged sobs until she was cried out.

Then she turned to him and said, "The most unbelievable thing is when something so unimaginable happens, a thing that kills you inside, you keep breathing and your heart beats and you still live. Time still goes on."

Joe had to fight his own feelings, and they were many. He

wanted to comfort her. He wanted to kill someone—Petrović. He wanted to cry.

Anna said, "It has been so long since I've told anyone, Joe. I'm sorry that you had to be the one. But seeing Petrović today, healthy, *prosperous*. I thought he was dead. I thought he was long dead."

"What can I do to help you?"

Anna and Joe sat in the parked car and talked for a while, Anna describing fantasies of killing him, detailing conversations she'd had with other women in Djoba. Hushed conversations in which they never said what had been done to them. They hadn't had to.

Finally exhausted, she said, "Please drive me home now, Joe. I need to be alone." He started the engine.

Ten minutes later Joe parked near the house where Anna was renting a studio apartment. He told her that he would bring the bike to get it fixed, not a problem, and carried her backpack upstairs. He gave her his contact numbers and said to call him when she wanted to speak again.

She thanked him, went inside, and closed the door behind her.

Anna's pain had permeated Joe's car.

He could still see the violent imagery she had drawn of old people hanging off the sides of trucks, the slaughter of children, the refugees who'd hanged themselves rather than suffer at the hands of Slobodan Petrović.

These images accompanied him all the way home.

CHAPTER 8

I'D GONE FOR a short run with Martha and was now home in our apartment on Lake Street.

The evening news was on the TV and the soup just beginning to simmer when Martha broke for the doorway, barking and shimmying, to greet Joe.

He bent to pet our good doggy, but his expression told me that he'd had a very bad day.

I said, "Hon. What's wrong?"

"Did you eat?" he asked me.

"No. Did you?"

He shook his head.

"I'm heating up some split pea. I can give the chicken legs another few spins in the microwave."

"Would you? I need to get out of my clothes."

While I "cooked," Jacobi called, and we updated each other on our lack of progress on the schoolteacher case.

"We've got zippo," Jacobi said to me. "I hate this."

We commiserated and talked over plans for the next day,

and I had just hung up as Joe came into the spacious kitchen/ living room. His hair was wet and he was wearing his robe.

He asked about my day, but I said, "You go first."

Between bites he told me about meeting Anna Sotovina, a Bosnian war survivor, a couple of hours before. Her chilling story had gotten to him. It was getting to *me*.

"What's she like?" I asked.

"Terribly broken. Her face is scarred. Her whole life is scarred. She survived the worst—torture, rape, the murders of her husband and child—and came here after the war. She has a good job and a rental apartment on Fulton. She had started over, Linds. And then she sees Slobodan Petrović coming out of a house a few blocks from her place."

"It was really Petrović? Is she sure?"

"She has no doubt."

I didn't need to tell Joe about eyewitness sightings—how the mind fills in memory gaps with convincing detail, so that every time a memory is pulled up for review, it is slightly overwritten in the present. We'd both had firsthand experience with witnesses making positive IDs on criminals who, at the time of the crime, were in maximum security at the Q.

"I considered that," Joe said.

He carried his half-full plate to the sink, refilled his wineglass and mine.

"Petrović," I said. "I remember what he looked like. A husky, red-faced hog of a man."

"That's him," Joe said. "He was charged with war crimes and crimes against humanity, and went to trial but wasn't convicted. It was a scandal at the time, but he was released.

"Then—he disappeared. A body was found in a river, I think, bloated and decomposing, and identified as Petrović. But identified by whom? Friends in high places? If Anna is right, he got out of town and ended up here."

"What's your gut tell you?"

Joe and I had been married for only a few months back then, but Martha loved him. She trotted over to him and rested her chin on his knee. Joe stroked her, drank his wine, and took long, thoughtful pauses that I did not interrupt.

Then he said, "I believe her, Lindsay. Enough to look into this. I don't know yet how or if I can help her, but I'll start digging into it tomorrow."

In Joe's place, I'd have done the same.

CHAPTER 9

JOE WAS DRIVING to work the next morning, thinking about Anna Sotovina, when she called.

"Can we meet?" she asked. "I have a couple of things to show you."

Twenty minutes later Joe pulled up to the three-story house on Fulton Street where Anna lived. He was about to ring the doorbell when she got out of a red Kia parked across the street. She was dressed for work, wearing a blue skirt suit and lipstick. Her hair was combed so that it fell in a way that covered the burn scar on her cheek.

She waited for traffic to pass, then crossed, opened the passenger-side door, and got inside, saying, "I have to apologize for last night. All that crying."

"Don't apologize. You have good reason to cry."

She said, "I was in shock to see Petrović."

"Of course."

"I told you. I chased him on my bike. Crazy."

"I'm glad you didn't catch him," Joe said.

37

She nodded. "I didn't even think it was crazy. I couldn't help myself. I saw him. And if I caught him—what did I think I would do? Call him names? But it was *him*. The Butcher of Djoba."

Joe said, "You were very brave, Anna. Crazy but brave."

She nodded.

"You wanted to show me something."

"Yes."

She opened her handbag, pulled out a plastic folder, 8½" x 11". Inside was a newspaper article that had been folded into thirds. She opened the yellowed and worn page with shaking hands and showed it to Joe.

The article was written in Bosnian. Anna tapped the photo at top center, just under the headline.

"That's him going into the ICC in handcuffs. See them? He was charged with war crimes and crimes against humanity, but the charges were dismissed. I don't know why. Thousands were killed. I saw the bodies. But he was simply *released.*"

She took out her billfold and pulled a photo from behind a rectangle of clear plastic, then held the photo so Joe could see the picture of a young man in his twenties, laughing, bouncing a baby in his arms.

"You see how much love?"

Joe said. "I do."

Anna said, "This is not in question, Joe. Petrović was the commanding officer of the destruction of my town. My poor husband was hanged," Anna said. "They cut my little boy's throat. Thousands were murdered, and Petrović killed many with his own hands. Why should my family be dead while he is alive and free?"

Joe said, "The words for these crimes are just inadequate."

She nodded and went on, "You know, after Petrović was released, there was a big protest. Then it was said that he was killed."

"I read that, too. His body was found quite decomposed in a river. Look, Anna, I'm just asking. Is it possible that Petrović was killed and the man you saw yesterday looked like him? Reminded you of him?"

"It *is* him, Joe. Don't you think I would know?" She held the palm of her hand a few inches from her face. "I've been *this* close to him. Under him. You understand?"

"Oh, God. I'm so sorry."

He was more than sorry. He wanted to kill the guy who'd done this to her. Kill him slowly.

Anna said, "I also believed that he was dead. Now I know it was a mistake or a lie or a covering up. Petrović left Europe. Someone must know how he did that and maybe helped him."

"I checked with Interpol last night, and there are no warrants out for him, nothing to prevent him from using his passport."

Anna said, "When he was military, he wore his hair very short. His hair is longer now. He's put on thirty pounds. Otherwise, he looks the same. He is fat and healthy. He has an expensive car. Seventy-five thousand dollars, Joe. Where is he getting his money?"

Joe couldn't answer her question. Ten minutes of research had told him that Petrović might have changed his name and flown legally to the United States. The FBI had no jurisdiction over an ICC-charged war criminal who, for whatever reason, had walked.

"Do you mind if we take a ride?" Anna said.

CHAPTER 10

THE DRIVE WAS three blocks down Steiner, three blocks on Fell, in under three minutes.

"Over there," Anna said.

Joe pulled up to the curb, and Anna rolled down her window, saying, "That's where I saw him."

She pointed to a Victorian house, pale yellow with dark blue trim, well cared for. "He was coming down the steps like he owned America."

Anna turned to Joe, pulled back the curtain of hair that had been hiding her scar. "He did this to me. After he raped me, when I called him all the names I could think of. I wanted him to shoot me. I wanted to die. He used his lighter...."

"You were in the hotel?" Joe said.

She shook her head. "I can't talk about that."

She didn't have to say more. Joe had been with the FBI in Virginia when the Serbs had slaughtered the men of Djoba, captured the women, and kept many in a school, calling it a rape hotel. The point had been not only to humiliate and dishonor these Muslim women and girls, but to impregnate them with the children of their enemies.

Anna's voice broke into his thoughts as she called his name and pointed to a Jaguar parked a hundred yards up the street.

"That's his car," she said. "He's home, inside his house. Can you just go in there and shoot him between the eyes?"

"No. I can't. Stay here."

Joe got out of the car and took a picture of the house, and then the man that Lindsay remembered from his photos as a husky, red-faced hog came out the front door of the fancy yellow house. He walked rapidly down the steps while talking into his phone.

Joe aimed the phone's camera at Petrović's face, but his features were largely hidden by the phone in his hand. And then he was getting into his car and pulling out onto Fell Street.

Anna was out of the car, crying out to Joe, "That's him. That's *him*. That's Slobodan Petrović. Now do you believe me? Follow him. *Follow him, please.*"

The car had sped off, and other cars quickly filled the gap between the Jag and where Joe was standing with Anna.

"Anna, no. I can't arrest him for crimes he committed in Bosnia."

Anna sagged against the car.

"Well," she said, "maybe I can do something. I need a gun. Then I can shoot him myself."

Anna stretched her neck so she could watch the Jaguar disappearing up the street.

All around them, normal life went on. Dogs being walked.

Joggers heading into the park. A grocery truck making a delivery. People going to work. But to a woman who'd survived a massacre, none of these activities meant a thing.

Joe understood. Anna had built a life again. And then Petrović had appeared. How could it not enflame her?

Joe spoke to her across the roof of his car.

"Anna, listen to me. You asked for my help. I'm a federal law enforcement agent. I'll do what I can legally do, the right way. Please. Look at me."

She dragged her gaze away from the disappearing car.

Joe continued.

"Do not confront this man on your own. You know if he feels threatened, you won't get away from him. Promise me you'll let me handle this. Promise me you'll do that."

"I promise," she said.

Anna got back into Joe's car.

CHAPTER 11

THIS ALL HAPPENED five years ago, but I remember it like it was yesterday.

That week I had a lunch date with Cindy Thomas. She was waiting for me at Fast 'n Good, a coffee shop two blocks from her office, and I was late. I was still ten minutes away, walking toward Fourth Street as fast as I could without breaking into a run.

Jacobi had called an impromptu meeting that morning. He stood at the front of the squad room and barked, "We have to get a grip on this case. A clue. A witness. A theory that holds water. As you know, Boxer is lead investigator. Boxer—no one goes home until we have something with legs."

We were all with him. Where were Carly, Adele, and Susan? No freaking idea. A death clock was ticking, and the dozen investigators in the homicide squad were working nonstop and hoping beyond reason that the schoolteachers would be found alive.

Cindy, one of my best friends, is a crime reporter at the

San Francisco Chronicle. The first time I met her, she was covering a savage double murder and had finagled her way into the crime scene. *My* crime scene. In the end, she helped me solve the case and we bonded for good. It was no surprise to me that she was now making a name as a talent with a big future.

Late as I was that day, I knew Cindy would make use of the found time to return calls, check in with sources, write notes, or draft her story. When I showed up, she'd jump right into the business at hand—or grill me until I gave her a scrap of printable news.

But in return she was likely to tell me something I didn't know.

The OPEN sign hanging in Fast 'n Good's plate-glass window was blinking. I pulled the door open and scanned the place from the vestibule until I saw the mop of blond curls showing over the back of a booth. I strode down the aisle, slid into the banquette across from Cindy, and said, "Hey. Sorry to hold you up."

I could already see the question in her cornflower-blue eyes.

"You anywhere with the schoolteachers?" she asked.

"Just what I had yesterday, girlfriend. Nothing. Please don't rub it in."

CHAPTER 12

CINDY PUT DOWN her half-eaten BLT and said, "I give the tomato rice four stars."

I ordered a cup of soup and a grilled cheese with bacon. Then I said, "Whatcha got for me?"

She poked at her cell phone and called up a photo of a woman stooping to hug a large dog that was washing her face with its tongue.

Cindy said, "Look *past* the girl and dog."

I enlarged the photo, bringing up the couple in the background walking across a parking lot away from the camera. The male was lanky, taller than the woman, and had spiky hair. The female had turned to look at the male. Her face was in profile. Yellow lines on the asphalt marked parking spots. I could see one side of a dark SUV and almost make out a building at the edge of the frame.

"Okay. What am I looking at?"

"It was sent to me by a confidential source," Cindy said. "A guy who reads my blog. The attached note said, 'Carly

Myers and friend. She's one of your missing teachers, right?'"

I looked closer. I'd seen only a formal head shot of Carly Myers. This snapshot was not in sharp focus and showed only the woman's profile. But it *could* be her.

I asked Cindy, "Who's the guy?"

"Don't know. Yet."

"Where's this parking lot? Is this the Bridge?"

"That's all I have. This picture. My source was taking a shot of his girlfriend and her dog. Later he looks at the picture and recognizes Carly Myers. He's seen her before."

"Cin. Don't publish this until we have Carly, okay? Let's not get her killed. And you have to hook me up with your source. We need the name of this guy walking with the woman."

"I get it, but he won't talk to you. He's got outstanding warrants."

"Okay, okay. I'll talk to him on the phone. That'll be fine." For now.

"Let me see what I can do."

"You can do anything, Girl Reporter."

She laughed.

She took back her phone and sent the photo to me and a text to her source. My lunch came, and while making the daily special disappear, I looked again at the picture Cindy had sent to me.

The shot had been taken at night. Fuzzy focus no matter what I did. Maybe it was Carly Myers. Who was the guy? Had he been the last person to see Carly when she left the Bridge? Had she told him where she was going? Had he abducted her?

I told Cindy what assistant dean Karin Slaughter had told me about the three missing women and about Carly Myers in particular.

"Carly's a sports fan and a history buff. She lives alone. Her parents…" I sighed, thinking about them. "They said as far as they knew, she wasn't seeing anyone right now."

I forwarded the photos of the three teachers to Cindy. She'd get them into the *Chronicle* today with a request to the public for help. This posting would bring out the kooks, flood our tip lines with 99 percent nonsense. But 1 percent might pay off. Maybe there was still time to bring the women home—alive.

Cindy said, "Hang on."

She showed me a text she'd just gotten. The sender's name was Kev32 and the message read, *I should have the boyfriend's name in 1 hr.*

We had apple pie with our coffee, and I insisted on paying for lunch. It was fast 'n good and, for a real lead, damned cheap.

CHAPTER 13

JOE WATCHED ANNA start up her car and head up Fulton and take a left on Steiner.

Only after she'd turned the corner did he drive to his office.

Joe believed everything Anna had told him about the brutalization, the terror, the repeated gang rapes, the murder of her family and nearly all of the men in Djoba.

He had only one question: Was the man coming down the front steps of a fancy house on Fell Street Slobodan Petrović, or had Anna superimposed her searing memories onto a person who resembled the monster she would never forget?

Joe didn't have enough information. But he would get it.

He parked his car on Golden Gate, walked two blocks to the FBI's office building, and entered through the glass doors. He passed through security and took the elevator to his floor, preoccupied with Anna's story, his mind on his computer.

Joe thumbed in the code to his office, flipped on the lights, hung up his coat behind the door.

His office was functional, no pictures or knickknacks, nothing personal about it. He had a standard wooden desk, a high-tech computer on the desk's return, a TV affixed to the facing wall, one side chair, a flag standing in the corner, and a window to his right with a thirteenth-floor view of the city.

He booted up his PC, transferred the picture he'd taken of "Petrović" twenty minutes before, and studied the enlarged photo. If this was Slobodan Petrović, then at 8:14 that morning Joe had been within yards of a monster guilty of genocide.

But the picture was disappointing.

He'd known that he'd caught Petrović at an angle, but what he saw on his monitor was a slimmer wedge of the man's face than he remembered.

Petrović's longish hair fell over his eyes, and worse, his hand and cell phone covered most of his cheek and ear. Petrović had been looking down, watching his step, causing folds of his neck to gather under his chin, further distorting his profile.

Joe was exasperated. He'd missed an opportunity, but still, if he'd stepped in to take a better shot, Petrović would have seen him do it.

No good would have come of that.

Joe focused on what he had.

The shapes of Petrović's head and nose were distinctive.

He opened FACE, the agency's facial recognition software, and imported the image of the "husky, red-faced hog." The program could identify a partial image with 85 percent accuracy. If Petrović's mug was in federal databases or those of sixteen states, FACE could nail him.

Joe stared at the screen as the program did its work, but when the run concluded, only three marginal matches had been retrieved. None were positive. None were Petrović.

Joe went back to Interpol's Criminal Information System, a global criminal database, and after typing in Petrović's name, he found several photographs like the one in the ragged newspaper clipping Anna had carried with her.

Documents and hundreds of pages about Petrović's military history and arrest downloaded, as well as transcripts of translated police interviews. The transcripts were heavily redacted. Why? A fast look through them told Joe that Petrović had denied every charge—the killings, the rapes, the torture—claiming that he was just a soldier.

He'd been misidentified. They had the wrong guy.

Joe had heard this same heinous crap from guilty criminals over the long history of his career. And without evidence, denials could work, even for red-faced, red-handed killers.

In Petrović's case, there were mountains of bodies. And there were survivors like Anna who surely would have testified. How had stonewalling gotten the Butcher of Djoba released for lack of evidence?

Only one thing made sense to Joe. Petrović had been the witness. He must have testified against higher-ranking officers who had, in fact, been tried for war crimes and convicted. If this was true, he'd made himself one hell of a deal.

After his release, Petrović might have changed his name and gone far away from the scenes of his crimes.

It looked to Joe like that's what he'd done.

CHAPTER 14

JOE'S DAY WASN'T going as he had hoped.

His concentration had been derailed by the briefing from Craig Steinmetz, the San Francisco field office supervisor. The meeting was about three private school teachers who'd been missing for two days—Lindsay's case, Joe knew. There was no clue as to their whereabouts, and the SFPD was asking for help.

Joe would have liked to jump on board, but other agents were willing and able, and he had made a promise to Anna.

When the meeting ended, he went back to his office and tried to get back to work. But there were more interruptions.

The director called from DC and got right to the point. A domestic terrorism plot Joe had uncovered months ago needed his attention. Now. The suspect was American born, connected through Syria to an actor high up in a terrorist chain of command. Phone messages had been deciphered. A truck had been rented. But nothing had pinned the tail on Greg Stassi, the American donkey.

Stassi was in custody but wasn't forthcoming. Without direct evidence leading to him or a confession, he would be released in forty-eight hours.

The director said, "Molinari, you know Stassi. He might talk to you."

Two days ago Joe would have gotten on the next flight to DC and met with the kid. Today he told the director, "Marty, this is a bad time. I might be able to kick free in a week or so, but I'm on the brink of something here. I can't get out of it. I'm sorry."

Petrović wasn't a case or even a file folder. Joe had never misled the director before. Then again, he'd never before promised a survivor of ethnic cleansing that he would try to nail a killer, let alone one as monstrous as the Butcher of Djoba.

Joe was 90 percent convinced that the man on Fell Street was Slobodan Petrović. But without independent verification, he couldn't prove it, even to himself.

Full stop.

He pulled the phone toward him and called Hai Nguyen, a top FBI forensics tech at Quantico, then forwarded two photos to him. One, Petrović's ICC mug shot; and the second, this morning's partial of Petrović's face.

"I'll take a look, Joe."

"Thanks, Hai. And—"

"I know. Right now."

After getting a fresh cup of coffee, Joe resumed researching the man who was accused of slaughtering hundreds if not thousands of Bosnian civilians.

File names filled his screen and Joe opened them all. Every

document added nuance, color, and data to what he already knew: Where Petrović had been born, his brutal upbringing and punishing military service, hints of what had led him to become a mass murderer.

Fact: After the end of the war Slobodan Petrović had been captured on the run, charged with war crimes and crimes against humanity, and indicted in the International Criminal Court. Then the charges had been dropped. He'd been released and his criminal record closed.

Supposition: Sometime later he'd come to America, where he'd bought or rented a house and a car in San Francisco.

Joe zeroed in on that.

He ran the poor-quality photo he'd taken of Petrović through the DMV database and wasn't surprised that he didn't get a hit. So he called Hai Nguyen again.

"How's it going, Hai?"

"Your mail, Joe. Open it."

Nguyen's reconstructed photo looked like the pictures of Petrović he'd retrieved from the military files. It was an astonishingly good likeness and quite usable.

Joe hung up and entered the picture into the DMV database. A driver's license appeared on his screen. It was the man he'd seen on Fell Street, but his name was not Slobodan Petrović.

It was Antonije Branko.

CHAPTER 15

JOE WAS FOCUSED, streaming along a tunnel of concentration, the zone where he felt most comfortable.

Once he had a name with a photo, it didn't take long to get into all that followed: tax rolls, parking tickets, and records of a house on Fell Street sold to Antonije Branko a year ago.

Now Joe had something tangible.

He enjoyed a few seconds of elation while analyzing this new information. Most likely before he'd left Bosnia, Petrović had changed his name to another Serbian name that gave him plausible deniability. If he was ever recognized here or there, he could say, "Petrović and I were from the same village. He might be a third cousin. Many of us *resemble* one another."

Joe's illuminating thought was supplanted by one more urgent.

He bent to his keyboard and quickly searched the SFPD database for *Antonije Branko*. He found him listed as a person of interest who had been seen affiliating with known criminals in "crime-prone locations"—bars, girly clubs, dodgy neighborhoods.

Branko had parked in those neighborhoods in his pricey midnight-blue Jaguar. He had been brought in for questioning on two minor drug cases, for purchasing Molly without intent to distribute. Seasoned narcotics investigators had failed to lay a finger on him. No arrests. No indictments.

It looked to Joe like Petrović used go-betweens and buffers in his work, and so far he hadn't left any fingerprints. That he'd obscured his face with his phone and hand while walking down the front steps of his house now seemed calculated and deliberate.

But Joe couldn't see any cause for the FBI to bring him in for questioning.

If Petrović had *legally* changed his name in Bosnia, gotten a passport and a visa as Branko, come to the USA and applied for a green card, and gotten a driver's license as Branko—none of this was a crime.

But in Joe's opinion, people didn't change very much.

Petrović hadn't left all of those bodies in Djoba and come to the US determined to live a new life as a choirboy. As Anna had asked, where was he getting his money?

The thing to do was to let the fish run. Watch him, track him, and if he was involved in illegal activities, reel him in. Beach him.

Joe leaned back in his chair, clasped his hands behind his neck, and stared at the acoustic-tile ceiling.

He couldn't stop thinking about Anna. Her story had gripped him, and he was worried for her. He wanted to put Slobodan Petrović away. If he attempted to make this case official without any reason to open a case on Branko, he'd be shut down.

But if he didn't help Anna, she could get herself killed.

CHAPTER 16

THANKS TO CINDY'S anonymous source, Conklin and I had a name and known hangout of a guy who may have dated Carly Myers.

Name: Tom Barry. Favorite lunch spot: a sports bar called Casey's on Fillmore.

I'd never been to Casey's before and took a good look from the doorway.

The room was narrow, dark, and clubby, with framed photos of sports stars on the walls. A long bar ran along the length of the place, and there were some tables and armchairs front and back. Three HD TVs were positioned at intervals, and all of them were locked in on a horse race running in Saratoga Springs.

The crowd was fervent—money was on the line.

Conklin and I looked at the men at the bar, and one of them fit the photo. White guy in his twenties, lanky, spiky hair, drinking his lunch. To be fair, he had a bowl of peanuts beside his beer.

We walked over and stood on either side of him, and from the look in his eyes, we were pissing him off by encroaching on his personal space. *Sorry, bud. This is police business.* We were ready to grab him if he tried to run.

I flashed my badge, introduced my partner and myself, and asked if he was Tom Barry.

"Why do you ask?"

I pulled my phone and showed him the parking lot photo. I asked him if he was the man in the picture.

"Looks like me. Yeah. That's my leather jacket."

"Who's that with you?"

"Uh. Carly?"

"You were with her a few nights ago," I said.

"Nope. I saw her last week, Tuesday. That's when we went out. What's going on?"

Conklin sidestepped the question, asking Barry if he knew where we could find Carly.

"Me? No. We're not that close. If we're drinking in the same bar, we sometimes go out for a bite and a roll."

"She's missing," Conklin said. "She hasn't been seen in a few days."

"I don't know anything about that," Barry said, drawing back, showing alarm.

The horses on the screen overhead were clearing the back turn and pounding into the stretch. The crowd in the bar broke out in yelling and rooting.

Barry glanced up at the screen, yelled, "Oh, come onnn, Fast Talker, come onnnn." Then he remembered we were standing beside him, and turned back to us in disgust.

"I don't know anything about Carly. You're wasting my time."

I said, "We believe you, Mr. Barry. But if you care about Carly at all, we need your help."

"Christ. I don't even have her phone number."

Conklin said in that nice, nonthreatening way he has, "Sometimes people know more than they think. We'd appreciate you coming with us to the station, Mr. Barry. You might be able to shine a light on this situation."

"Look, I have to be at work at two, okay? I manage the car wash over on Third."

"You'll be back in plenty of time," I lied.

Barry slapped a ten down on the bar, and I noticed his knuckles were scraped up. He'd swung at someone or something recently and connected. While he struggled into his leather jacket, Conklin snaked a hand around him, picked up the beer glass by the rim. While I further distracted Barry by putting the photo of him back in his face, asking, "This is the parking lot at the Bridge, right?" Conklin got a plastic bag from the bartender.

"I guess so," Barry muttered.

With his prints on a bagged glass under Conklin's Windbreaker, we escorted him out onto the street and into the back of our car. As Conklin drove, I checked out Thomas Barry on the MDC built into the console.

Barry had a minor-league record: an arrest for drunk and disorderly one night at Casey's a couple of years back, a fender bender last year, and a DUI. His juvenile record was sealed.

I had an image in mind of Carly Myers and Barry, and he didn't look, smell, or feel like a match for her. What did she see in him?

My interest was piqued. So much so that I was cautiously optimistic that Tom Barry held a key to the whereabouts of the missing schoolteachers.

CHAPTER 17

THE HALL OF Justice was a large, rectangular granite building on Bryant Street, home to the criminal court, the DA's office, a jail, and the Southern Station of the SFPD, which included the homicide squad, where Conklin and I worked in the bullpen on the fourth floor.

Despite its storied past and understated charm, the HOJ was rat-infested, prone to flurries of asbestos and sewage leaks, and seismically unstable.

We'd been working here for so long that Conklin and I hardly noticed that the Hall was hazardous to our health. Whenever we talked about it, we agreed that we would miss the old wreck when it was eventually demolished.

But at that moment, with a possible suspect in tow, we were only thinking about the missing schoolteachers.

Conklin, Tom Barry, and I were seated at a metal table inside a small interrogation room down the hall from our squad room. Lieutenant Warren Jacobi, our old friend and commanding officer, was behind the glass.

I took the lead in the interview and began by asking Barry to help us out. He responded by pushing my buttons, first denying knowing anything about Carly yet again, then becoming argumentative and belligerent. He had quite an act. And the truth was, we had nothing on him.

He could walk out anytime.

Conklin took a turn.

"Mr. Barry, cut it out. This is very damned serious. We're trying to save lives here, and you're acting like you've got something to hide. If you're innocent, act like it, okay?

"You went out with Carly, spent time with her, so give us something to go on. Where would she be if she went somewhere on her own after work and after dark?"

"I. Do. Not. Know. Look, I wasn't attached to her. At all. We talked baseball, football, and especially soccer. We screwed. Once in my place. Once in hers. I didn't buy her a Valentine. I didn't introduce her to my mother. The relationship was casual. What don't you get?"

After an hour of this combative back-and-forth, I thought I'd wrung everything out of Thomas Barry that he had to give; not only his work schedule but also the name of a woman who could vouch for him the night Carly, Susan, and Adele went missing. He gave us names of two other women he'd rolled with on the two nights after that. Thomas Barry was a player. We would send his prints to the lab, my thought being that maybe his prints would be found on Carly Myers's car.

It was quarter to two in the afternoon.

Barry said, "Can I go now? I don't want to get fired."

I said, "I'll have an officer give you a lift."

"Okay. Finally."

He stood to put on his jacket and gave me a peculiar look, which I read as a sign he was about to do us a favor.

"Sergeant, I had nothing to do with Carly being missing. Or any of them. If I were you, I'd be looking into Carly. My take is that she's no angel. She has a dark side. That much I can tell you."

There was a knock on the door and Jacobi came in, looking stricken.

He said, "Mr. Barry, I've got you a ride. Thanks for your help. Boxer, Conklin, I need to see you right away."

I handed Barry off to Officer Mahoney and headed back to Jacobi's glass-walled office at the back of the squad room.

He and Conklin were waiting for me.

I pulled out a chair, saying, "Waste of time. We don't have enough cause to get a warrant—"

Jacobi cut me off.

"We've got a body. Might be Carly Myers. Big Four Motel, room 212. Call me when you get there."

CHAPTER 18

RICHIE LOST THE coin flip, so I drove.

We reached Ellis Street in record time, then closed in on the Big Four, slowing only for the aimless druggies wandering down and across Larkin.

I pulled into the parking spot at the front of the seedy, rent-by-the-hour, no-tell motel, switched off the engine, and took a breath. We weren't alone. A dozen homeless, impoverished, drug-dependent residents of the Tenderloin were camped out on the macadam between the parked cars.

They were about to lose their campground.

The parking lot was a secondary crime scene and would have to be vacated and taped off from the street.

Conklin and I got out of the car. My mind was racing with questions, none of which would be answered until we got into room 212.

Question one: Was the dead woman Carly Myers?

Questions two and three: If the DB was Carly, what had killed her? And why here?

A handful of the motel's guests stood under the awning outside the manager's office, complaining loudly that they needed to get into their goddamn rooms.

The manager said just as loudly, "Cops said when they're done, they're done. Nothing I can do."

I interrupted the dispute to get the manager's name, Jake Tuohy, and to tell him to stick around. We'd be back.

Room 212 was at the rear of the motel. My partner and I rounded the corner of the three-story stucco building and saw a small fleet of first responders: two cruisers, an ambulance, and two CSI vans, all empty.

We badged the uniform at the foot of the stairs, ducked under the crime-scene tape, and headed up to the second floor, where Nardone, another uniformed officer, was waiting for us. At that time, Officer Robert Nardone was a beat cop with ambition and promise. He told us that he was the first officer on the scene.

"Tell me what you know," I said.

"Housekeeper, Nancy Koebel, went to clean 212 at twelve thirty or so and found the DB hanging by the neck from the shower head. She reported the body to the manager, Jake Tuohy, who took a look in the bathroom, closed the door, and called it in."

"Where is Koebel?"

Nardone said, "By the time I got here, she'd taken off."

Conklin asked him, "You checked out the room?"

"I was very careful not to contaminate anything. It was dark. I flipped on the light switch with my elbow and stepped into the bathroom. Saw the victim and went to check her vitals. She wasn't breathing. I touched her leg. She was ice cold."

Nardone looked sad, maybe ill. I pictured him in that bathroom, hand against the wall as he reached out to touch the victim. His prints were likely on the wall and definitely on the doorknob. Doorknobs had also been handled by the housekeeper and the manager, probably smearing whatever the perp had left behind.

"Keep going," I said.

"I looked into the main room from the hallway. The curtains were closed, but I could see a little bit by the bathroom light. No one was in the room, living or dead. I called the lieutenant."

"Okay," I said. "Good job, Bobby."

We talked protocol for another few minutes.

I directed Nardone to get plate numbers of every car in the lots front and back, clear and seal off the parking lots, and set up a media liaison post on Ellis.

"No one but law enforcement goes in or out of here until I say okay. I'll get you some help to collect the guests and sequester them in the reception area."

"They're like crazy people," he said.

"They're going to object. Be nice but firm. This is a police investigation into a possible homicide, okay?"

"Got it, Sergeant."

I called Jacobi.

"I need uniforms and investigators, boss. We have to question guests who are not going to volunteer."

Jacobi said he was on it.

Then Conklin and I headed to room 212 and the scene that was waiting for us.

CHAPTER 19

I WAS VERY glad to see Charles Clapper standing outside room 212, thumbing his phone.

A former homicide lieutenant with the LAPD, Clapper was a hands on criminalist, ran a great shop, and was neither a showboater nor a politician. He was rock solid and I called him a friend.

We exchanged greetings, and then Conklin asked Clapper if there was security footage.

"Wouldn't that be a treat," said Clapper.

"I take it that's a no," said Conklin.

"It's a maybe. The customers here don't like cameras, but I've got two guys checking the ATM across the street. I'm curbing my enthusiasm."

The door to room 212 was open, and LED lights blazed in the small room beyond the doorway. Clapper talked as we gloved up and fitted booties over our shoes.

He said, "I could teach a university course in forensics on this scene. But then, don't take that to mean I've got a handle on it."

We followed him over the threshold and got our first look at the room. In many ways 212 was typical, about eighteen feet long from the door to the window at the far end, nine feet wide, the width largely taken up by the bed. The bathroom was to our immediate left, right off the entrance.

The Big Four Motel had been a fixture in the Tenderloin for thirty years and, during that time, had aged disgracefully. The carpet was dirt gray, original color indeterminate. The curtains were threadbare, and the spread was all that plus stained and soiled. The double bed was still made, but the pillows were disturbed.

Conklin and I stood inside the doorway, watching the CSIs taking photos of everything, sketching the layout, and dusting for prints, the last being a fairly futile activity given the three decades of accumulated splooge. But it had to be done. Maybe one clear print or even a partial would find a match in AFIS.

The CSIs had put markers down next to folded items of female apparel on the floor: a dark garment, either pants or a skirt; a lacy top with long sleeves; an underwire bra. High-heeled shoes stood next to the bed, a light coat hung over a chair back, and at the foot of the chair was a large handbag of the tote bag variety. It was unzipped and looked plenty big enough to hold electronics, books, and the kitchen sink.

As crime scenes went, this one was tidy. But we hadn't seen the body yet; the two techs in the bathroom were blocking our view.

I asked Clapper, "Did you find a note?"

"Not yet. I opened her bag to check her ID. Her license says Carly Myers, and her face matches the photo. We'll take the bag back to the lab and let you know what we find."

If the bag contained a phone and a computer, he'd also check her incoming and outgoing calls, get her text messages and emails, too. A phone could crack open everything from before she went missing. Pray to God it would lead to Susan Jones and Adele Saran.

Noting that, Clapper said, "We've only been in here for twenty minutes, so this is still a prelim. What I can tell you is that the victim is a Caucasian female found hanging by her neck by an electric cord noose. The other end of the cord was wrapped a number of times around the stem of the shower head and the curtain rod for added support. The cord was cut from a standing lamp in the other room. Scissors are on the floor."

Clapper went on.

"She's wearing an extra-large men's shirt. Looks new."

"What do you make of that?" I asked.

"Nothing yet. We'll test it. I saw no defensive wounds on the victim's arms, but I haven't checked her hands. Her wrists were bound in front with a pair of panties. The ME will take her liver temps, but I can tell you she's just coming out of rigor. So I'm estimating that she died twenty-four to thirty-six hours ago."

Bodies were different. Environments were different. But it was safe to use Clapper's guesstimate for now.

Carly was last seen on Monday night. So she'd died probably late Tuesday night or early Wednesday morning.

Clapper said, "We're just beginning to process the bathroom, but you can have a look. Are you ready, my friends?"

He knocked on the doorframe. The techs came out with their kits, and Clapper toed the door wide open.

Conklin and I went inside.

CHAPTER 20

I ENTERED THE small tiled room knowing that I was about to see something that I would never forget.

Clapper moved the shower curtain aside with the back of his gloved hand, revealing the body of a woman wearing a men's white shirt large enough that the tails hung to her mid-thigh.

As Clapper had said, the ligature was an electric cord wrapped around the stem of pipe between the shower head and the wall, and knotted under the victim's jaw. Her wrists were secured in front of her with pink ladies' underwear. A few twists of stretch lace could not withstand even Carly's feeblest thrashing to get her hands free. Her feet hung over the drain, just below the spigots.

There'd been no sign of a struggle in the main room, and I didn't see signs of disturbance here, either. The curtain hadn't been pulled down, the bath mat was flat to the floor, lined up with the tub.

I tried to picture Carly Myers, a woman who was well

liked, attractive, successful, and athletic, getting undressed, putting on a men's white dress shirt, making a noose with an electric cord, and slipping that noose over her head and pulling it tight. She would have had to secure the other end to the shower head and then loop her panties around her wrists in a couple of figure eights.

And then what? She'd stood on the lip of the tub and jumped a couple of feet toward the drain?

No way. She would have reflexively kicked at the tub rim and the wall, pulled at the cord, and the shower apparatus would have pulled out of the wall—no, no, no. She'd been murdered first, and very likely after that, her killer had strung her up. This was a staged suicide. The panties were a flourish. I'd bet my badge on it.

Conklin edged in for a better look.

"There's a bite mark on her neck," he said.

"Good catch. And it looks like two bath towels are missing," I said.

Conklin said, "He used the towels to clean up and took them with him."

My partner took snapshots of the body and the rest of the small room. When he was done, Clapper asked us to back out, and he summoned Hallows, his number two, to help him cut the body down.

Hallows laid a clean white sheet on the floor between the tub and the wall. Clapper supported the body while Hallows leaned in and cut the electric cord at the midpoint to protect possible DNA on either end.

I was guessing Myers weighed 115 pounds. She fell heavily when the cord was cut, but Clapper took the weight,

Hallows grabbed her legs, and the two of them laid her down on the sheeted floor.

Hallows bagged Myers's bound hands to preserve evidence that might be under her nails, and Conklin and I stepped outside to the walkway for some air.

I said to Conklin, "You okay?"

"Not really. You?"

We leaned on the railing and watched squad cars slow and pull up to the curb. Cappy McNeil and Paul Chi, two of the best homicide investigators in the state, got out of a gray Chevy and ID'd themselves to the uniform at the tape. Bystanders and looky-loos crowded the Ellis Street side of the line.

I wanted to talk with the manager, Jake Tuohy. Now. I had questions.

Who had checked into room 212? I wanted to see the register and run the names of the guests. I wanted to talk to the housekeeper who had found the body.

And I wanted Chi and McNeil to interview the motel guests sequestered in the lobby. A guest's name could light up the criminal database. Someone may have seen something—a questionable person, an altercation, a license plate. It crossed my mind that whoever had strung up Carly Myers in the shower was staying here at the Big Four.

Despite my feeling of urgency, it was well worth the time spent to kick around theories with Conklin.

"Let's play it out," I said to my partner.

CHAPTER 21

"RICH, DO WE agree that this was not a suicide?"

"Agreed. Her tongue wasn't protruding," he said. "The panties and the shirt are someone's idea of a joke. She was dead when she was hanged in the shower."

My turn to agree.

"If she was suicidal, she wouldn't kill herself in this hole. She'd do it in her apartment. She'd take pills. She doesn't want her parents to picture what we saw in that bathroom. So let's back up to the beginning."

"Right. Starting with where she was last seen," he said. "Killer sees her walking back to her car after she and her girls leave the Bridge on Monday night."

I said, "He comes up behind her with a gun and forces her into his car."

"Or she knew him," said Conklin. "She gets into his vehicle and he drives her here. There's a fight and it all goes wrong for Carly. But what about her two friends? Where were they?"

"Let's focus on Carly for now," I said. "Most likely, the guy picks her up, and class act that he is, he checks them into this dump. That was his plan all along. He kills her in the room Tuesday night or Wednesday morning and strings her up. He figures when she's discovered, the cops will think that her death was self-inflicted."

"That works," said Rich. "The killer washes up and gets into his car. He could be in Vancouver by now."

I said, "But there will be evidence of the murder in 212. What about the shirt?"

Conklin shrugged. "Let's just say this freak likes a woman in a big man's shirt. Maybe he left some of himself on that shirt." He nodded at the road. "Look. We have company."

Press trucks and a satellite van had double-parked along Ellis, and reporters hoping for quotes were crowding the line.

I saw Cindy. She waved. I waved back but made no move to let her through.

She would hold that against me.

Conklin said, "We should notify Carly's parents before the press does."

"Right. But first we talk to Tuohy."

CHAPTER 22

CONKLIN AND I were with Jake Tuohy in his grubby office, sitting across the room from his dump site of a desk.

He looked to be in his sixties, a heavy bulldog of a man with black tufts of hair sprouting in a horseshoe pattern around his balding scalp. His hands were calloused, his clothes were baggy, and his general appearance was consistent with the entropic ambiance of the Big Four Motel.

He also had an aggressive, one-note personality.

While his demeanor and appearance didn't make him a murderer, I tried him on as a suspect.

He looked physically strong. He had access to the rooms. His prints and DNA would be all over 212 and could easily be explained away. Would the bite mark on Carly Myers's neck match an impression of Tuohy's teeth? Was the saliva his?

Tuohy gave us the registration book—he had to. It was the law. But I had no right to demand a bite impression or a cheek swab, and we had no probable cause to arrest him.

Time was speeding by and our investigation was stalled. I

drummed my fingers on the narrow plastic arm of my chair as we waited for Tuohy's boss to call and give him a go-ahead to talk to us without a lawyer present.

The silence was killing me.

I stared over Tuohy's head at the large sepia photograph hanging behind his desk, a reproduction of the four railroad tycoons who'd built the Central Pacific Railroad, funding their endeavor with what was widely described as questionable means. They were called the Big Four.

Also hanging on the wall was a photo of a younger Jake Tuohy in some wooded section of Northern California. He was standing beside a deer that had been strung up in a tree by a hind leg. Tuohy was grinning. He had a knife in his hand and was about to gut his kill.

That photo of the dead animal and the pleasure on young Tuohy's face gave me a very bad feeling.

His phone vibrated.

He read a text, tapped the phone, read another text, then put the phone down.

"All right," he said. "The dead woman checked in on Tuesday night with cash."

"Tuesday," I said. "Not Monday night? You're sure."

"It's in the book. Tuesday. She didn't say anything to me, just pushed the money across the counter. Two tens and a twenty."

Conklin leaned forward and asked the motel manager, "She was alone?"

"That's right."

"At what time?"

"Around the same time as usual. After ten, something like

that. And like always, she put a 'Do Not Disturb' sign on her door. We honor that around here. Up to a point. Due to a laundry strike yesterday, that point was an hour ago."

Conklin pressed on. "How'd she look?"

"I don't understand the question."

Conklin said, "Did she seem normal? Or was she stressed?"

"Fuck if I know," Tuohy said. "I was on the phone. She pushed the cash at me. I gave her the key card to 212."

I said, "You said 'as usual.' You've seen her before."

"Sure. Like, every few weeks. Cinnamon was some kind of working girl."

"Cinnamon? No, I think you're talking about someone else. I'm asking about Carly Myers."

"Look, I don't know and I don't care what her real name was. You showed me her picture, and I'm telling you now. The only way I know that girl is as Cinnamon. And from what I can tell, her customers liked some spice."

My mind spun. Carly Myers was a working girl? A prostitute?

No way. How could that possibly be true?

CHAPTER 23

TUOHY SAID THAT Carly Myers had checked into the motel on Tuesday night and that her name was in the register.

I checked it myself.

As Tuohy had said, her name was right there, wedged in between other guests who'd checked in on Tuesday night. So where had Carly been for twenty-four hours after leaving the Bridge on Monday?

This didn't make sense.

I pulled up Carly's picture on my phone, walked it across the room, and showed it to Tuohy.

"This is the dead woman?"

"Yeah. That's her. She went by the name of Cinnamon. Usually, her pimp drops her off in the parking lot, but I didn't see him when she checked in the other night."

Conklin asked, "What's the pimp's name?"

I expected Tuohy to say again, "Fuck if I know." But he said, "Denny or Danny. I've heard her say, like, 'Later,

Denny.' And don't ask me if I know anything else about him, because I don't. Never saw him close up. Couldn't pick him out of a lineup, don't know what kind of car he drives, or if he has any 'stinguishing marks.'"

There was a knock on the door.

Tuohy groaned, leaned heavily on his desk, and got up. He went to the door and opened it.

Officer Nardone came in and gave me a report; he'd taken guest names and photographed their IDs. A few of the guests were feisty. One had told him he was out on bail and an arrest would sink him. Another had thrown up on Nardone's shoes.

"I told you. It's nothing but wild animals out there."

He shook his head, then said, "None of them saw anything or anybody, including the deceased. Also, Inspectors McNeil and Chi just got here. They're taking over the interviews."

This was good. The ball would be moving now.

I went into our holding room and talked with McNeil and Chi, and together we set up a phone relay between them and Nardone. Nardone would run the guests' names on the car's computer, while Chi and McNeil stayed with the guests. Nardone would let them know who had a rap sheet.

Einhorn was manning the door. I told him to go out to the street and take pictures of the crowd. The doer might come back to the crime. It happens.

I looked at my watch as I went back to Tuohy's office. It was 6:00 p.m. We'd been here for three hours. A big twenty-four-hour gap had opened in our timeline. Carly had been somewhere before she was brought here. Where were her two missing friends?

I told Tuohy that I'd need the housekeeper's contact info.

He tapped on his phone, scribbled a number on the back of a card, and handed it over. "That's all I've got. Anything else I can do for you?"

His growl was heavy with sarcasm.

"Do you have a record, Mr. Tuohy?"

"I've been pristine for twenty years."

"Then you have nothing to worry about. We're going to need you to come with us down to the station. You spoke with the dead woman. Your fingerprints are on the doors. This makes you a material witness to a homicide. Let's get your statement on the record."

"Son of a bitch."

Tuohy glowered at us. My gut tensed up. I could see him killing a prostitute, easy.

It might have been a murder of opportunity, then he'd staged a cover-up. Or maybe it was personal and he thought he could get away with it.

I watched Tuohy think through his options. Guys in jobs like this were streetwise. He knew he didn't need to come to the station, but if he didn't, we would double down. Get a search warrant for his home and car while we were at it. We could take his life apart.

Tuohy texted his boss.

Then he put on his hat and jacket, and we walked him out to our car.

CHAPTER 24

CONKLIN TOOK THE wheel, and as we crawled through rush hour to the Hall, I checked Tuohy's arrest record on the MDC.

Jacob "Jake" Tuohy had spent time at Folsom for possession, holding up an all-night convenience store armed with his finger in his pocket, and around that time his ex-wife had gotten a restraining order against him.

I expected more and worse, but as he'd said, his sheet had been clean for twenty years. "Pristine."

While I liked Tuohy for Carly Myers's murder, I didn't see him as organized, a master planner, or a serial killer. But Jake Tuohy was all we had.

We left the squad car parked on Bryant in front of the Hall and escorted Tuohy upstairs to Homicide. The squad room was nearly empty, all hands on the street, talking to their informants, trying to locate the missing and possibly dead schoolteachers.

Conklin made Tuohy comfortable in Interview 1, while I

went out to the observation room behind the glass and watched with Jacobi as Conklin questioned our person of interest.

He started off with softball questions, then mixed in the harder ones—pitching them right across the plate.

Tuohy stuck to his story; he had not killed Carly Myers and didn't know who had. He hadn't seen anyone go into her room. Furthermore, he'd never heard of Susan Jones or Adele Saran. He scrutinized their photos and said he didn't recognize either of them.

I didn't see a tell. I didn't smell a lie. But men who ran no-tell motels were streetwise and cop-wary. They made deals with their guests, sex in exchange for drugs or a free overnight. Lies came easy to them.

Conklin joined us behind the glass, and Jacobi took his place in the interrogation room. Jacobi was a pro who'd spent most of his career in a squad car, and much of that time in the Tenderloin. Some of that time I'd been sitting next to him in the car. He was tough.

At this time, Jacobi was just over fifty, and any sympathy he may once have had for down-and-out psychos had disappeared.

Jacobi took a turn at Tuohy, with one new result.

Tuohy now remembered that he might have seen a man standing in the parking lot when Carly checked in. He only saw the guy from the back. Tuohy said he was big, with square shoulders. He didn't remember seeing him before. He wondered now if Carly had freelanced this date.

A big man, seen from behind. Christ.

Was he throwing Jacobi a bone so we would let him out of the box?

Jacobi asked Tuohy, "Did you see his vehicle?"

"No."

"What was he wearing?"

"Fuck if I know."

"I want to clear you, Mr. Tuohy. I need your prints, et cetera."

Tuohy sighed, nodded.

Jacobi got up from the table and left the room.

CHAPTER 25

TWO HOURS AFTER bringing Tuohy in to Southern Station's Homicide Division, we had his statement, a ten-card of fingerprints that matched his prints already in the system, a cheek swab, and a bite impression.

He had also submitted to Conklin taking photos of his naked arms and upper torso. His body was clean, but Tuohy wasn't happy.

I thought he might bite *me*.

I assigned a uniform to drive the motel troll home and stashed all the physical evidence we'd collected from him into the overnight pouch for the forensics lab.

There was takeout Italian dinner in a bag on Jacobi's desk when Conklin and I went in to tell him good night.

I asked my boss and former partner, "What do you think?"

"I'm not convinced either way," said Jacobi. "He had means and opportunity, and if he's a psycho, opportunity could've been his motive. He knew the girl. She could have let him into the room. They got into something. He killed her. But

82

that's 'what if,' Boxer. Pure speculation. Until Washburn and Clapper weigh in, I'm not putting down any bets."

Which meant he wasn't going to ask the DA to get an arrest warrant, or search warrants for Tuohy's domicile, office, and car. There was no probable cause. We were lucky to get exclusionary prints and DNA.

I nodded my agreement. Any guy walking past Carly's door could have pushed her in and killed her. He might've even had a clean white shirt in his suitcase.

"You did good," Jacobi said to me and Conklin.

It was after 9:00 p.m. when Conklin and I got into our car and headed out toward Russian Hill.

Carly Myers had been murdered. How, by whom, and why were still pieces of a mystery, and that was devastating. We weren't quite back to square one, but we might as well have been.

Where were Susan and Adele?

No freaking clue.

Conklin and I parked on Filbert Street in front of a nice apartment building where the Myers family lived, waiting for us to bring them good or at least hopeful news.

Tragically, all we had was that Carly had been murdered in a motel frequented by prostitutes on possibly the skeeziest block in the city. We didn't have a suspect, but to stem the grief over Carly's death, we would promise to find her killer.

Right now that promise wouldn't hold a drop of water.

My partner and I got out of the car and psychologically buckled up. What we had to tell Carly's parents was going to change their lives forever.

CHAPTER 26

I'D LEFT JOE sleeping when I headed out of our apartment before seven this morning.

Now, fifteen hours later, I was done and done in. All the lights were on in the living room when I shuffled through the front door. I dropped my keys onto the console, stowed my gun belt in the cabinet, and hugged my dog.

I called out to Joe, but he didn't answer.

I wanted to tell him all about my day. The leads that had run us into stone walls, a killer who'd scrubbed away evidence, and maybe worst of all, parents who wanted to die rather than live without their murdered daughter.

When Jacobi gets stuck on a case, he turns it upside down, looks at it from a different person's point of view, or from an opposite angle. I turned my case over as I unlaced my shoes.

Three women had last been seen leaving a restaurant bar after having a good time. They'd been drinking, but none of them had been stumbling drunk.

One of them had been found three days later, a day and a half postmortem, hanged from a shower head in a motel that she'd frequented in her part-time night job as a prostitute.

That was a mindblower from any angle, but I turned it over in my brain. Was Carly broke?

A drug addict?

Under someone's thumb?

Her sometimes date, Tom Barry, had told us that Carly had a dark side. Jake Tuohy had said she was turning tricks—not what I'd thought Barry meant by "dark side."

Was this possible? Schoolteacher by day, whore by night?

Karin Slaughter, the assistant dean, was Carly's friend. She would have rung the bell if Carly were using drugs. Carly's parents weren't wealthy but surely could have helped her out if she couldn't make do on her $70K annual salary. As far as I could tell, she had a safety net. So—why turn to prostitution?

In fact, we had only Jake Tuohy's word for that.

Similarly, Adele and Susan had friends, jobs, parents. They, too, seemed to have safety nets. But you never knew what was going on beneath the surface. Had their support systems failed?

Were they alive, in mortal danger? Or were they in similar creepy motel rooms, hanged by their necks, as yet undiscovered?

The search warrants for all three of the women's apartments had been executed, and no additional phones, laptops, or tablets had been found.

I had interviewed Adele's roommate, Patricia Sanders, who was torn up by fear. She had no idea what could have happened to her friend. According to Patricia, Adele had left for work on Monday morning, running late. She'd said she was going out for dinner and thrown a kiss as she raced out the door.

The roommate confirmed that Adele carried her phone and a laptop in a shoulder bag.

CSI had the electronics, and so far nothing had jumped out of them, making it more certain that the women had been nabbed by a person or persons they hadn't known.

At the same time, there had been no ransom notes or calls to any of the women's parents, and the hounds hadn't picked up a scent of any of the three women beyond the Bridge's parking lot.

If this was an abduction, how had it happened? By force? Willingly? And if willingly, what had the kidnapper used to bait the hook?

My shoes were off and lined up under the coatrack.

Martha was wriggling in front of my knees and telling me she'd missed me. I grabbed her up and kissed her and snuggled her. After telling my sweet doggy girl how much I loved her, I went into the living room to find Joe.

CHAPTER 27

I FOUND MY Joe reclined in his big chair, papers stacked around him, his laptop open on his thighs, and deep in sleep.

It was after ten o'clock and I wanted to sleep, too, but I wanted to talk to Joe more. Maybe my own special agent would see a flaw in my reasoning or a door I hadn't opened.

I called his name, walked over, and kissed his head, and he started awake.

"Joe, honey," I said. "I really need to talk to you."

He righted his chair into a sitting position and said, "I really need to talk to you, too. In fact, I may need to talk to you more."

"You first," I said to my man. "But I have a confession. I stink."

"Do not."

"*Do.*"

By the time I'd showered, gotten into pj's, and made ham

and mayo sandwiches with tea for two, Joe was back with Martha from their nighttime walk around the block.

I brought our dinner over to the coffee table, and Joe and I relaxed into the inviting embrace of the long leather sofa. I urged Joe to start talking. And he did.

"It's about Anna," he said. "Anna is the woman I met sitting on Golden Gate Avenue."

"I know who you mean."

"Well, here's the thing. I didn't open a case file on her that night. She looked like she'd been through hell, and I was right. In fact, I didn't know a fraction of it. So I said 'screw protocol' and gave her a lift home."

"That doesn't sound so bad, Joe. You can walk the protocol back, right?"

Joe picked up his sandwich, looked at it as though he'd never seen such a thing before, and put it back down on the plate.

"I should have done it before I started investigating Slobodan Petrović. I didn't know if Anna's story was for real or if she was having flashbacks to the nightmare of nightmares. If I'd opened a file, she would have had to meet with a duty officer and she would have been questioned. Extensively. What if he didn't believe her? There was a good chance of that. And Bosnia isn't exactly on our patch.

"I didn't think it through."

I remembered Joe's face when he told me Anna's story on the night he'd met her. He'd been this close to breaking down when he told me about the scorched-earth destruction of her town. The savage murders of her husband and child.

"You did the humane thing, hon. Subjecting Anna to an

FBI grilling without first vetting her story could have been worse for her, and you, too."

"That's what I told myself. But what I'm doing now, having people in other offices do research, digging into government files on behalf of my concern for this woman…I'm acting like I'm a PI, not a federal agent. It's inexcusable. Let me be more precise: I could get beached."

Joe Molinari was a straight arrow. Solid. Honest. Some would say a hero. He'd taken a hell of a chance for a stranger. A woman. I tried not to let that bother me.

I asked, "What can you do to fix this?"

"Now that I've gone this far, I want to bring this to the supervisor as a real thing. If Petrović is living on Fell Street legally, I want to know how that happened. Why is he here? Is he in a witness protection program? Is he being managed? What's his deal? If Anna is wrong and this is a Petrović look-alike, I'll talk her down and save her the grief of being interrogated by the FBI. And I'll fess up."

"That shouldn't take too long," I said.

He shrugged. "I have to work this myself, not get anyone else involved. Anyway, your turn. Tell me."

He didn't have to convince me. I was dying to tell him about my day.

CHAPTER 28

JOE AND I changed positions on the sofa. I lay down with my head in Joe's lap, and he stroked my hair. I told him how good it felt. He smiled, but it didn't quite take. He looked as wrung out as I felt.

I put it out there; that we'd found Carly's dead body, that it appeared to be homicide.

"I heard something about a dead woman found in the Big Four."

"That's her."

"Oh, man. Too bad, Linds."

I filled Joe in on the details, including the shocker that she'd checked into the motel alone, and that according to the manager, she'd done it before.

"He said she was a prostitute."

"No kidding. The schoolteacher?"

"So said the manager. Right now I have nothing to support that. But, Joe, if Carly was a party girl, *anyone* could have killed her."

Joe commiserated, encouraged me to keep talking.

I said, "The manager says he may have seen her date, but only from the back. He says Carly had a pimp named Danny or Denny, he doesn't know. Our night shift is showing Carly's picture around, talking to their CIs about her and this possible Danny or Denny. And here's a surprise. None of the hotel guests heard or saw anything suspicious while Carly was at the Big Four.

"These three women were having good lives by nearly any standard. What am I missing?"

Joe said, "Maybe it wasn't them. It was him. What kind of person would have done this?" His anger was right there, just below the surface. Was he thinking about Petrović and Anna? What kind of man had committed this shocking crime?

I said, "I think her killer was careful. Organized. This wasn't an amateur job. My guess is he's killed before."

"I couldn't agree more."

I pictured the three women leaving the Bridge feeling happy, maybe a little tired, tipsy...what had happened?

"Joe, there's no sign of a struggle in the parking lot outside the Bridge. Assuming the women were offered a lift back to the school after dinner. Say the driver saw an opportunity. Why did these women get into that car?"

"Was it raining?"

"Nope."

"Maybe they trusted him."

I smiled at him, squeezed his hand.

"Or one of them did."

He said, "You're in the early stages of the investigation. You need more information, Linds. Want to go to bed and sleep on it?"

Sounded good to me. I cleaned up while Joe stacked the dishes in the dishwasher. A few minutes later I met the man I loved in the bedroom. We got under the covers, and Martha climbed in between us.

We all slept.

CHAPTER 29

MY EYES FLASHED open at some dark hour.

I couldn't remember the whole of my dream, but the fragment that remained was a picture of Carly, Adele, and Susan climbing into a vehicle outside the Bridge.

Now my conscious mind kicked in.

If the three women had gotten into a car with a killer, how was it that twenty-four hours later, Carly had checked into the Big Four Motel alone?

Big question: Where had she been during that time?

If Carly had been tricking, *any* smart and careful psychopath could have killed her in room 212.

I was scared.

I was afraid that this case could be an endless ball of string that would be unsolved for the next twenty years. Or it could go cold forever.

Next unrelenting question: Where were Adele and Susan?

Joe said, "You can't sleep, either?"

"Oh, damn. I didn't mean to wake you up."

"I was awake. I can't turn off my brain."

Martha rolled onto her back and I mindlessly rubbed her belly.

"I've got unsolved murders running through my head," I said.

"And I've got voices talking to me," said Joe.

He rolled toward me. "The voices are saying, 'Get it together, you dumb shit.'"

"That's just *mean* of your voices."

Joe sighed and reached for me.

Martha jumped off the bed and I went into Joe's arms.

We comforted each other, and then we made love, and fell asleep again until the sun came through the bedroom window.

It was Friday morning. I was primary on a sickening case, and I still had no clues. I had to go to work.

CHAPTER 30

BY EIGHT THIRTY that morning Conklin and I were at our facing desks trying to get a lead on Nancy Koebel, the housekeeper who'd come upon the gruesome scene in room 212.

Then she'd vanished.

Her phone number came up as a prepaid phone, a burner. I called Tuohy, and he told me once again that it was the only number he had for her.

"She's only been here for a coupla months."

"Thanks," I barked at him. This guy really pissed me off.

I went back to my computer.

Koebel's name was absent from the DMV, SFPD, NCIC, and other available criminal databases. Did she get payroll checks from the Big Four—or was she paid off the books? Did she pay taxes? I doubted it. I couldn't find a trace of her.

"She's undocumented," I said to Conklin. I was taking an educated guess.

That's when Clapper called.

Maybe he'd found evidence on Carly Myers's body.

"Hold a sec," I said, "I'm putting you on speaker."

I stabbed the button on my phone console.

Hellos were exchanged, then Clapper said, "What do you want first? Bad news or good?"

"Bad," I said. "Don't cushion it."

"Inventory of Carly's handbag: two textbooks, American history, Western civ. Hefty makeup kit. Pair of sneakers and two white socks. Miscellaneous pads and pens. A strip of condoms. Phone and charger. Laptop and charger. We've run down the numbers and email; she shops and pays her bills online. Nothing pops."

"Shit."

Clapper kept going.

"Meanwhile, here's something to keep hope alive. We've impounded the ATM from the Stop 'n Go facing across Polk toward the back of the motel," he said. "We're taking it apart and should know shortly if the camera was working, the disk was usable, the lens was clean. If all that's a go, we'll see if it captured anything useful."

"Good," I said, crossing my fingers.

Clapper said, "I'm being paged, but we finished processing Carly Myers's body down at the morgue last night. Claire has my detailed notes. Call me if you have questions."

I had questions. Lots of them.

I shouted, "Charlie, wait."

"Can't," he said. "Boxer. Go to the morgue. Claire's waiting for you. And keep the faith."

He hung up.

I looked at my partner. "Ready?"

"You go. Take notes. I'll keep working on Koebel."

Fine.

I jogged down the four flights of stairs to the lobby and out the back door, and then power walked three hundred yards to the ME's office. I pulled open the heavy glass door.

It was closing in on 9:00 a.m., and the waiting room was filled with several cops and civilians who were likely family members waiting for autopsy results.

I opened my jacket, flashed my badge at the new receptionist, and told her that Dr. Washburn was waiting for me.

The receptionist pressed the intercom button on her phone and said, "Doctor, Sergeant Boxer is here." Then, to me, "Go ahead."

She buzzed open the inner door.

Several people who were waiting their turn saw this exchange and gave me hard looks.

Well. I was on the job.

I headed back to the autopsy suite. It was still early in the investigation, but maybe Claire would give me one tidbit or even, God willing, a eureka that would lead us to a killer and maybe from there to the two still-missing women.

Claire, San Francisco's chief medical examiner and my best bud, was suited up in baby-blue gown, cap, and gloves. She said, "I've got you a set of clothes over there, Lindsay. See it?"

There was a pile of blue cotton scrubs folded on a metal stool, necessary attire to prevent contamination of Carly Myers's body.

When I was properly dressed, I moved in.

Claire and I bumped our gloved fists, what Claire's little girl, Rosie, calls an elephant kiss. We grinned and then turned our attention to Carly Myers. She was draped with a sheet from her knees to her armpits.

Claire told me, "Obviously, I haven't begun the internal autopsy yet, but I have a few useful notes and one thing that has me completely stumped."

"Start there," I said.

"What? You want to spoil all my fun?"

"God forbid. Start where you like. It's your party and I'm in your house."

CHAPTER 31

CLAIRE OPENED THE victim's mouth and shined her flashlight inside.

She said, "Look here, Lindsay. Call this confirmation of what you suspected. In a death by hanging, you'll usually find the tongue is cut from biting."

Carly's tongue looked intact to me.

I said, "So she was dead when she was hanged."

"Yes, that's my opinion. I found petechial hemorrhaging in the eyes and bruising around the neck. The cricoid cartilage in the neck was fractured. This doesn't happen with ligature strangulation."

"What then? Manual strangulation?"

"That is correct, my dear sergeant."

Claire showed me the bruises around Carly's throat that had been covered by the collar of the white shirt.

Claire said, "And look here. Abrasions on her knees, forearms, and here, the base of her palms. This might have happened if she tried to get away from her attacker and fell when he overpowered her."

Those abrasions had been hidden by shirttails and pink panties around her wrists when I saw Carly's body in the shower. If she'd been attacked in the motel room, carpet fibers might be embedded in her scraped knees. If she'd been attacked outside, she should have traces of dirt from a lawn or a road or a parking lot, or even carpet from the inside of a vehicle.

That kind of evidence could be a break for the good guys.

I asked, "What kind of trace did CSI find in the wounds?"

"Linds, I hate to tell you this, but Clapper himself swabbed those abrasions last night, and it's his opinion that the body is squeaky clean."

I asked, "How squeaky? You're not saying she was washed?"

"Clapper thinks so. When the DNA tests come back, he'll be able to say with certainty, but from the first pass, this is what he got. They combed out her hair and found no foreign particles. No trace under her nails. They swabbed the bite mark on her neck, and that swab has gone off to the lab. The shampoo bottle that was found in the bathroom was empty, and even with decomp, you can smell the soap on her. Chamomile."

"Nuts. Her killer really cleaned up after himself."

"He's smart enough. If he had sex with her, he used a condom and left no trace on the bed—or anywhere."

"There were towels missing," I said.

"So he put them on the bed to protect the spread. Huh. Possible."

"What else?" I asked.

Claire told me that she had sent out the sexual assault kit and the blood samples, that there was zero chance that results would come back until after the weekend—if then.

"We're looking at weeks for the DNA. I can only ring the fire alarm so many times," she told me, "and I've rung it quite a lot recently."

I remembered the many times I'd stood in this room with Claire, using logic and forensic pathology to puzzle out what had happened to the person on the table who couldn't tell us anything.

Claire waggled her fingers in front of my face.

"You still with me, Linds?"

I snapped out of my thoughts and said, "Absolutely. We have to wait for the sexual assault kit to come back."

"Correct," she said. "But I'm not done here. Not by far."

CHAPTER 32

"OKAY," CLAIRE SAID. "CSI found nothing at all on the shirt. It's a common brand, all cotton, size 2XL, available for purchase in twenty thousand stores all over the country and online, priced between twelve and twenty bucks, made in China."

I sighed, long and loudly.

Claire didn't notice. She said, "The shirt hadn't been worn until Carly's dead body was dressed in it."

"Great," I said sadly.

If the doer had a new shirt handy, it pointed to a premeditated crime, either specific to Carly or in general if a choice opportunity arose.

"And what about Carly's own clothes that were left on the motel room floor?"

"They were worn, but there was no blood or dirt or anything that would lead anywhere. I do have something for you, though."

"Please, Claire, make my day."

She smiled. She was enjoying herself. But hell, this was a rough job, and if someone had to oversee twelve hundred autopsies a year, best if it was someone who enjoyed her work.

"I've taken photos of her injuries," said Claire, "including these."

She pulled down the sheet, exposing Carly's torso. She had large bruises on her body from chest to hips, and there was more: a half dozen discrete wounds in Carly's flesh, three inches long, like knife wounds in a random pattern.

Claire said, "She was beaten over a couple days' time, but these wounds are fresh. She's got similar wounds on her back and buttocks."

"What the hell are they?"

Claire said, "I'm asking the same question. The incisions are shallow and were made by an unusual kind of blade. Check this out. There's no collateral bruising at the point of entry."

"Meaning?"

"The blade was beveled and double-edged and super sharp. I can't yet identify the implement—that's good. It wasn't any kind of knife I've seen. So if you find the weapon, you may find the killer."

"Were the cuts made premortem or post?"

"She was alive," Claire told me. "And that also supports Clapper's opinion that this body was washed. Even though these cuts were shallow, Carly had to have bled. But there's no sign of blood.

"That said, keep in mind that these wounds didn't kill her, Lindsay. She was strangled. That's a man's crime."

"So, unofficially . . ." I said, prompting her.

"Unofficially, manner of death: homicide. Cause of death: asphyxiation by manual strangulation. I'll call you," she said. "Right after I do the internal post."

CHAPTER 33

CLAIRE'S RECEPTIONIST ELBOWED the door open and said, "Sergeant, Inspector Conklin called. He's waiting upstairs for you."

I told Claire, "Thanks. Talk to you later," and left the ME's office, taking the breezeway to the back entrance of the Hall's garnet-colored, marble-lined lobby. An elevator was waiting, and I rode it to four and then walked the short, brightly lit corridor to the homicide squad.

Conklin was sitting behind his desk—and Cindy sat behind mine. Even at that time, before they'd gotten together, there was chemistry between my friend and my partner, known by women in and around the Hall as Inspector Hottie. I'd liked seeing it.

Cindy said, "What can you tell me?"

It was quite bold of Cindy—coming to our house, taking my chair, making demands. She's infuriating and funny, often at the same time.

I smiled and said, "This is absolutely all I can tell you,

Cindy. You can say that the deceased is, in fact, Carly Myers and that the authorities are looking for anyone who may have seen her or her killer."

"Cause of death?"

"Still undetermined. Claire is doing the post now."

"So, a positive ID of Carly Myers, deceased. What about the other two women? By my calculations, they're still missing on day four."

"We're working on it. All of us." I waved my hand to encompass the squad room, which was largely empty.

"Okay. I'll do another blog post about the missing women."

"Good. Thanks. And here's something we haven't released," I said. "Nancy Koebel was a housekeeper at the Big Four. She disappeared. Can you say on your blog that the SFPD needs to get in touch with her? She may have seen or heard something regarding this crime."

I spelled Koebel's name, hoping that going public with that wouldn't drive her further underground.

Cindy closed her tablet and gathered her possessions, saying, "I've got some work to do. I'll speak to you later. That means both of you."

She waved in our direction and headed out.

Conklin followed her with his eyes.

"Back to work, Tiger," I said to him.

I filled him in on what I'd learned from Claire and Clapper.

"First and worst, Richie. No trace evidence has been found on Carly's body. Clapper thinks and Claire agrees that the body was washed to destroy evidence. There's also nothing of interest on Carly's phone or laptop as far as Clapper can tell. Blood and DNA swabs are out for analysis."

"Shit. The killer rolled up his trail," said Rich. "He threw her in the shower before he strung her up."

"Yep. And washed her down with the freebie shampoo. The shirt she was wearing is a generic men's cotton shirt that could have been purchased anywhere. Claire is positive—unofficially—that Carly was strangled manually. The electric cord wasn't the murder weapon."

"It was window dressing?" Conklin asked.

"Exactly," I said. "A distraction. A feint. An artistic touch."

I told my partner the Claire-stumping news that Carly had been cut in a dozen places front and back with a sharp unidentified blade that left an unusually shaped slit. I showed him the photo. "Narrow on both ends and broader in the center."

"What does Claire make of these…injuries?"

"She says that Carly was alive when she was cut. Some of the incisions were made like this."

I used a letter opener to demonstrate a slice to my forearm.

"Others were at an angle. One of the cuts just grazed her shoulder, opening a flap of skin."

"If the wounds weren't lethal, what was the point?" Conklin asked.

"I think he wanted to scare her, Rich. Or force compliance. Either way, Carly was tortured."

CHAPTER 34

JOE TAILED PETROVIĆ'S blue Jag from the yellow house on Fell, hanging back behind several cars at all times.

When the Jag pulled into a spot in front of Tony's Place for Steak on California, a valet appeared and ran around to open the driver-side door.

The man in the Jag was getting celebrity treatment.

Joe glimpsed only a blue-trousered leg and a shoe as he passed the driver disembarking from his car.

Blending into the stream of traffic, Joe drove east for another couple of blocks before turning right onto Mason Street. Then he wrapped around the block again and one more time until he was back on California.

He parked on Taylor and walked one long uphill to the steak house, entering at quarter to one. He took in the whole of the room from the entrance. It was densely carpeted, mirrored on both long walls, with chandeliers overhead casting a flattering light over the well-dressed lunchtime crowd seated in the red leather booths and at round tables down the center of the room.

There was a closed door to his right that looked like it went to a private dining room.

The maître d' approached.

Joe said, "I don't have a reservation. Can you fit me in?"

"I can give you a small table in the back."

"That'll be fine."

As he followed behind the maître d', Joe looked for the man who might be Petrović, but didn't see him. He took his seat with his back to the kitchen doors. A waiter introduced himself as Giorgio and asked Joe for his drink order. Joe went with sparkling water and accepted the menu.

It was a nice place, reminding him of the Palm in New York. The kitchen doors behind him swung open as elderly waiters in uniform came in and out with trays. Soon Giorgio returned and asked Joe if he was ready to order.

Joe asked for a New York strip steak, medium, with creamed spinach and a baked potato. When the waiter had gone, he thought about his conversation with Lindsay last night.

She'd advised him to get on the right side of this Petrović investigation. He knew he had to do it. But he didn't yet see how to get a green light from Steinmetz.

The kitchen doors swung open again and two men came out, passing by Joe's table.

One was of average height and build, wearing a gray suit. He had a thin mustache and gray hair. The other man was big, bulky, wearing blue serge, a white shirt, and a striped tie. Joe saw his face in profile as he said a few words to the man in gray. They were speaking Serbian.

There was no mistaking the bulky guy for anyone else.

He was Slobodan Petrović.

The man in gray was saying in Serbian basic enough for Joe to follow, "Tony, I just heard about it a minute ago. I can take care of her tonight."

Tony. Antonije Branko was Petrović's pseudonym. The two men were walking toward the front of the restaurant when Petrović paused midstep and pivoted back around.

Joe felt a shock to his heart.

It was clear that Petrović, too, had cop or military attentiveness. Petrović recognized him. It had just taken a moment for the cogs to engage, for him to place Joe's face.

Petrović took a few steps back toward Joe and stood at the table, looking down at him.

He said, "Well, hello. Nice to see you here. We've only just opened up again as Tony's. I'm Tony Branko," he said, sticking out his hand.

Joe shook Petrović's large hand, saying, "Nice place. Congratulations."

"And you are?"

"Molinari. Joe."

The man in blue released Joe's hand and asked, "Where's your girlfriend? The one who rides a bike past my house on Fell."

Shit. Petrović had seen Anna. Did he know who she was?

The waiter came to the table with Joe's lunch, saying, "Excuse, Mr. Branko," and put the plates down in front of Joe. "Can I get you something else?"

Joe said, "No, thanks. I'm all set," and the waiter disappeared.

Petrović remained at Joe's table. He didn't introduce the

man in gray standing uncomfortably a few feet away from him. He said to Joe, "You're a cop?"

Joe said, "Good call."

Petrović smiled. "Now I think *federal* cop. Hey. Molinari. If you need a girl, I mean another one, let me know. I think we could be friends."

And then he was gone.

Joe forced himself to eat, but he felt like an ass. He shouldn't have stopped. He should just have kept driving. What the hell was wrong with him?

He asked for the check, paid in cash, then, throwing down his napkin, he headed to the front of the restaurant. As he passed the private room just off the entrance, Petrović/Branko stood up from a table of male diners and leaned out of the room. He called after him, "I hope you found everything to your satisfaction, Joe Molinari. Come again."

Joe's face burned as he left the restaurant and walked downhill to his car.

CHAPTER **35**

IT WAS SATURDAY morning, five days since Carly Myers, Susan Jones, and Adele Saran had gone to work at Pacific View Prep School for what may have been the last time.

The task force on this case had taken over the squad room. Besides me and Conklin, McNeil and Chi, it now included two additional career homicide inspectors, Samuels and Lemke. Also present were a dozen volunteers from Robbery and Crimes Against Persons. Even our squad assistant, Brenda Fregosi, had come in this morning to make sure we had fresh coffee and eats.

At that moment we were watching the television hung high on the wall of the bullpen and centered directly over my desk and Conklin's.

On-screen, Jacobi was being interviewed by Kathy Cabot, a reporter from an NBC affiliate. Cabot was asking him to fill in the public on the missing schoolteachers.

Jacobi looked reassuringly in charge when the reporter said, "Lieutenant, people are frightened. What can you tell us about the Carly Myers murder?"

Jacobi said, "As has been recently reported, Carly Myers is a victim of a homicide. I'm sorry that I can't give you any details on our investigation, which is in progress."

"Do you have any information about Susan Jones? Adele Saran?"

Jacobi took two photos from inside the breast pocket of his coat and held them so that the camera could get a fix on them. "Susan Jones and Adele Saran have been missing since late Monday night. The entire police force is looking for them. The mayor has just authorized a twenty-five-thousand-dollar reward for information leading to the arrest and conviction of Carly Myers's killer, and the same amount each for information leading to the recovery of Susan Jones and Adele Saran. Call our hotline…" Jacobi read off the number.

Ms. Cabot had prepared for this announcement. The information appeared on the screen. She asked the public for their help, thanked Jacobi, and signed off, returning the viewing audience to the studio.

The camera took a parting shot of Jacobi climbing the stairs to the Hall. The shot was wide enough to take in the patrol cars blocking the press from coming into the building.

Back in the squad room, over a dozen worried and restless cops were feeling the pressure of the complicated unsolved homicide, plus our two missing persons.

I picked up the remote and muted the TV, gesturing at Conklin to take the floor.

CHAPTER 36

CONKLIN LEANED THE whiteboard against the easel we'd set up at the front of the room.

Behind me, cops had wheeled chairs into the aisle of our small, crowded bullpen. They all knew the faces of the schoolteachers, but even so, I clipped their photos to the top of the board.

Lemke moved closer and said, "Damned shame, Boxer. We're going to find them."

Cappy McNeil stood and faced the group. A heavy, bald man with a bulldog face and a gravelly voice, Cappy sounded depressed as he summarized the notes he and Paul Chi had gathered from their interviews with twenty-six motel guests.

"The interviews fall into three types," he said. "'Don't know anything about it,' 'Didn't see anything,' and 'Was in my room minding my own business. Can I go now?'"

There was a smattering of laughter, then Cappy summed up the guests' rap sheets. None of the twenty-six were totally clean, but there were no suspects convicted of crimes against persons.

Paul Chi took over for his partner. Chi had a sharp mind and a mild manner. Many saw him as having a big future in the SFPD.

He told the group that news of the murder and presumed kidnappings had gone viral. The parents had been interviewed and had made pleas for information, telling their daughters, "If you're watching, we love you. We want you home."

From the blanket coverage in all media, including social, the tip lines had yielded a flood of phone traffic but very little actionable information.

Chi said, "As of an hour ago we have one promising lead.

"Edna Gutierrez, who works at a nearby laundromat. She called in a description of a man in a dark-colored SUV who had dropped off a woman who looked like Carly Myers in front of the Big Four Motel at around 10:00 p.m. last Tuesday night.

"Ms. Gutierrez came in to see the lieutenant this morning. Boxer, you have the tape?"

I cued up the audio of Ms. Gutierrez relaying these facts to Jacobi, boosted the volume, and let it roll.

Ms. Gutierrez told Jacobi that the SUV looked new and it was black or blue. The windows were too dark for her to see the driver, and she couldn't give any kind of description. But she firmly believed that the woman he'd dropped off in front of the motel's office was Carly Myers.

"I'm sure it was her. Almost sure."

Hardly bulletproof testimony, but it was something.

I had diagramed the whiteboard, pinpointing the dates and highlights of the case. I used a laser pointer to give me something to do with my hands.

I took the squad through the last five days, from the time the three women ordered dinner and drinks at the Bridge. I'd inked in a big black star on the board over the words *Day Three, Thursday.*

I said, "This was the day that the motel manager, Jake Tuohy, called us to report the dead body hanging in the shower of room 212. He told us—and this is unconfirmed—that Carly Myers was turning tricks. Also reported by Tuohy, she may have had a pimp called Danny or Denny. He can't or won't describe him."

I asked the room, "Anyone know of such a person?"

No one answered, but I saw some taking notes.

I said, "There's another missing person. Nancy Koebel is the housekeeper who found the body."

I laid it out.

According to Tuohy, after Koebel told him about the body, she was hysterical, grabbed her purse, and ran out to the street, never to be seen or heard from since. We had no picture of her. Her phone was a prepaid burner, and she wasn't answering our calls.

Conklin added, "She may have been spooked by the murder, or maybe the doer saw her and she has good reason to be freaked. She's a critical witness."

Inspector Joy Robinson piped up from the back. "Or the killer knows her and offed her to stop her from talking."

Conklin nodded, put down his pointer. "Alive or dead, we need to find her. Alive is preferable."

We all looked toward the squad room entrance when someone entered, standing off to the side of Brenda's desk.

"Sorry to interrupt," he said into the silence.

John Clark was a senior video tech from our forensics lab. I knew him, and when I read his expression, I felt a small surge of hope.

"You've got something?" I asked.

"Maybe," Clark said. "I think maybe I do."

CHAPTER 37

AS SOON AS Clark made his report, I called an impromptu working lunch with my best friends and members
of the Women's Murder Club.

We were all working that weekend—that's how alarmed
we were that the women were still freaking missing.

The Women's Murder Club met at MacBain's, the bar
and grill located across and down the street from the Hall of
Justice. We had all arrived by quarter to twelve, before the
lunchtime crush, to snag our favorite spot: the small table
with high stools by the window at the front of the room.
With luck, we'd get our order in to the kitchen before it was
overwhelmed.

We'd done this for years, since Cindy helped me solve a
gruesome double murder back in the day. She had jokingly
named us the Women's Murder Club and it had stuck. Now,
whenever any of us had a knotty problem, love or work or
what not to wear, the four of us would get together and kick
it around.

I signaled to Sydney MacBain, our favorite waitress, and she hustled over to take our order, the usual—burgers, fries, and beer times four. She gave a rare smile, told Claire she looked pretty in pink, and headed off toward the kitchen. Meanwhile, the room was filling up. The jukebox was rocking. And laughter ricocheted from wall to wall.

This was a conference, but apart from being geographically desirable, MacBain's was nothing like a conference room. We put our heads together, literally, so that we could hear and be heard. Cindy was sworn to keep everything we said off the record, and she snorted her annoyance. "When are you going to trust me, hmmm? How many more years?"

"We trust you," we said in unison.

I added, "If I don't say it, I'm negligent in my duties. Don't take it personally, Cin. Please. Okay?"

She tossed her head, said, "Okay, okay," then asked me, "What news on Carly Myers?"

I said, "An hour ago I would've said we'd hit a wall."

"And now?" Cindy asked.

I filled my friends in on the hot news delivered to us direct from our forensics lab.

"The ATM at the deli across Polk Street and facing the back of the now infamous Big Four Motel captured three images of a man who might be a suspect in Carly Myers's murder."

Yuki said, "Can you show us?"

"Here you go."

There, on my phone, was the lab's photographic reconstruction of ATM snapshots taken from a hundred yards away of a man moving along the motel's second-floor walkway. A floodlight in the parking lot illuminated this individual, but he was captured by the camera at an oblique angle. The reconstruction had sharpened the man's features.

I said, "From what our lab techs can determine, he's in his mid-thirties, sandy-colored hair, five ten, and fit. They've refined his facial features as much as possible, but they don't match with anything in ViCAP or DMV."

Yuki asked, "What makes you think he has anything to do with Carly Myers?"

"Only this," I said. "It looks like he's leaving the second floor, and the photo is time-stamped Tuesday night, 11:23. Carly was probably killed right around then. And one other thing. A woman called the hotline saying she saw a dark-colored SUV drop Carly off at the motel on Tuesday night. I pointed to one of the photos of Mr. X, which included a lengthwise section of a dark-colored SUV parked a few yards from the subject in question.

"Crap," said Cindy. "The license plate isn't showing."

I said, "You stole my line. Cindy, I'll give you this photo of an unnamed male when it's cleared for takeoff. But right now we need to find him, not send him running over the border.

"But," I went on, "I do have something for you to run with your reward-for-information story. No one else has this."

"Now you're talking," Cindy said.

"The assistant dean at Carly's school, name of Karin Slaughter, gave it to me to use as we see fit."

I showed Cindy a sweet photo of Carly, Adele, and Susan taken at the Bridge the previous week. The women were relaxed at a table and had pulled their chairs close enough to put their arms around one another.

Last week when this picture was taken, a tragedy was waiting for them in the wings.

But at that moment they all looked very happy.

CHAPTER 38

AFTER LUNCH WE said our good-byes outside of MacBain's. Cindy cabbed it home, Yuki walked up the street to an off-site meeting, and Claire and I headed back to the Hall together.

As we walked toward the intersection of Bryant and Harriet Streets, Claire said, "I've got some breaking news for you."

"Really? I'm listening."

"The tox screen came back. Carly was drugged with Rohypnol. Large dose."

"Carly was roofied?"

Claire went on. "The sexual assault kit came back, too."

I grabbed her arm and looked at her.

"Give me something good."

The traffic light changed and we crossed the street. I couldn't wait for Claire to start talking again.

When we were standing on the far side of the intersection and Claire was about to take the turn to her office, she said, "There was no semen present, but we did find condom lubrication. On a hunch, I gave her a pelvic exam. I found one pubic hair. One. And it's not Carly's."

I said, "Wow. That could be a breakthrough."

Claire said, "It's very good news, but I don't have to tell you, that piece of evidence is going to have to get into line for DNA comparison."

"Claire. Can't we jump to the front of the line? Use your considerable influence, will you?"

"Linds. Every cop in the city is trying to shove to the front of the line. But I will definitely lean on a few people."

I thanked her, hugged her, waved good-bye, and carried on down Bryant to the main entrance to the Hall.

I crossed the mostly empty lobby and headed for the elevator, thinking about Claire's news, imagining Carly's last moments.

I saw her waiting outside the Bridge, getting into a car with or without her girlfriends. Twenty-four hours later she checked into the Big Four. Where had she been during that twenty-four hour gap, and had she been with whoever had picked her up at the Bridge?

Maybe her driver or date or customer had driven her to the Big Four the next night and waited there while she checked into room 212, then parked his car at the back and met her upstairs.

If I was seeing this right, whoever this guy was, he'd planned his night with Carly. It was premeditated. Up in the room, he'd given her a drink of something that had been loaded with the powerful knockout drug Rohypnol.

She'd gone down.

While she was unconscious, Carly's attacker had spread towels down on the bed and done horrific things to her. He'd sliced her, raped her, strangled her, dressed her in some items from his sick imagination, then hanged her corpse from the shower head.

He was good. But not perfect.

He'd left his calling card behind: a short hair with a skin tag, a neat little bundle of his telltale DNA.

We finally had a real lead.

I hoped like mad it would take us to Carly's killer.

CHAPTER 39

JOE HAD MET with Anna over the weekend to prepare for their Monday-morning meeting with supervisor Craig Steinmetz.

At 9:00 a.m. they sat at right angles to each other on the squared-off leather sectional in the FBI's thirteenth-floor reception area.

Joe glanced over at Anna.

She seemed unperturbed, buds in her ears, eyes closed. A curtain of brown hair hid the terrible scar on her face. Joe flashed back to last week, Anna telling him in the dark of his car how Petrović had burned her with a cigarette lighter, men holding her down as he raped her.

Then and now, Joe felt enraged. It was all he could do to sit still in his seat. He thought about Anna and the hundreds of other women who had lived and died in that "hotel."

He drummed his fingers on his knees and turned his eyes to the FBI seal hanging on the wall opposite the sofa. The medallion was round, blue and gold, with the words

Department of Justice and *Federal Bureau of Investigation* encir-
cling the outer rim, enclosing a circle of stars. At the center
of the seal was a shield made up of red and white stripes and
the scales of justice.

Beneath the scales were the words *Fidelity, Bravery,* and
Integrity.

Another way of spelling *FBI.* These were the values he'd
built his life around since joining the Bureau.

He was startled out of his thoughts as he heard his name.

Supervisor Craig Steinmetz came through the doorway
and asked him to come in. "Joe. Just you."

Joe followed Steinmetz down the hallway to the corner
office and took the chair across from his desk. Like his own
office, this one was uncluttered, had a flag in the corner, and
featured the seal on one wall, a couple of framed certifi-
cates and pictures with past presidents on another. In the
picture with President George W. Bush, a younger Captain
Steinmetz wore his USMC uniform with rows of ribbons
over his left breast.

Joe knew Steinmetz's history.

After his last tour in Afghanistan, Steinmetz had joined
the FBI to head up an antiterrorism division for a dozen
years at Quantico, where Joe had met him. Then he'd led the
San Francisco branch for the last five years.

Steinmetz was unlikely to cut Joe a break for old times'
sake, and Joe had prepared himself for the possibility that
he could get jammed up for conducting an unauthorized
surveillance, which he'd done. Without an open case or a
preliminary inquiry, he'd probably get time on the beach
without pay.

Putting that possibility aside, Joe looked across at his supervisor and laid his weak cards on the table, knowing the conversation had to be recorded.

"A nationalized American, Anna Sotovina, originally from Bosnia, was riding her bike on Fell Street last Wednesday afternoon and sees a war criminal, Slobodan Petrović, coming down the steps of his house and getting into his car. She's sure it's him, and she follows him. On her bike. Several blocks later she gets sideswiped by a car. Walks the bike a couple of miles to us.

"I saw her sitting outside the building. She was banged up, and her bike…" Joe threw up his hands and then continued. "She wanted to make a report, but our security turned her away. She was hysterical, looked like she'd been in a fight or was living rough, and maybe she seemed irrational. Anyway, I asked her name and what was wrong. She told me she'd seen this war criminal from her past life. I drove her home, and while in the car, she told me that she had lived in Djoba and survived Petrović's massacre."

Steinmetz said, "Can you hang on a minute?"

He stepped outside his office, asked his assistant to postpone his next meeting, then returned to his desk.

He said, "I know what happened in Djoba. I'm listening."

CHAPTER 40

JOE PICKED UP where he'd left off.

"Anna is sure the man she saw that morning was Petrović. She seemed credible, but I couldn't know. Was she right? Or having flashbacks because of a man who resembled Petrović? I decided to vet her story and see if we should look into it."

Steinmetz looked at his watch, then told Joe to keep going.

Joe said, "Almost done. Day after running into Sotovina, I met with her near the place where she'd seen this man. He appeared, coming down his front steps. I took his photo, but it was in profile, and his hand and phone obscured much of his face. He looked like the pictures I've seen of Petrović, but I couldn't be sure.

"I reached out to Nguyen in Virginia to make the shot usable, and then I got a match. The man Sotovina saw is, in fact, Slobodan Petrović, now using the name Antonije Branko."

Steinmetz's eyes widened. Joe guessed he was alarmed

that Joe had gotten Nguyen involved without having a case number. Or maybe he was reacting to the frankly shocking news that Petrović's ID and fake ID had been confirmed.

One thing seemed sure. Steinmetz couldn't be happy that Joe had begun running an operation without clearance.

The branch supervisor shook his head, ran his hands through his hair, and swiveled his chair right to left and back again, settling in Joe's direction.

He said, "I get the feeling there's more."

"Well, yes. Yesterday I followed Petrović into a steak house on California. I ordered lunch. Ten minutes later he comes out of the kitchen, and he's clearly the boss. It gets worse. He made me from when I took his picture. And he connected me to Sotovina."

"Oh, that's just great," Steinmetz said. "And after you choked on your steak, what did you do?"

Joe apologized. He couldn't remember ever having to do such a thing professionally, but he knew making contact with Petrović had been a serious error in judgment.

"What I know now is that Petrović was tried for war crimes and crimes against humanity at the ICC and released. Now he's living high and he opened this restaurant. According to police records, he's been questioned twice in the last two years for associating with drug dealers but so far hasn't crossed the line."

Steinmetz said, "So you have nothing on him."

"Not exactly nothing. I've confirmed that he's a mass murderer using a fake name and flying as free as a bird in San Francisco. Craig, what's he doing here? Do you know?"

Steinmetz didn't answer, but he asked Joe a dozen

questions, all of them about Joe's motive for taking on a possible career-ending flier outside the Bureau's bounds and regulations.

He established that Joe hadn't taken money or used Anna to advance his career, hadn't betrayed the Bureau or the government, and had brought this off-road investigation to Steinmetz before going any further.

Steinmetz said, "Assure me that you're not having a relationship with this woman."

Joe said, "There's nothing between us and there will never be."

Steinmetz dotted some i's on his notepad, crossed a couple of t's, then turned off the recorder.

He said, "I'll be ready to see the witness in a half hour."

CHAPTER 41

ANNA HAD PLUGGED back into her music when Steinmetz opened the reception room door and said, "Ms. Sotovina, I'm ready to see you now."

Joe made the awkward introductions, then returned to his seat on the rigid sectional. He stared ahead through the wall-to-wall glass at a gray sky and replayed his meeting with Steinmetz. Of course, he hadn't been able to read the supervisor's mind. He didn't know if he'd be working the Petrović case even if Steinmetz found Anna believable.

Joe had promised Anna he would get Petrović off the street, but even with a green light, it wouldn't be easy. As far as he knew, Petrović hadn't done anything criminal. Red-faced hog opens steak house: not exactly the crime of the century.

There was a good chance Steinmetz would shunt this investigation to the DC branch, and if so, Joe would have to roll with that and break his promise to Anna. This worried him. She'd told him more than once that she would shoot Petrović herself. He believed her.

Joe read a left-behind copy of the *Chronicle* until Anna returned to her seat and Steinmetz asked Joe to come back in. They stood together in the corridor, where Steinmetz said without expression or inflection, "You're approved to open a case on this suspicious person."

Joe felt a surge of relief. Steinmetz told him to keep him posted, and that if a case against Petrović didn't come together in the next thirty days, that would be the end of it.

Joe shook Steinmetz's hand.

"Craig. Thanks."

The door closed and Joe walked over to Anna, touched her arm.

"You did great. I'm officially working the case," he said.

Anna got to her feet and hugged Joe. "Thank you. I can't say how happy this makes me."

Joe said, "I'm glad. I'm very glad to be able to help. There's our elevator. Let's go."

CHAPTER 42

JOE WALKED ANNA out of the building and up Golden Gate Avenue three blocks to her small red Kia.

They talked about the meetings, and Joe commented that it was a small miracle that Steinmetz had gotten behind this. After all, Petrović hadn't committed a crime on US soil, as far as they knew.

"He will," Anna said.

"I'll try to be there when he screws up, and I'll let you know when I have news to report. But Anna, Petrović knows you ride past his house on your bike."

"He said that?"

"He saw us together last week. I don't know that he recognized you from Djoba, but don't give him a chance to think about you. For now, drive to work. And don't chase him."

Anna lowered her head and said, "You don't have to remind me. That was my last chase."

"I'm sorry. I didn't mean to scold. I'm worried that he could pop you from his front step. You know that better than I do."

She nodded vigorously. Then she hugged him again, hard.

Joe patted Anna's back, opened her car door, watched as she buckled in.

She said, "Thank you so much," with a breaking voice. "I thank you for my son and my husband."

Joe said, "Be safe," closed her door, and stood on the sidewalk as she drove away.

He headed back to the FBI building. Once he was inside his office, he locked his door, texted Lindsay: *It went well. I'll tell you all about it tonight.*

He booted up his computer and dug back into the files he'd begun collecting on the ethnic cleansing that had devastated Bosnia in the mid-1990s. The images came up on his screen and flooded his mind; stories told by the women separated from their families and brutalized, men detained and forced to sing Serbian songs and to commit sex acts upon one another as they waited to be executed.

There were fresh images now; Anna's half-told story of her imprisonment in a cell-like room in the rape hotel as the very men who'd killed her husband and child repeatedly assaulted her. One of them had been Petrović himself.

He remembered Anna's expression as she told him about the horrific assaults, and could almost feel her terror and revulsion, with the threat of imminent death something to wish for.

He got up, walked down the hall to the coffee room. Ten minutes later he was back at his desk, going through his files, looking for something that would reveal more about Slobodan Petrović.

Petrović was mentioned in hundreds of the documents Joe

had accumulated. His military career was all there; a soldier moving up steadily through the ranks, peaking with his command of the massacre at Djoba. There were photos of him in uniform inspecting a barn where dozens of people had hanged themselves from the rafters, choosing suicide over the torture and humiliation of death by Petrović's hands.

Joe stared at those bodies and at the shadows they cast on the floorboards, Petrović's sadistic smile and his triumphant expression.

There had been witnesses at Petrović's trial, but while Filip Nikolic and his top commanders had received life sentences, Petrović had been sentenced to only five years, despite the number of witnesses against him and the incontrovertible proof of his unspeakable crimes. Then Petrović had been released.

Joe got up from his desk, crossed his office, and leaned against the window frame as the sun sank below the shabby buildings across the street. His mind was still swimming in the horrors of the war in Bosnia, but it was time to narrow his focus to the commitments he had made. He was one man working from an office in San Francisco. He could probably get Steinmetz to assign another agent or two to this case, but unless or until he had something worth the manpower, he was working alone.

He'd promised Anna he'd try to neutralize Petrović. The other commitment, the official one, was to Steinmetz, either to make a case quickly or to walk away.

As of this moment, Joe didn't know if he could do either.

But he was determined to do his best.

CHAPTER 43

JOE WAS AT his desk at the San Francisco branch of the FBI, but his thoughts were in Quantico, Virginia.

As clearly as if he were there now, he remembered sitting at a long table in the basement conference room at Quantico. He had been a profiler with the Behavioral Science Unit. With him at that meeting had been a dozen and a half officers from the counterterrorism watch center: FBI, CIA, military.

He hadn't been thinking about Petrović when he'd been sitting in that subterranean room, watching the video that legal attachés from the American embassy in Sarajevo had sent by pouch—a video of the ICC tribunal handing sentences down to the convicted war criminals that stood before them.

The worst of them was Filip Nikolic, the commander responsible for eight thousand deaths in Srebrenica. More than five hundred witnesses had testified against him. More than ten thousand exhibits had been presented to the court, and after four years at trial, Nikolic was convicted and sentenced to life in prison.

Several high-ranking officers of the Serbian Army were also sentenced. The victims' families had crowded the courthouse and the streets around it to glimpse the monsters who had assassinated a hundred thousand civilians.

One of those grief-stricken wives, a young mother, told a reporter, "They had to be held responsible. But even with the justice done, there is nothing the tribunal could do that would be sufficient punishment for these men."

Joe was sure that Anna's feelings were the same.

There had been a more prominent person on trial, and her photos had flashed across the curved face of the old TV on its stand at the head of the table.

Jelena Jovanovic looked completely ordinary, a stiffly coiffed white woman of a certain age who would've been at home behind a counter in a department store or at a cocktail party in Georgetown. But the seventy-two-year-old woman was the former president of Serbia, known as the Iron Lady. Jovanovic had been an unapologetic proponent of ethnic cleansing of non-Serbs, Muslims in particular, calling the eradication of non-Serbian people a "natural phenomenon."

After governance issues and confrontations with her cronies, Jovanovic retired from politics. But she didn't get far enough to avoid scrutiny by the International Criminal Court.

The year following her retirement, Jovanovic learned that there was a sealed indictment against her containing numerous counts of genocide and crimes against humanity. She denied the crimes and voluntarily turned herself in to the ICC to stand trial.

While waiting for trial, Jovanovic had an apparent change of her so-called heart. She pleaded guilty on all counts and even recanted her earlier position, stating that the victims of her purge had been innocent.

Back at Quantico, Joe, along with members of the counterterrorism agencies, had watched the announcement of the trial chamber's decision. He had been stunned to hear the court announce that Jovanovic's confession and admission of guilt would be more meaningful to the survivors of the still war-torn country than a guilty verdict after a many-years-long trial.

Where was the justice in that?

In return for pleading guilty to war crimes, the genocide charges had been dropped. Jovanovic had been sentenced to fifteen to twenty-five years for crimes against humanity, but before serving a day, her sentence had been reduced to eleven years, to be served in a Swedish prison that featured all of the amenities of a first-class resort.

Later her sentence had been further reduced to five years for time served and good behavior, and at age seventy-nine, after six years of imprisonment, she had been released.

How had this happened?

Had Jovanovic gotten her break not just in exchange for her confession but for giving up information on other military officers, in this mother-of-all-grande-dame deals? The unbelievable kicker was that once she was free, Jovanovic retracted her confession in full, saying that she had confessed only in order to get a lenient sentence.

No kidding.

After reviewing the disposition of Jovanovic, Joe felt more

certain that Petrović was free because he, too, had gotten a plea deal.

Petrović had been a colonel. He had taken orders from generals who'd gotten life sentences for genocide and crimes against humanity.

Bigger fish.

If they were obtainable, Joe wanted both the facts on Petrović's deal and the terms of his release. For God's sake, how had it come to pass that the Butcher of Djoba had opened a steak house in San Francisco?

CHAPTER 44

JOE WAS HUNGRY, but he didn't want to stop his work to go home and eat.

It was still afternoon in DC.

Joe punched numbers for the State Department into his phone, and when his call was answered, he asked to speak with deputy director Brandon Reilly. The call was switched over and Reilly picked up.

After some catching up, Joe said to Reilly, "Do you remember a colonel in the Serbian Army named Slobodan Petrović?"

"That evil scumbag. I remember. He drowned or something, didn't he?"

"If only."

Joe sketched it in for Reilly, that Petrović was living in San Francisco, very much alive and well. Once he'd caught Reilly up, Joe made the ask: information on how the bastard had skated on a life sentence for war crimes and crimes against humanity.

Reilly said, "Hang on."

Joe did and was relieved when Reilly got back on the line.

"Molinari, still there?"

"Yes. What do you know?"

"It looks like Petrović rolled on a few people in the high command in exchange for immunity. There were seven indictments and convictions as the result of the information he turned over to the ICC."

"Son of a bitch."

Reilly went on.

"That's why he got a deal. Due to the number of enemies he acquired, he was given a new identity, passport included, and allowed to leave the country. He's now known as Antonije Branko."

Joe said, "What were the conditions of his release?"

"Only one," said Reilly. "If he commits a felony anywhere from Bosnia to the moon, the original sentence of life imprisonment will be reinstated."

"So as I understand you," Joe said, "if Petrović is convicted of a major crime, he goes back to the ICC, and he'd have to serve the sentence they set aside in return for a guilty plea and information."

"Yep. Of course, it might not fly. In order to deport him, you'd have to nail him to the wall."

"Thanks, Reilly. That's what I needed to know."

Joe made notes to the file and closed down his computer. As long as Petrović ran a clean business and didn't flaunt the conditions of his agreement, he was free to zip around town in his Jaguar and be the big man of Tony's Place.

But if he laundered money, or transported drugs, or trafficked children, he could be sent back to The Hague, and from there to prison—where any number of his former fellow officers would be happy to murder him.

CHAPTER 45

ANNA HAD PROMISED Joe not to chase Petrović, and she would keep that promise.

But nothing had been said about parking on Fell Street, where she could see the Butcher come and go, observe his movements in the hours when she was not working, and make sure that if he did spot her, he wouldn't get a good look at her face.

It was after 8:00 p.m. and Anna was in her car, parked on Fell. The traffic was light, and she could easily see the row of Victorian houses, especially the yellow one with the blue trim where she'd seen Petrović coming down the front stairs twice before.

The fancy houses were lit up inside, and Anna could see the blue glow of televisions and the silhouettes of the homeowners against the curtains.

Once, she had lived in a beautiful mountain town with pretty houses and TVs and cars, and parks and shops, bridges over cool waters, and an ancient fortress. She and her friends had read books and gone to work and dressed in Western clothing, like in any European country. It had been like a dream, but she hadn't known she was only dreaming.

Now she opened a nut-and-chocolate candy bar and ate it as she stared out at the picture-pretty street. She thought about a time not so long ago when she and her husband had had their own house on the outskirts of Djoba.

The house was not big, but it was cozy.

Built of brick and stucco and wood, it was pale blue outside and white inside, with exposed beams overhead and a brick stove in the kitchen. She loved cooking on that stove and felt completely at home in that earthy kitchen, with its sweet touch of decorated plates hanging on the walls.

When she was just married, her friend and Tina, her older sister, taught her to cook their recipes on that small stove, and they gave her some good tricks to make delicious dinners.

There was a sweet dessert called *krempita*, cream pie, that they made for holidays and birthdays. Anna remembered her first attempts at rolling out the puff pastry dough and making the custard filling. Her friend and sister had laughed so hard at the flour sticking to her hair and her face and hands and every surface, but she had learned and grown to love serving *krempita* on her grandmother's blue cake plates, using the forks that had been in her family for generations. And it was her husband's favorite dessert, though his mother made a different type: *sampita,* in which the custard was replaced with meringue. He would tease her in a sexy voice, "Anna, my sweet, I love your *krempita.*"

The way he said it always made her laugh.

Anna hadn't made pie since Petrović's army stormed Djoba. Her family had been buried in a mass grave, except for her baby. She didn't know where his poor bones had come to rest.

Tears came down her face, but she didn't sob and she didn't even blink. She wiped them away with the back of her hand and kept her eyes on the fancy house where Slobodan Petrović lived.

CHAPTER 46

ANNA SAW HEADLIGHTS in her rearview mirror first but didn't realize until after they'd passed her that the car was a blue Jaguar.

There was an empty spot in front of the yellow house, and the car swept into it, parked, shut off the lights.

It was dark again, and Anna exhaled. She looked at her watch and saw the time, just after midnight. She'd fallen asleep and hadn't known it. Petrović's restaurant must have closed, and he was home for the night.

She watched him get out of his car, phone to his face as usual, and head up under the decorative woodwork of the front porch to the front door. Lights came on in the front hall, then the parlor.

Anna switched on her ignition as another car came down the street, the headlights shining into her eyes. She waited for this car to pass her before pulling out, but instead it pulled parallel to a parked car behind her and stopped. Double-parked.

The driver-side door opened, and a man with silvery hair in a gray topcoat got out, slammed the door to his dark SUV. Anna knew cars. It was a Cadillac Escalade.

Who was this?

An FBI man tailing Petrović?

A friend or colleague paying a call at midnight?

The man in gray walked to Petrović's house and climbed the stairs. The door opened. Anna saw the dark hulk of Petrović stand back so that the man in gray could go in. The front door closed again.

Anna shut off the ignition, took a swig from her water bottle, and put it back on the seat. She would wait until the man in gray left the house. She'd promised Joe not to chase Petrović, but technically, following his associate wasn't chasing *him*.

The more they knew about Petrović, the better.

And she didn't have to wait long.

About five minutes after going inside the yellow house, the man in gray came out, got into his car, started it up, and drove up from behind her at a slow speed, coming alongside her and then stopping. Right next to her.

The man in the car waited for her to turn her face to him, and then made the universal signal for rolling down the car window.

She didn't do it. Anna was actually paralyzed. She pictured a gun pointed at her. She imagined ducking to the floor of the car. She saw herself bolting out of her car on the sidewalk side and just running, running, running, bullets coming at her as she ran.

Anna heard the man yelling through his open window.

"You need help?"

She shook her head no. And reached for the key, turned her engine on. There was room to pull out and drive past him. Barely. She turned the wheel, and as she rolled out into her lane, she looked toward the driver of the Escalade.

He was smiling at her. It was the kind of smile she'd seen before in the darkest days of her hell on earth. The smile was an expression of power.

He was letting her know how confident he was of his power to hurt her.

The tires of Anna's Kia grabbed asphalt, and the car squealed as it shot off and up the street. As Anna reached the intersection of Fell and Broderick, she checked her rearview mirror.

The Caddy wasn't following her. But if he looked for her, he would recognize her car. She parked blocks away from her front door and stuck to the shadows as she made her way home.

CHAPTER 47

NANCY KOEBEL, THE housekeeper from the Big Four Motel, had taken off to parts unknown after finding Carly Myers's dead body.

Not only had she discovered the body, but because of her presence around the motel on the days surrounding the murder, she might also have information about Carly's killer. So Conklin and I were surprised and *very* glad to see Koebel when she came through the entrance to Homicide on Tuesday morning and asked for me.

We escorted her into Interview 2 and asked her if she needed anything. She declined and told us that she couldn't stay long.

Nancy Koebel was young, between eighteen and twenty-two, and thin, with choppy brown hair and dark circles under her eyes. She explained that she had come to San Francisco from Canada almost three months ago with her boyfriend, Roger Lewis.

"It was supposed to be a vacation," she told us. "But we

weren't getting along. I said some things. Roger said some things. Then he ditched me. I had very little cash, no car, a used-up credit card, and my visitor's visa was about to expire. I lived with my parents and had been raving about this jerk. I've been staying with my uncle, who lives in Pacifica, but I was too embarrassed to borrow money from him, so I decided to get a job and work until I had enough money to go home with a little dignity."

Conklin and I commiserated and Koebel went on, telling us that she'd seen a HELP WANTED sign outside the Big Four Motel. She had taken the job for a couple of weeks, which expanded into a couple of months.

Conklin's famous way with women wasn't all about his good looks. He was kind, he listened, and he used the magic words. He'd taken the lead in the Koebel interview, and I was happy to sit back and let him do it. He said, "What can you tell us about finding the body and any information you may have about Carly Myers's death? Don't edit, please, Nancy. We'll listen and ask questions."

She nodded, and I sat on the edge of the rickety metal chair as she began to tell her story.

Inside the first hour, Koebel told us, "I was working my usual shift—from noon checkout time to 10 p.m.—and room 212 was supposed to be empty. But the 'Do Not Disturb' card was still on the door. I knocked a few times, and then I had to go in. The room had to be cleaned.

"I went to the bathroom first. That's how I do it. I take the towels and toss them into the cart, then I go for the bedding. But the towels weren't on the rack or the floor, so I opened the shower curtain."

Koebel covered her face with her hands. I'd seen what she'd seen—so I knew that the sight of the victim had given her the shock of her life.

She told us what she'd done after that, and it matched Tuohy's version of the events. She'd gotten her bag from the office, run out to the street, and not been back to the Big Four since, not even to get her paycheck.

She said, "That's how messed up I was about what happened."

I showed her on my phone a photo of the man seen on Tuesday coming down the stairs at the back of the motel.

Koebel thought she might have seen him, but not on the day she found the body. She also said she had never spoken with Carly Myers. She claimed that she had done her job, kept her head down, and saved her money so she could go home.

"I just came in to tell you what I know. That when I opened the door to room 212, no one was there—only that poor woman hanging in the shower."

CHAPTER 48

AN HOUR AND a half after first meeting Ms. Koebel, my hope that she was going to lead us to a killer, or two missing schoolteachers, had dimmed considerably.

Conklin said to our iffy witness, "But you recognize the man whose picture we showed you?"

"I don't know. I just don't know. I didn't pay that much attention."

Conklin said, "Okay. It's okay. Nancy, let me get you that tea I promised you."

When he'd left the room, I said, "One more time, please, Nancy. You were working from noon until ten. Did you see Carly Myers check into her room last Tuesday night at around ten?"

"No, like I said, I didn't see her at all on Tuesday. I've seen men going to her room on other days, two or three times. But I didn't know her name until I saw her picture online."

"Did you ever speak with her?"

"She asked for more towels once. She asked for batteries for the remote control. For the TV."

"And what about these men you saw with her on separate occasions? What can you tell me?"

"Like I said, Sergeant, I didn't look at their faces. They went to 212. She let them in, and a little while later they left. I didn't look or try to remember any of the guests. It was none of my business, and Mr. Tuohy made sure he got his six dollars an hour out of me. I had stairs. I had vacuuming. I had laundry. I wanted to keep my job."

"I understand. Did you ever hear or see any signs of violence? Broken furniture, bruises on Carly's arms or face?"

"Never."

"Did you ever find anything disturbing in Carly's room after she checked out? Blood? Anything like that?"

She said "No" emphatically.

Conklin came in with a mug of tea for Nancy. I smelled Chinese herbs. Paul Chi's private stash.

He pulled out his chair and said, "I know this is stressful, Nancy, and you've been very helpful. You're our last hope to find Carly's killer."

She shook her head, out of desperation or regret, I couldn't know. But the video camera was still rolling; the witness was still in her seat. And I still had questions.

CHAPTER 49

CONKLIN WAS RIGHT: Nancy Koebel was our best hope.

She'd seen Carly alive and then dead. And before Carly's death Koebel had seen men coming and going from the victim's motel room. One of those men *might* have been Carly's killer. But *might have* was miles away from proof.

I didn't want to admit it, but Nancy Koebel was believable and not panning out at all. But as my mother used to say, pressure makes diamonds. If I had to lean on Koebel, I would do it, because I wasn't ready to give up on this witness.

I said to Koebel, "Nancy. Look at this picture once more."

"Okay," she said, resigned.

She blew on the tea, and I pulled up the best of the pictures the ATM had shot from across the street of the rear of the Big Four the night Carly Myers was killed.

"Here are some additional shots of him from a slightly different angle. Do you recognize him now?"

She took the phone out of my hand and really gave the images a good look.

She squinted, then said, "You know…let me see the other shot again."

I complied.

Koebel took my phone and squinted at it.

"That could be Denny. I can't swear on a Bible, but that might be Denny."

Jake Tuohy had said Carly's pimp was named Danny or Denny.

"You saw him a number of times," I pressed.

"The time I remember, Carly checked in. He waited in the front parking lot near the office. They walked around back together."

I said, "Go on," and Koebel added a new layer to the story she'd been telling us all morning.

She said, "Carly waved and shouted out, 'Bye, Denny,' and he watched her while she went up to the second floor."

Koebel clamped her mouth shut and closed her eyes.

She was probably thinking about the last time she'd been in room 212, a life-altering experience. And from the way Koebel was gripping the edge of the table, I thought she was ready to bolt.

If she did, we couldn't stop her.

Conklin saw it, too. Fear of something. Maybe fear of us. She was in the USA with an expired visa.

Conklin said, "You're not going to be asked to testify. We are trying to find this woman's killer because two other women are still missing. You're helping us, Nancy, and we're very grateful to you for coming in."

She nodded and said, "I need to get home."

I wasn't done, so I pressed on.

"Nancy, we're not there yet. We have a hypnotist on call. Dr. Friedlander can come in and put you into a hypnotic state. You'll be able to visualize the moment you saw this man and freeze the picture. Get a good look at him through the lens of your own memory."

"How long will that take?"

"Do you want to call your uncle and tell him that you're helping the police find a killer and you have to stay here until you give them a clue?"

She looked genuinely distressed.

"I have to go. I don't want to be hypnotized."

"Then answer my questions, Nancy. Truthfully. Do you think that Denny was Carly's client or a friend? Or do you think she worked for him?"

"Oh, my God. Now that you mention it, another time I think I saw her give him—or someone like him—a wad of money."

It was another *might have* statement, but it felt like I'd finally gotten somewhere. And I thought of the woman who worked at the laundromat across from the Big Four. Edna Gutierrez. She'd told Jacobi that she'd seen a man drop Carly off in front of the motel in what she thought was a black or blue SUV.

I asked Koebel, "What kind of car did Denny drive?"

"I didn't notice a car. Look. I need to get back to my flat and pack my two sets of clothes and my toothbrush. My uncle is coming to get me in a couple of hours, and we're driving to Toronto."

Conklin looked at me as if to ask, *Anything else?*

I sighed.

I asked Nancy for her phone number and thanked her again for helping out the SFPD. I left her in the box with Richie, putting a statement together, and headed back to the bullpen and my desk.

Before I reached the swinging door, Conklin called me back.

I turned. He said, "There's more."

I went back into the interrogation room. Nancy Koebel was sitting where she'd been when I left the room.

"I remember something," she said. "I'm not 100 percent sure."

I sat back down.

"Tell Sergeant Boxer what you told me."

"I saw them standing next to a car when she handed him the money. It was a boxy kind of thing, like an SUV, and if this is the right car, there was a decal on the side, a logo for Taqueria del Lobo. And once when I was cleaning out room 212, I found a paper bag with the same lettering on it. I think the address was Valencia Street."

Did Denny work at the takeout taco joint on Valencia? I danced back to my desk. Maybe we had a lead made of diamonds. Maybe, maybe, maybe.

Susan Jones. Adele Saran. Hang on, please. We're doing everything we can do to find you.

CHAPTER 50

I TOLD JACOBI what I had and my feeling that it all added up to a lead.

Nancy Koebel was almost sure she'd seen Carly Myers giving a roll of money to a guy named Denny, a man known as Carly Myers's sometime pimp. She had further linked that meeting and cash payment to an SUV with the logo of a take-out taco joint on Valencia Street called Taqueria del Lobo.

Jacobi exhaled and said to me, "Go get him."

Once Koebel was on her way home, I searched the DMV database for a vehicle registered to the taco shop on Valencia Street. I got a hit on a blue Chevy Tahoe belonging to the taqueria's owner, Jose Martinez.

The records told me that Martinez was thirty-four, had been honorably discharged from the army, and lived on Shotwell Street, a few blocks away from his shop. He had no police record, and his DMV photo didn't match the ATM shot of Denny. That was too bad, but I was still interested in the taco truck's connection to Carly Myers.

I called my girl Yuki and spelled out the short version of the story. She said, "Stay right there."

Yuki came up to Homicide, and after Conklin and I filled her in on the Koebel interview and what it meant to our case, she jogged back down to the DA's office and got busy. Yuki is fast and thorough; by 6:00 p.m. I had a search warrant for the Chevy Tahoe in my pocket.

The six o'clock news came on as Conklin and I got ready to leave the Hall. I buttoned my jacket, left a message for Jacobi, shut down my computer, and boosted the volume on the tube.

The top-of-the-hour broadcast began with the heart-breaking pleas of Harold and Marjory Jones and William and Cora Saran, the parents of the missing teachers. They wept, begged the kidnapper to bring back their daughters, and offered rewards with no questions asked for information leading to their return.

After the grieving parents spoke, the mayor made a no-news announcement that every member of the SFPD was on the job, and that the FBI was also on the case.

So far there was nothing to report.

I felt sick to my stomach. My gut told me that those girls were dead and their bodies had been dumped. But for the sake of my mental health, I looked at the positive side. Until we found their bodies, there was hope.

We hadn't shared Denny's low-resolution ATM photo with the FBI. He was a local character, and this was still our case.

Conklin jangled a set of car keys until I turned to face him.

"Ready, Sergeant?"

I followed him down the fire stairs and out the front doors to Bryant, where we picked up our regulation gray Chevy squad car. Conklin took the wheel, and we made good time as we sped from the Hall to the Mission, a diverse and vibrant neighborhood with a bustling nightlife. It also had sketchy areas known for crime: crack houses and drug dealers, streetwalkers and gangs, criminals of all types and customers looking for some type of good time.

The Mission is gentrifying now, but five years ago, when we were working this case, it was dangerous after sunset. Even armed, I was on edge as the light faded out and the fog that usually evaded the Mission rolled in.

Rich slowed the car and we crawled down Shotwell, both of us searching the darkening streets for a taco delivery vehicle and a man called Denny, last name unknown, no verified ID, who was maybe a pimp and was definitely a person of interest.

We passed the intersections of Sixteenth, Seventeenth, and Eighteenth.

Men with hoods obscuring their faces clustered on the unlit street corners, drug deals going down in plain sight. We passed Nineteenth and came upon Shotwell's, on the corner of a seemingly quiet street known as the prostitution hub of the area.

CHAPTER 51

SOMETHING ABOUT THIS area—or maybe it was just the darkness of this case, the specter of a man who got off on torturing women—was stirring up memories for me. I'd worked the Mission as a beat cop, and I'd spent a lot of time on these streets. San Francisco had been a different city then. After years of gentrification, the city barely had anything that qualified as a "bad neighborhood." Although the building had some polish now, I remembered Shotwell's being a lot grittier.

It was a personal landmark for me. When I was still a rookie, this tavern was an off-site HQ used by female cops. It was a meeting place to discuss how to deal with being ignored, belittled, and sexually harassed by the men of the SFPD.

And with the fonder memories of those nights drinking with some of the toughest women I'd ever known, Shotwell's brought back vivid images of a crime I'd worked when I was still green. Still unaccustomed to the shock of human savagery.

I recalled every detail of that night that had begun with a crackling radio call. "Calling all cars. Homeless down at Shotwell and Twentieth."

My partner, Lisa Frazer, and I had answered the call.

Lisa had ten years on the job and was a wife, mom of two, and top marksman. As she proved often in the squad car, she could also carry a tune. Lisa was singing and driving as we patrolled the Mission that night, and when dispatch called at midnight, we responded.

We were two blocks from the location and arrived in under a minute. Frazer braked the car, turned off the engine. The headlights went out. Without the headlights, the only illumination was one small light coming from a high window in a nearby apartment.

It threw just enough wattage to shadow the victim, lying spread-eagled in the street.

I jumped out of the car and got to the victim first. I took one look and called our street sergeant, Pat Correa, saying that we were on the scene and needed clear air, an ambulance, and CSI.

She said, "I'm on it. I should be there in three, four minutes."

Thank God it was Correa. She was an old hand and a role model.

Meanwhile, Frazer and I had work to do. By our flashlight beams, what I could see through the dark and fog looked to be the work of a serial psycho known around the Hall as the Bloodsucker. No one had ever seen him up close, so the man was also a myth, but he did cut throats, drink his victims' blood, and leave his signature behind.

My hand was shaking as I shined my light on the victim and said, "I'm Lindsay. I'm a cop," and I asked her to hang in. An ambulance was en route. She groaned softly but didn't open her eyes and didn't move.

The victim appeared to be a street person, middle-aged, with knotted hair and rags for clothes. The plastic bag she used to carry her possessions was still looped over her left wrist.

I sorted through it for ID and found an apple, a wad of tissues, a ball of tinfoil, and miscellaneous odds and ends, but no wallet, no ID.

The four-inch-long gash to the side of victim's neck looked like a knife wound, and an artery had been cut. No mistake about it, she was bleeding out. So much blood was puddling around her, it was separating, and the iron smell of it blended with the urine stink coming up from the street.

Frazer was quick to render aid, pressing her gloved hand to the victim's pulsing wound.

She said, "I've got her, Boxer. Preserve the scene."

The victim was still alive. Just.

Was the Bloodsucker hanging back, watching us?

I looked at the faces of the gathering crowd of bystanders. Gangbangers who ran the neighborhood, I thought. We didn't have cell phones then, so I took pictures with my mind, memorizing what little I could see of the rubberneckers even as I ordered them away from the immediate area.

One of the onlookers was a husky guy with big hands, and he just wouldn't step back. I warned him off. I got in his face and blocked his access, but he mocked me, crouched into a boxer's stance, and danced on the balls of his feet, daring me to take him on.

And then he rushed me.

My father was a bad father, a worse husband, and also a dirty cop. Maybe I was trying to make up for all that by becoming a cop myself. One thing Marty Boxer did teach me: "With the name Boxer, you better know how to box."

I thought the husky guy could hurt me, but I was more afraid that he'd corrupt the scene. So I drew back my fist and punched him in the face with all my strength.

He howled, staggered backward holding his hands over his nose. The crowd I had shooed away reassembled and began hooting, catcalling me and Frazer, "Here, piggy, piggy."

I was worried that this mob was going out of control. Two of us. More than a dozen of them. I fired a shot into the air to get their attention. I remembered, too late, that warning shots were illegal, but I figured I'd explain later. We were outnumbered and I was afraid for my life.

It was almost pure bravado when I yelled, "Who wants to go to jail for interfering with law enforcement?"

There was laughter. This was bad. A menacing scrum of kids was having a good time with the lady cop. They might have weapons. I would be surprised if they didn't. The crime scene was still exposed, and it was just me holding off gangbangers, and Frazer standing between the victim and death.

I pushed through the hecklers, and when I got to the car, I called dispatch, demanding backup forthwith.

Correa's voice came over the radio. "I'm on Mission and Twentieth. Watch for my lights."

The gangbangers heard Correa's voice over the radio saying that she was three blocks away, and it backed them off. I'd bought a minute to tape off the street and I got to it.

Frazer said, "I'm sorry I can't help with this."

I said, "Do you see *that*?"

I flashed my light on the brick wall, and there, finger-painted in blood, was the Bloodsucker's signature, the sketch of a grinning face, blood running down his chin.

Frazer was asking the victim for her name, telling her to stay with us, repeating her promise that she would be all right.

The guy I'd punched out was sitting with his back against a car, holding his nose and howling. I prayed that we'd gotten to the victim in time. That someone had seen the victim's attacker.

I took out my notepad and shouted to the ominous and growing crowd. Not just young men anymore, thank God. "Did anyone see the attack on this woman?"

One old man raised his hand. He was wearing a Giants cap and a plastic bag over his clothes. I felt mist on my face. It was starting to rain.

"I saw him," he said.

I said, "Come with me."

CHAPTER 52

I STILL REMEMBERED how it had seemed to me, then, as though everything were working against Lisa and me, and most of all, against the victim, who hadn't yet been able to tell us her name.

But there *was* a witness.

I steered the elderly man to a place where we could speak outside the tape. I stood with my back to the wall.

I asked him for his name and address.

He pointed to his chest and said, "I'm Sam Winkler." Then he pointed to a large cardboard box halfway down the block, leaning against the wall of a building, and said, "My centrally located, eco-friendly, multipurpose abode."

He was deadpan, but I had to smile.

While keeping my eyes on the street, I asked Sam to tell me what he had seen.

He said, "This strange guy passed right by me—four feet away. He was talking to himself, very loud and very crazy. I didn't understand him. I don't think it was English. Maybe

Swedish. I never saw him before. I was just glad he kept going. I didn't mess with him."

"Tall? Short? Black? White? Young? Old?"

Sam Winkler shrugged, then said, "Medium-sized and skinny."

I made a note. "And you saw the attack?"

"Some of it. I stood up to make sure he was gone, and Rona was sitting right there against the building when this dude came up to her. He hunched down. She cried out, and I couldn't see what he did from where I was. But I saw when he wrote on the wall with his finger."

"You did?"

Sam said, "That was him, right? The Bloodsucking bastard?"

"The victim's name is Rona?"

"Yeah. That's what she calls herself."

"Last name?"

He shrugged for the second time.

I said, "Do you see that man here now?"

"No, he took off thataway." He pointed southbound toward Twenty-First Street. "I didn't get a good look at him."

"Would you recognize him from a picture?"

"I wanna help," Sam told me. "But my eyes aren't good. And it's blacker than black here, right?"

He was right. Almost total darkness with a chilly froth of fog.

The bystanders were getting rowdy again and a half dozen of them began to rock our car. It was a dangerous situation. I pictured ordering them to line up with their faces to the wall, frisking them, cuffing them.

166

I'd never pull that off. It was not a one-cop job and Frazer was occupied.

Where was our sergeant? Where was backup?

I turned to see Frazer still keeping pressure on the fire hose that was Rona's severed carotid artery. She was saying, "Hang on, please, dear. Help is on the way. I promise."

I thanked Sam for his time and went on to a witness found after I'd left the scene. This one was high on drugs and had not seen the crazed, bloodsucking psycho. Of the six men and women I questioned, only Sam had seen the actual assault, and his eyewitness report was almost useless.

To my great relief, Sergeant Correa arrived with lights and sirens on full blast and a cruiser drafting behind her. The ambulance pulled up, and after a moment the victim was lifted in and the bus took off.

Once the victim was gone, the crowd dispersed, and Frazer, Correa, and I waited for CSI with our hands on our guns. Correa went back to her car and took the call from dispatch, who informed her that Rona had died in the bus en route to the hospital.

Correa told Frazer, "I hope yours was the last face Rona saw before she died, not her killer's."

I felt sad and mad. He'd been right here, and for all any of us knew, he was still here, one of the shadowy figures just out of reach.

He was never caught. The killings of this type stopped, and that meant that the Bloodsucker had gotten scared, or married, or moved on. But unless he was dead, the odds were good that his blood lust was only dormant.

Another killer the SFPD chased, a sadist, committed a dozen

murders. Then he put himself on the shelf for thirty full years, holding a regular job, belonging to the neighborhood watch and family-type organizations. Until he missed the attention and began to kill again.

Had the Bloodsucker retired? Or was he still living in the Mission, hiding out, working as a barber or a librarian, watching cartoons with his kids on the weekends, biding his time?

Was he watching us now?

My reverie dissolved when Rich said, "Chevy Tahoe at three o'clock."

The Tahoe was dark blue, a full-size SUV with logos spelling out the taqueria's name and phone number on the side doors. Across the street from the vehicle was the Taqueria del Lobo, a small walk-in takeout taco shop.

"That's it," I said.

I called in our location, and my partner double-parked beside the Tahoe, blocking it in its spot.

Conklin and I got out of our car into a neighborhood of bad old memories and ghosts that were still quite alive in my mind.

We waded through the fog.

CHAPTER 53

THE BLUE TAHOE had the Taqueria del Lobo logo on both sides.

The vehicle was locked, but I shined my light through the windows to look all around the interior. It was clean and tidy. There wasn't even a taco wrapper in the footwell. Richie checked the tags and called out to me that the number was the same as what we'd gotten from the DMV.

Across the street and down a few doors was the taco shop. The sign overhead was a line drawing of a grinning wolf saying "Bite me" in a voice balloon. The sign hanging in the window read OPEN. We crossed the street and Rich pushed the door. A bell tinkled and I followed him in.

The place was small and brightly lit, and smelled delicious. That reminded me that I hadn't eaten anything since coffee and toast with Joe this morning, eleven long hours ago. Something dancy was playing over the sound system, and three men in work clothes were hunched over one of the small tables, eating tacos and refried beans.

The woman behind the counter was in her late twenties, with auburn hair in a ponytail and various tats on what I could see of her arms, mostly of the hearts-and-butterflies variety.

She looked at us, but her big brown eyes swung to my partner.

"What can I get for you?" she asked.

"We're with the SFPD." Conklin smiled, introduced us, asked the woman for her name.

"Lucinda. Drucker."

He said, "We have a few questions for you, Ms. Drucker."

"Questions for *me*?"

I stepped in and showed her the photo of Denny on my phone. I asked, "Do you know this man?"

She scrutinized the photo, and I swiped the screen, showing more photos from the same set the ATM had shot of the parking lot. Finally she said, "I think that's Denny."

"Last name?"

"Lopez."

I said, "Denny works here?"

"Denny's my boyfriend. What's wrong? Why do you need to know?"

I said, "Denny was seen with a vehicle like the one across the street. It was parked near a crime scene. He may have seen something that could help us with our investigation."

A dark-haired man with a tattoo of a wolf on the side of his neck came out of the kitchen and into the small main room. He wore a stained white apron over his T-shirt and jeans and was drying his hands on a dish towel. This had to be Jose Martinez, the taco shop's proprietor and owner of the matching SUV.

Conklin and I were both wearing SFPD Windbreakers. Martinez noticed, scowled, and said, "Can I help you?"

Lucinda said, "I got this, Jose. It's personal. I need to take a smoke break, okay?"

The boss said to me, "This is my shop. Did she do something wrong?"

"We're doing an investigation, and Lucinda may know a witness who can help us out."

He was going to go nuts when I told him we were going to impound his vehicle, but I wasn't ready to disclose that yet. First we needed Lucinda to talk about Denny.

He said to Lucinda, "Your boyfriend get into an accident with my car?"

"No, no, Jose. No, he did not."

Martinez looked at her, walked to the front window, peered out until he saw the SUV. Then he flapped his dish towel over his shoulder and glared at Lucinda, saying, "Five minutes, Lucy. You gotta help me out here."

Martinez went to the cash register as the three men stood, balled up their trash, and dunked it into a bin. Lucy ducked under the counter and came around with a pack of cigarettes and a lighter.

Given Lucinda's noticeable anxiety, I thought she might refuse to give Denny up. Regardless, I was betting that Carly Myers had left a print or a trace of DNA inside the SUV. Maybe Susan and Adele had also left some trace.

I'd almost forgotten what it was like to be optimistic, but I felt this close to bagging Denny Lopez.

CHAPTER 54

I WAS HIGH on hope as we followed Lucinda Drucker out to Valencia Street.

I watched and waited as she fumbled with her lighter, lit her cigarette, and took a long drag. She exhaled. Then she said, "I don't know where Denny is. I called him a couple times today and he didn't call me back yet."

Conklin asked for Denny's number and hers, and she reluctantly complied. He asked, "Under what circumstances did Denny use the company car?"

"He does lunchtime deliveries. Sometimes I let him take it after we're closed."

"Martinez is okay with that?"

"Please don't...look, he'll fire me."

Conklin asked, "Do you know where Denny was last Tuesday at about this time?"

"Oh, hell no. I don't ask him his business."

She rubbed her shoulder as if she was remembering something that had happened when she'd asked him his business before. She asked, "What kind of crime was he supposed to have seen?"

"Does Denny do other kinds of work?" I asked, side-stepping her question by inserting one of mine.

"I told you, I don't ask him his business. Here's what I want to say: I love Denny. He loves me. I dropped out of high school ten years ago, and he was my first boyfriend and my only. I really know him. Understand? He would never do anything wrong."

I said, "But you don't ask him his business."

She scowled, took a drag on her cigarette, flicked ashes.

We weren't alone on the street.

Traffic came slowly up Valencia, and streetwalkers leaned into cars at the lights. Shopworkers walked to their cars. Bars opened and stores closed.

It was getting dark, but the big white letters on our backs, spelling *SFPD*, were bright enough to draw attention from passersby. Drucker cast a look up the street, threw her cigarette down on the sidewalk, and stepped on it.

The last three customers came out the door, accompanied by the jingling of the bell. She stepped out of their way.

"I've got to go," she said. "Jose is waiting. I have to close up the front—"

"I've got a better idea, Lucinda," I said. "Let's take a ride to the station and talk where there's less distraction."

"I'm *cooperating*. I've told you *everything* I *know*."

I said, "Do you know if Denny runs girls?"

"I don't know what you mean."

I showed her my phone. I pulled up pictures of Carly and

her friends. "Have you ever seen this woman? Or her? Or her? Is Denny pimping these women?"

"*No way.* Jeez. I don't know them. I just *said* I don't ask Denny his business."

Funny thing. I believed her and I even felt sorry for her. She showed signs of emotional abuse. She was fearful and pretty clearly lying to herself. But we weren't done here.

I said to my partner, "Let's serve the warrant on Mr. Martinez and get the vehicle to the lab."

"Wait," Lucinda Drucker said. "You have to understand. If you tell Jose that I let Denny drive the car after hours, I'm going to lose my job."

"Look, Ms. Drucker. We don't want you to get fired, but see it from our side. We're investigating a *homicide.* A woman was *killed.* Two more are *missing.* If Denny has seen something, he has to tell us."

I thought I saw tears in her eyes, but I turned away from her and called Dale Culver in Impound at the lab. I gave him the location, the warrant number, the description of the vehicle, and the tag number. Culver said, "It's gonna be twenty-five to thirty minutes to get a flatbed out there."

I was looking up Twentieth Street as I spoke with Culver, when I saw someone who might be Denny Lopez approaching on foot. He was smaller than I'd pictured him, maybe five seven, narrow shoulders. He had his hands in his pant pockets, head down, apparently deep in thought.

Lucinda saw him at the same time.

That was *Denny.* That was *him.*

I turned to Conklin, and that's when Lucinda yelled, "Denny! Cops! Run!"

174

CHAPTER 55

LOPEZ LOOKED UP, saw us, and split, turning on his heel and running back the way he'd come.

I yelled, "*Stop! Police!*"

He kept going. I was the law, and by running, he'd crossed a legal line right into a gray area called reasonable suspicion.

I yelled again for him to stop. He didn't even turn his head. Conklin and I ran behind him, and then after streaking along Twentieth, he ditched down Lexington. Although Conklin had a couple of inches on me, my legs were as long as his, and I was fit from running with Joe and Martha.

But I knew we couldn't risk Drucker or Martinez disappearing with the possible evidence inside that vehicle. I had enough air to yell to Conklin, "Rich. Here. Take the warrant and wait for the lab."

Conklin faded back and I picked up speed.

I was fast, and on a straightaway I would have had the advantage, but Denny Lopez could pivot like a quarter horse.

One minute he was pounding the asphalt ahead of me, and then he was just *gone*.

He seemed to have slipped into another dimension.

Did he live on this block? I thought about Susan and Adele. Where had he stashed them? Were they only yards away?

I checked out the back doors on Lexington Street. Some were gated with iron grilles, some were wood, one was a roll-up garage door. Next to that one was a pair of double doors with metal studs, and beside that was a slim metal grille with peeling green paint and a dead bolt. Behind the grille was a matching green-painted wooden door.

But the dead bolt was unlocked, the grille slightly ajar—as if someone had run through and hadn't had time to throw the bolt.

I pulled my gun, yanked open the grille, and kicked in the wooden door.

I was expecting anything. A gun pointed at me. A room full of naked men weighing heroin, packing glassine envelopes. But it was nothing like that. I was inside a basement room lit by a bare bulb hanging from the ceiling. It looked like something between a knickknack shop and a hoarder's lair.

I called out, "Lopez. This is the police. Come out with your hands up."

Something stirred from behind a six-foot-tall stack of newspapers. I had a two-handed grip on my Glock, hoping like hell I wouldn't have to use it.

A woman's voice called out, "Helloooo, Janice?"

A weedy-looking faerie of a woman wearing a gauzy floral frock, looking between seventy and ninety years old, appeared from between the newspapers and a rickety china closet.

"Janice," she said, looking delighted to see me. "You're early, aren't you? Is it time for bed?"

I lowered my gun and said, "I'm Sergeant Boxer, ma'am. Did you see a man come in here a moment ago?"

I was breathing hard, managing to speak to the elderly woman while taking in the whole room. I wasn't sure that Lopez was here. He could have gone through any door and out the other side. I pictured him fleeing on Eighteenth, circling back for his girlfriend, who might still be standing outside the Taqueria del Lobo.

I tapped the radio on my shoulder mike and called Conklin, gave him my location, and told him to call for backup.

And then a lamp toppled and crashed at the back of the jumbled room. I yelled, "*Hands in the air!*"

A slight man of about thirty, with regular features and wearing a pullover, worn jeans, and run-down sneakers, stood up and showed me his palms.

This was the guy from the ATM photo. I was positive.

I said, "Denny Lopez, put your hands on the top of your head and turn around."

"You have the wrong guy. You have the totally wrong guy."

"You're not Denny Lopez?"

"I'm Denny Lopez, but I didn't do anything wrong."

"Are you carrying a weapon?"

"No," he said. "I have a ballpoint pen in my shirt pocket."

I said, "Running from the police is breaking the law. I'm bringing you in on reasonable suspicion of committing or about to commit a crime."

"*Bullshit!*" he shouted.

"Don't make this hard on yourself, Denny. Do not move, or I'll add resisting arrest to the charges."

I patted him down; found the pen, keys, phone, wallet. I put the wallet on a wobbly end table, pulled Lopez's hands behind his back, and cuffed him for my safety.

I opened the wallet. Bank card. Credit card. Driver's license. All in the name of Dennis L. Lopez.

When he spoke again, his tone was conciliatory. He said, "Believe me, Officer. I've done nothing wrong. Nothing."

And I was suddenly filled with doubt.

I could say with some certainty that he was Carly's pimp, that he'd been seen near the scene of the murder. But had he killed Carly? Had he kidnapped and maybe killed the two other women? Had this puny guy done all of that?

He'd run from me.

Reasonable suspicion was a gray area, and that's how the courts had ruled. Sometimes yes. Sometimes reasonable suspicion was an excuse for a bad cop to fire on an innocent person.

I weighed it all—quickly.

Was Denny Lopez's flight from police cause enough to bring him in? Or was I grasping at the only available straw?

CHAPTER 56

JOE WAS AT his desk that evening with all the lights on, going over photos while he waited for Anna to arrive for their meeting.

Twelve hours ago, at seven thirty this morning, Anna had called him at home to confess that she'd been doing her own stakeout of Petrović's house, against Joe's express directions to leave surveillance to the FBI.

She said, "I have to tell you what happened."

Her Bosnian accent weighed down her English, but Joe listened hard and understood that Anna had been watching the Victorian house when Petrović arrived home last night at around midnight. She described the gray-haired man who had visited. "He looked well off, Joe. He had very good posture and a strong step."

Anna then recounted what he'd done.

She said, "I disguised myself. I had a scarf on, and there was no moon. But still, he saw me and stopped his car."

"He stopped next to you?"

"Yes. That's right."

"Jesus," Joe said. "What did he want?"

"He asked if I needed help. Pure evil was…radiating? Radiating off him. I know what you're thinking. I have a panic fear of evil. But I tell you, it was as if he could see through me and wanted me to know that he had all the power."

Joe could almost see the dominant smile Anna had described. He muttered "Jesus Christ" again, then said, "You told him that you didn't need any help."

"Yes. Just shook my head. I started my car and drove to my house, and then, you would be proud, Joe. I parked several blocks away in case he was following me. I watched carefully. No one was following me."

Joe sighed. She couldn't know that for sure. Petrović knew that Anna was watching him. He might well know her as a survivor of his atrocities in Djoba and his personal attacks against her. Her scar, the size of a handprint, was unforgettable. Petrović might have had someone surveilling her house, and he might have a plan to take out this witness to his old life who knew his real name. It was possible, and it made Joe angry and frightened for this woman he hardly knew.

He said to her in this early morning phone call, "Do you understand me now, Anna? Stay the fuck away from Petrović."

"Joe. No shouting."

"Sorry. Please. Anna, you're looking for trouble."

"Joe, listen to me. I woke up at dawn with my heart pounding. I knew the man in the Escalade. I've seen him before."

"You're sure?"

"I think so. I think he was in the Serbian Army. I don't know his name and I never knew his name. I think he was a regular soldier. But I also think he was one of the men who came to the hotel."

CHAPTER 57

JOE HAD ENDED the call by saying, "Stop by my office when you get off work. I'll pull up as many pictures as I can of the invading force in Djoba. Maybe you can pick out that man in the Escalade. Are you up for that, Anna?"

"Yes. I get off at six."

"So you can be here by six thirty or so," he said. "Call me if you get hung up at work. I'll let security know I'm expecting you."

It was now 7:30 p.m. No call from Anna.

Damn it. Goddamnit. She'd been confronted by someone she thought might be a man who had attacked her, and he'd let her know that he'd seen her hiding in the dark.

Now she was late. Where the hell was she? Had something happened to Anna?

Joe called down to security to double-check that she wasn't waiting downstairs. The guard at the desk was sure. No one had come to see him.

Joe went back to the photos.

They were still shots printed from videos of the Serbian troops entering Djoba in tanks and trucks and on foot. The soldiers wore fatigues and helmets, carried Zastava machine guns, and had bandoliers strapped across their chests. Most of the footage had been taken by civilians.

One of the videos had been shot from a balcony thirty feet up, showing soldiers mowing down fleeing civilians, shooting at random, the bodies jerking, falling, dust coming up on the street like a brown cloud. Women in head scarves held up their arms and cried out at the sight of the slaughter.

The still shots lacked sound, and for that Joe thanked God.

The last piece of footage felt like a jackpot.

It was a group shot of a hundred men gathered around a monument on the main street. The troops had formed rows, like a class photo, the tallest in the line at the back, others seated on the lower three tiers of steps around the monument.

At one end of the grouping, taking a strong stance, was Slobodan Petrović. He was red-faced, uniformed, in a gold-braided hat, and heavily armed. He waved at the camera, grinning and proud.

Joe was staring at Petrović when a thought struck him.

He pictured the gray-haired man in Tony's Place, walking a half pace behind Petrović. He'd had a mustache, and he'd been speaking with Petrović in Serbian.

Could this be the same man who'd paid a call on Petrović at oh dark hundred last night? The same one Anna thought she recognized from the prison brothel?

Joe couldn't help but remember in crisp detail when Petrović had called him out in the restaurant last week. He had mentioned Anna, referring to her as his "girlfriend."

Maybe, as Anna suspected, the gray-haired man knew her, too.

Joe grabbed his phone and called Anna's cell phone again. Still no answer. He got the number of San Francisco Tesla, where Anna worked as a bookkeeper, and called there. He asked the woman who answered the phone to put him through to Anna Sotovina.

The receptionist said that Anna wasn't there. She thought that Anna had gone to lunch at one and hadn't come back. The dealership was closing now for the night.

Joe said, "Was anyone concerned that she didn't come back from lunch?"

The woman said, "Not really. If she finished her work, no one would care if she went home. It was a slow day. Is there anything I can do to help you? Shall I leave a message for Anna?"

Joe said, "No. Thanks anyway."

Anna wouldn't have stood Joe up without calling. Had she been abducted by Petrović or the man in the Escalade?

Joe folded his hands on his desk.

This was unusual for him. He didn't know what to do.

CHAPTER 58

IT WAS AFTER 7:00 p.m. when Conklin and I escorted Dennis Lopez from the back of the cruiser into the Hall and gave him a brief elevator ride to Homicide.

We had detained Lopez on reasonable suspicion, but that was short of probable cause, which would have allowed us to get an arrest warrant and toss his butt in jail.

Reasonable suspicion meant that anything he said could be used against him, but after questioning him for a short time, like twenty minutes, we would have to charge him and read him his rights, or let him go.

I hoped he'd break under pressure, confess to killing Carly, or give us something that would lead to the two missing schoolteachers. And that they'd still be alive.

Interview 2 was available. Conklin pulled out a chair for Lopez, and I kept my hand on his shoulder until he sat down. Time was blowing past.

Conklin removed the cuffs I'd slapped on Lopez in the basement, saying to him, "Okay? You should be more

185

comfortable now. Can we get you something to drink? Soda?"

But Lopez had had experience with the police before. He turned down our offer and answered "No," "No," and "I don't know" to our questions. Ten minutes into our interview, he asked, "Am I under arrest?"

"No," I said. "We've brought you in for questioning. We're detaining you on reasonable suspicion of having committed a crime. That's because when I ordered you to stop, you stepped on the gas. You can't do that. Like I told you, you broke a law."

"Oh. But to be clear," Lopez said, "can I leave?"

"Not yet," I said. "That's the detaining part. But you're correct that you're not in custody."

"If you decide to hit the street," Conklin told him, "we're going to upgrade you to suspect. We'll be taking a much harder look at you. We'll work with the DA on getting probable cause, and that means search warrants and cops watching you until you screw up. Which I think we can count on."

"Actually, I want to help," said Denny.

I said, "Okay, good. Let's get to it."

So I asked Denny for the third time, "When was the last time you saw Carly Myers?"

"I don't know her."

I almost lost it. He was screwing with us, and I had no power to turn him around.

I leaned in, and speaking in a hard, cold voice, I said, "I swear, Denny, either you help us or you become the focus of my life until you're in jail."

Lopez used a minute of our precious time to think things over. Then he said, "The last time I saw Carly was a couple of weeks ago. I guess. I don't keep a calendar."

"You're sure you didn't see her last week? Let me give you a hint," I said. "Carly and her two friends were seen leaving a bar called the Bridge on Monday night."

"*I. Didn't. See. Her.* How am I supposed to prove that? I got a question for you. How many hookers get killed every year in this city? A dozen? Do you know? Do you want to grill me about them? Do you think I go around killing working girls? Are you out of your minds?"

When he'd finished venting, Conklin said, "Let me help you out. You were seen on Tuesday night at the Big Four, where Carly was murdered. Your taco ride has been seen there frequently. The Big Four manager knows you were pimping for Carly. That's what the DA is going to tell the judge. You were the dead woman's pimp. You were seen at the crime scene around the time she was killed. We're asking you about a woman you knew and did business with. Follow me?"

Denny nodded and all of the air went out of his balloon.

Conklin said, "Right now our forensics lab is going over the tacomobile, and the DA is getting a warrant for your DNA. A foreign hair was found on Carly's body, and if the DNA on that hair matches yours, you're our guy. You're it."

"I didn't kill Carly," Lopez told my partner. "I've never had sex with her. I've never even touched her."

"Then you have nothing to lose and everything to gain by telling us every single thing you know," I said.

Conklin asked, "How about it, Denny?"

187

CHAPTER 59

DENNY THOUGHT OVER the win-win suggestion I'd made, while looking into my hard blue eyes—and he took it to heart.

He said, "I met Carly at the Bridge one night about three months ago. I was sitting at the bar. Carly was a couple stools down, and I started talking to her. She was very cute. I moved over next to her. I bought her a drink. I asked her what kind of work she did and she told me. She said she didn't make a lot of money and was trying to pay off her college loans."

He shrugged. I drummed my fingers on the table. I wanted him to get to it. Faster.

Lopez said, "I told her I'd be happy to help her work off the loan and I'd give her a pretty good deal, a fifty-fifty split after taking out for expenses. She laughed. Asked me what I meant. I told her and she told me I was crazy.

"So about a month after I made that offer, she called me and said she wanted to do it."

Conklin said, "She agreed to be a prostitute?"

Lopez said, "She had *decided*. I didn't pressure her. Not at all. She said she wanted to try. I made a date for her. I drove her to the Big Four. I like that place because they don't ask any questions.

"I stayed in the parking lot while Carly was having her date. I had told her I would be lookout in case of trouble. She made a couple hundred bucks and told me to make another date for her."

"And you did?" Conklin asked.

Lopez said, "Once or twice a month. That was all she would do. Hey. To be honest, Sergeant, I don't know for sure that she even liked guys."

"Explain," I said.

"Just a feeling I had. Look. A lotta girls who turn tricks hate men, don't you think?"

"Go on with your story, Denny. There's a line forming outside, people waiting for this room."

He looked up at the two-way mirror and waved.

I slapped my hand down on the table and his attention came back to me.

Lopez said, "I picked guys who weren't too gross, and she seemed fine with it for a month or so. Then, a few weeks ago, she said she didn't want to do it anymore."

I said, "Is that right?"

I took out my phone, showed Denny the pictures of him coming down the stairs at the back of the motel.

"You recognize this guy?"

He looked at the picture, eyes moving over the small screen, pausing, clearing his throat, then saying, "That's me."

"That was a week ago," I told him.

"I was there," he said, "but not with Carly."

I was ready with my follow-up questions. I asked him if he knew Adele Saran and Susan Jones. I showed him the picture I had of all three of them together at a table at the Bridge.

Lopez said he'd seen them there but never spoken to Adele or Susan.

He added, "Those are the missing women I heard about?"

"I think you know that."

He stood up from his seat and yelled in my face, "You've got the wrong man. You've got the wrong man! I didn't hurt anyone. And now I'm getting out of here. Adios."

CHAPTER 60

CONKLIN STOOD UP and said to Lopez in his very reasonable and patient voice, "Hey, Denny, you're free to leave, okay? But come on. We're not trying to pin anything on you. We're trying to save some lives here."

I left Denny to Conklin and went to get our person of interest a soft drink. By the time I had returned to the box, Lopez was chatting with Conklin as if they were old friends.

That was a good thing and I hated to break the mood, but I was still half crazy worrying about two missing schoolteachers. I took my seat, pushed the can of soda over to Lopez.

He popped the top, took a swig.

I pulled out my phone again and said, "Denny, here's the timeline. Carly checked into the Big Four on Tuesday night a week ago. On Thursday she was found dead in room 212. Murdered. This picture of you is time-stamped 11:23 p.m. Tuesday, the night we think she was killed. You were coming down from her room. What were you doing there? Make me understand."

Lopez heaved a sigh.

"I didn't go to her room," he said. "Actually, I was waiting for Daisy, my new girl. Daisy was in room 314, the top floor. I was in the parking lot, and I saw some man in a sports jacket leave 212, the room Carly always booked. It's on the corner. She liked that because the room is a little bigger. I figured she might be in there alone. It was a hunch, that's all. I knocked on the door. She didn't answer. I went back down to the car and waited for Daisy."

He looked at my face and said, "That's the fucking truth. You want to talk to Daisy? Because I don't have her number."

Lopez was getting worked up again.

Conklin said, "Keep going, Denny. You waited for Daisy to be finished."

"Yes. Thank you. When Daisy was done, we did our financial transaction inside the car, and I drove her back to Mission and Eighteenth Street."

I said to Lopez, "Can you describe the man you saw leaving Carly's room? The man in the sports jacket."

"It was a nonevent. He was moving fast."

"Did you see his car?" I asked.

"No. I was in the back lot, and I think what he did was walk around to the front. Sometimes I park in the front, too."

I said, "Could you describe him to a sketch artist?"

"Doubtful. I could try. If I do that, will you kiss me good night and drive me home?"

Conklin said, "First, the sketch artist. Then I'll talk to our lieutenant, and if you've been cooperative—no kisses. But we'll get you a ride home."

Denny spent a few minutes with our sketch artist, who showed us the resultant drawing of a rectangular face with regular features. It could be anyone.

I didn't want to release Denny, but we'd gone past reasonable suspicion already. We could charge him for pandering, but there was no point.

We'd done our best with our only suspect—and damn it, we'd come up empty.

CHAPTER 61

IT WAS JUST after 8:00 p.m. when the lab tech picked up the soda can with Denny Lopez's DNA on the rim to compare with the lone pubic hair Claire had retrieved from Carly Myers's body. It was after 9:00 when I sent my report to Jacobi, and as I closed down and packed up for the night, I ran the Lopez interview through my mind again. Was he a small-time criminal guilty of pimping out willing females in exchange for a cut? Or was he far worse, a clever, psychopathic killer?

I was leaning toward the former, that Lopez was a common parasite who was supplementing his by-the-hour taco delivery job, when my desk phone rang.

Yuki's name flashed on my caller ID.

What was keeping her in her office at this time of night? I picked up the receiver and Yuki didn't wait for me to say hello.

"I just heard something," she said. "You're not going to believe this."

"Hi, Yuki. What's up?"

"I gotta talk to you. Your place or mine?"

Yuki's office was one floor down, so either place was easy enough, but I had one foot out the door, and I asked her, "Can this wait? I'm on my way home."

"How about we talk in your car?"

I phoned Joe and reached him as he was driving home.

"Have you eaten dinner?" I asked.

"I was thinking we could go out for Thai food."

There was a restaurant we loved on Clement, located two blocks from our apartment. It was a good idea, but from the sound of Yuki's voice, I calculated that I was going to be occupied for a while. Joe and I made a plan and a backup plan, and then I took to the fire stairs and headed down.

Yuki was waiting for me on the second-floor landing.

"What took you so long?" she said.

It had been thirty or forty seconds since I'd hung up the phone. I said, "Ha, ha. This had better be good."

We continued down the stairs to the lobby, exited through the back door, walked along the breezeway past the ME's office to Harriet Street and the parking lot under the overpass. I unlocked my trusty Explorer and we both got in. I reclined my seat, and Yuki did the same with hers.

"Start talking," I said.

Yuki said, "Have you ever heard of a Bosnian war criminal named Slobodan Petrović?"

This question was a stunner.

I turned my head to look at my friend. Joe had told me about Petrović, but even though I trusted Yuki *completely*, I couldn't just spill Joe's beans.

Yuki had fixed me with her sharp brown eyes.

"Do you know who I mean?" she asked again.

"The Butcher of Djoba," I said. "He was tried for war crimes and crimes against humanity at the ICC, but as I recall, the case against him was kicked. It was said that after he was released, he drowned. How'd I do?"

"Impressive," said Yuki. "Do you know about his particular crimes against humanity?"

"Fill me in," I said.

I dug around in the console, found a couple of PowerBars, and gave one to Yuki. She took a bottle of water out of her bag and passed it to me.

We took half a minute to satisfy our snack and hydration needs, and then Yuki was back on Petrović.

She said, "As you may have heard, this mofo ordered the killing of a couple thousand civilians. The men were locked in burning barns, slaughtered with machine guns, or randomly executed. Babies were pulled from their mother's arms and tossed alive into fires or bayoneted; the lucky ones had their throats cut. The women and girls were raped, impregnated, destroyed from the inside out . . ."

Yuki choked up, then after a moment went on with this horrible story of Serbian military atrocities. She told me that she'd seen film of Colonel Petrović taking a child of about six onto his knee.

"He kissed his forehead and said everything would be fine. Then he cut the boy's throat."

"That's...beyond monstrous," I managed to say. "Simply inconceivable."

Yuki said, "There's more. From witness reports, Petrović

liked to choke women and girls while he raped them. He'd let up so they could breathe, then choke them some more. When they were dead, he hanged them. Actually, whether they were dead or alive is unclear."

I was dying to know why Yuki wanted to tell me about Petrović so urgently.

And then, finally, she told me.

CHAPTER 62

YUKI SAID, "I guess you're wondering why I'm telling you about this dead Serbian war criminal, right?"

I laughed, wondering whether I could tell Yuki that I knew exactly who she was talking about. "You could say that again."

"Well, just hang on," said Yuki. "He's not dead."

She grabbed her bag from the footwell and pulled out a page torn from a newspaper. It was an ad with the headline, STEAK HOUSE OPENS UNDER NEW MANAGEMENT. MEET TONY BRANKO.

There was a photo of the new owner, Antonije Branko, standing outside the door under the awning with TONY's PLACE FOR STEAK spelled out in flashy gold script.

Yuki said, "One of my coworkers showed this to me. He had family in Bosnia during the war. He knows this Tony as Slobodan Petrović. I looked up the photos of Petrović when he was on trial at The Hague. The names don't match, but the photos do. Apparently, Petrović got out of Bosnia some-how and opened an upmarket steak house on California Street."

I didn't have the expected response.

"You're nodding your head?" Yuki said. "That's it? War criminal living in San Francisco and you nod your head?"

"I'm trying to take it in," I said. "It's a lot."

She took my lack of astonishment as a rebuke.

"Are you *kidding*? I thought this would blow your mind. It did mine. But never mind. I'm clueing Parisi in in the morning, and then I'm going to take this to the FBI. They've got to know that a mass murderer is a local restaurateur, now open for business."

"I hear you," I said.

Joe would have to understand my sharing information with Yuki when I told him that she was already in the know.

"Okay," she said, "I'm waiting."

Yuki took back the water bottle and slugged half of it down.

I said, "I already knew. Joe's working on this."

She whipped her head around and gave me a startled look. Then she said, "Share a few more words, if you don't mind."

"The FBI has been duly notified and is aware of Petrović. A survivor from the massacre at Djoba came to Joe, and he's looking into all of it—how and why Petrović's case at the ICC got kicked, why he's here, what it means."

Yuki shook her head. "*Now* you tell me."

Yuki was an assistant DA, a prosecutor. She was dogged, and yet if there was no case to dig into, she'd drop it. The FBI was on it. There was nothing for her to do.

I said, "Sorry for not volunteering this, Yuki, but its Joe's case. I needed to know first what you knew before divulging what Joe told me in confidence. Okay?"

She nodded, disappointed but understanding.

I stuck my key into the ignition, and Yuki opened her door and started to get out. I was thinking fast. Was Yuki's news of a mad-dog war criminal who enjoyed hanging his victims purely coincidental?

Now it was my turn to say, "Wait."

Yuki got back into the car.

I said to her, "What you just said about Petrović. Follow me on this. Torture. Rape. Hanging. Does this ring a bell with you—or am I totally out of my mind?"

"You're thinking Carly Myers?"

"Do you see it?"

"How do you connect them?" Yuki asked me. "She's a schoolteacher. He owns a pricey steak house."

"She was a schoolteacher who turned tricks on the side—in a motel. Petrović imprisoned women in a building that, under his occupation, was called the rape hotel. He enjoyed hanging people, didn't he? Carly was found manually strangled, then hanged."

"Keep going," Yuki said.

"I'm thinking out loud," I said. "I admit I don't know how Petrović would know Carly—or any of them. But it's not impossible, right?"

"No, this is all good," Yuki said. "You could be onto something. Want to toss this around with Claire and Cindy?"

"Another good idea," I said. Sometimes we amazed ourselves.

Yuki and I hugged good-bye, and I drove home thinking about Petrović, wondering if it was possible that he'd gotten his hands on the three schoolteachers from Pacific View Prep.

I'd do anything to find out if and how.

CHAPTER 63

THE NEXT MORNING I left home early so I could meet the girls for breakfast at MacBain's before work.

When I hit Bryant and Langston, I heard shouting and saw that Bryant Street was cordoned off from Seventh to Harriet and mobbed by protesters.

I made the required detour and a few turns before I could park under the overpass on Harriet Street, then I walked up the block to the intersection and saw the protesters. They were mostly high-school kids, hundreds of them. They wore maroon-and-gold PacificView sweat shirts and were surging toward the Hall of Justice, carrying signs with the faces of Carly, Susan, and Adele, and chanting, "Do your job. Do your job."

I felt sick to my stomach.

I was doing my job, as was Conklin and the homicide crew, and the volunteer cops, our first-class ME, and the crime lab. But even the manpower, the twenty-four-hour days, the interviews, and the deep research hadn't produced a live suspect.

Yes, I felt defensive, but there were no acceptable excuses.

The Pacific View student body, the parents of the three women, and all of the city's citizens had every right to demand answers.

Someone shouted my name.

I turned to see Claire coming toward me, only yards away on Harriet. She tossed her head in the direction of the demonstration and looked as distressed as I felt.

We put our arms around each other's waists and crossed the street together. Cindy and Yuki waved to us from the entrance to MacBain's, and we burst through the door together.

Syd MacBain said, "Take any table you like."

No discussion needed, we went for our favorite table.

We ordered coffee and tea, and I swore Cindy in, as usual, officially notifying her that this meeting was off the record. She rolled her baby blues, shook her head, making her blond curls bounce, and said, "Gaaaaahhhhhh."

Claire laughed, Yuki joined in with her rolling, merry giggle, and then we were all laughing, because you cannot hear Yuki's laughter without falling apart.

I had to give it to Cindy. She broke the gloom into pieces.

Once the hot drinks arrived, Yuki took charge and briefed our group on Slobodan Petrović's suppression of Djoba, Bosnia, two decades ago.

"He's here now," she said, "going under an alias, Antonije Branko."

"Petrović is in San Francisco?" Cindy asked.

"Looks like it," Yuki said. "A man presumed to be Petrović just opened a steak house on California."

"Tony's? The one that used to be Oscar's?" asked Claire.

Yuki said, "That's the one."

Claire and Cindy were shocked. They listened avidly as Yuki described an aspect of Petrović's modus operandi—his documented pattern of rape, torture, and murder. I'd spent a restless night talking it over with Joe, comparing Petrović's MO to the strangulation and hanging of Carly Myers in a motel shower.

I wasn't yet convinced that the dots, in fact, connected.

When Yuki turned the meeting over to me, I explained that Petrović was known to have kept women prisoners in a rape hotel, and that he had sadistic tendencies.

Cindy said, "Go on," and I did.

I said, "Myers was found in a motel frequented by prostitutes. With nothing more than what we've said, I can't help but wonder if this bizarre torture and hanging of Carly Myers was committed by Petrović. And if so, is he on a roll? Has he stashed Saran and Jones in other motels around town? Because we don't know where they are. We don't have a clue."

I thought of those students chanting "Do your job" just down the block. Was Petrović a lead? Or was I just hoping for something to give us a handle on this kidnapping and murder?

Claire's voice broke into my thoughts.

She said, "I just got this back from the lab last night. These are impressions of those unusual premortem cuts on Carly's body."

Cindy hadn't heard about those cuts. She jumped in with questions.

"What kind of cuts? Can I see the pictures? Oh. Oh. Those don't look fatal. Were they, Claire?"

Claire said, "No, they weren't fatal. These wounds were probably inflicted to scare her and make her compliant. Sometime after that, she was asphyxiated, and then, when she was dead, she was hanged. Seems to me that the hanging was for effect. She was dressed in a men's white shirt—probably just to hide the wounds, make a better-looking corpse."

Claire and I have been close friends since we were both rookies, and I can read her pretty well.

From the look on her face, I was sure that Claire was about to drop some kind of news we hadn't heard before.

CHAPTER 64

MY PHONE BUZZED, Richie texting me that Jacobi wanted to meet with us right away.

I texted back. *Ten more minutes. Maybe fifteen.*

Then I tuned back in to what Claire was saying. She had opened another folder of photo enlargements, saying, "These pictures are of the latex molds pulled from the slashes in Carly's torso. See here: thin slabs of latex and a ridge where the latex material seeped into the wounds. The report suggests that the wounds may have been caused by throwing stars."

"Are those the same as ninja stars?" Cindy asked.

Without waiting for an answer, Cindy began googling *throwing stars* on her phone.

"Here we go," she said. "Actual name of throwing stars is *shuriken*. They're of Japanese origin but used in other countries. 'Historically, *shuriken* are made out of almost any metallic found objects'...dah-dah-dah...'star-shaped, five-pointed, swastika-shaped,' and so on."

She swiped on her phone, read another page, and resumed her summary.

"The stars are not meant as a killing weapon—to your point, Claire. They're used more to injure and distract and to supplement swords and other weapons . . . Uh, they're usually five to eight inches in diameter, very thin, thrown with a smooth movement so that they slip effortlessly out of the hand. Okay, paraphrasing here, the victim often doesn't see the star and thinks he's been cut by an invisible sword."

Claire said, "Yeah. That thin blade sounds right. One of the wounds was a slice on Carly's forearm. Like defense against a glancing blade."

Cindy showed us an image of throwing stars of all shapes tacked to a display board. Then she put down her phone and said, "Throwing stars are illegal in many countries and some states. They're illegal in California."

I remembered what Claire had said when I went to the morgue to see Carly Myers's body: "If you find the weapon, you may find the killer."

Forensics had homed in on the most probable weapon. But how were throwing stars a link to Slobodan Petrović?

The check arrived. Cash dropped on the table from four hands. We hugged and headed off to work.

I moved fast, edging through the demonstration and taking the front steps, wanting to get to that meeting with Conklin and Jacobi.

I had a lot to tell them about the genocidal war criminal living near the Panhandle. That he had a documented history of torture, rape, and mass murder.

And that, according to postwar witness reports, Petrović was a sadist: he made a point of hanging his victims, and it seemed like he just loved to do it.

CHAPTER 65

SECURITY CALLED UP to Joe, saying that he had a visitor, Miss Anna Sotovina.

"Send her up," Joe said.

Anna had stood him up for last evening's six-thirty meeting, turned off her phone, and not returned his texts and calls. He'd been worried about her all night, and now he was pissed off.

When she knocked on the doorframe, he checked her out. She was dressed for her job and didn't seem scared or injured. He asked her to come in and indicated a chair.

She started speaking as she crossed the room.

"I turned off my phone," she said. "I didn't want it to ring when I was waiting in my car."

"You didn't think to call and let me know where you were?"

"I know. I know. I had a sudden idea to follow Petrović home from the restaurant."

"You've lost me."

"After lunch I went to Tony's. I used a car from the lot so that he wouldn't recognize me by my car. I waited for hours and he didn't leave the restaurant. I stayed there all day. I peed in a bottle. I didn't leave or move."

Joe was fuming, but he nodded, then said, "Go on."

"I saw the man with the evil smile. He left at 7:00 p.m. That's why I didn't come here. I saw him and had to decide what to do. If I followed him, maybe he would recognize me."

"Oh, you think so?"

"You're being sarcastic with me? Really, Joe?"

He waited her out as she stared at him with an angry, hurt look on her face. She continued to glare as she debriefed him.

"I decided to stay outside the restaurant. I watched customers come and go, come and go, and then I still waited, until all the lights went out. Petrović never left. So I drove past his house. I didn't see the Jaguar. There was only one light on upstairs. I drove home and I circled the block."

Anna went on.

"No one was watching me. Still, I parked two blocks away, and then I walked home and came in through the backyard. I am sure that I wasn't seen."

Joe said, "And did you drive by his house this morning, on your way here?"

"Yes. His car wasn't there."

"And you drove by the restaurant?"

"They don't open until noon," she said.

"So what are you doing, Anna? Are you studying law enforcement online? You think you should get an honorary FBI badge and a gun? Do you think you can sneak up behind

Petrović at a traffic light, yell 'Hands up,' and bring him in? What the hell are you thinking?"

She stared at him and he didn't flinch. It was unbelievable that this woman, so completely out of her depth, unarmed, untrained, had been tailing a notorious war criminal and now was trying to stare *him* down.

Her lack of fear was alarming. If she kept this up, he'd be called to identify her body lying in the street, his card in her handbag.

She said, "You don't scare me, Joe. And you don't tell me what to do. I survived this fat man when he was fucking me on the floor. I survived what he did to me."

She pulled her hair away. In daylight the burn scar was like shiny cloth, bunched up and glued to her cheek from eyebrow to jawline.

Anna said, "I saw what he did to my friends and my sister, and I found my dead mother, naked, in a shallow grave. My beloved husband, same. My baby in a ditch. I got away. By night. By foot. By boat and train and more by foot. So do not tell me I can't watch him. Don't tell me that. Either help me. Or leave me alone."

She got up from the chair and headed for the door.

Joe called after her.

"Anna. Come back. I have pictures for you to look at. Do you want to identify your soldier in the Escalade. Or do you not?"

CHAPTER 66

ANNA STOPPED IN the doorway and, without answering, walked back to the side chair and sat down.

Joe swiveled the computer screen so she could see the enlarged photo of the soldiers grouped around the monument at the center of Djoba's main street. Beyond the monument, scattered bodies lined the road.

Anna looked at the photo, searched from the left side to the right. Her eyes stopped on the image of Petrović, then swung back to the other end of the row.

She reached out a shaking finger.

"That's him. The man in the Escalade."

Joe said, "You're sure?"

Tears sprang from her eyes.

"I'm sure," she said. "That's him. I can still smell his stinking breath. He's a twisted bastard. But I don't know his name."

Joe said, "Okay, Anna, okay. I'll get an ID on him. Not

today, but we have access to the identity papers of these troops. I'm sorry for what I said before. I'm scared for you, understand? Let me walk you to your car."

"I can find it," she said.

It was a struggle, but he didn't say "Stay away from Petrović" as he walked with Anna to the elevator. His office was on the thirteenth floor, and it took long, uncomfortable moments for the elevator car to travel up from the ground floor. During that time Anna stared at the elevator doors and Joe stared at Anna's profile.

He pictured the cruel episodes in her life as if they had happened to a relative or a dear friend, and it pained him. He was taking this case too personally, and that worried him. Still. He would tell Steinmetz he was assigning a 24/7 tail on Petrović.

The elevator ground upward and lurched to a stop. The doors slid open. Anna stepped in, turned around, and punched the button for the ground floor. She looked up at Joe as he told her he'd call her when he had new information. She thanked him and the doors closed.

Joe walked back to his office and took a good look again at his screen capture.

He paid most attention to the soldier Anna had identified as the man who had confronted her on Fell Street. As she had told him, the man was a regular soldier, not an officer, and he was in uniform—fatigues, the dark-colored beret, smooth-shaven. He had been adjusting his beret, and in this frame his face was blurred.

Joe cued up the thirty-second video of the men posing in front of the monument and cut screenshots every second.

He reviewed his work and found the clearest image of the man Anna had pointed to in the second row.

He printed out the still shot for his file and drew a circle around the unidentified soldier.

And funny thing, the more he looked at this man, the more certain he became that the soldier in the photo was a younger version of the gray-haired man he'd seen with "Tony" in the steak house last week.

This man had been saying something to Petrović. Like, "Yes, I just heard. I'll take care of her." Something like that.

Joe had been shocked to see Petrović come out of the kitchen and had focused on him. He hadn't been listening closely to Grayhair at that time. But in retrospect, the odd phrase had a terrible ring. It could have meant anything; that a payment was due to the hostess or the linen company—or something darker.

Petrović had said to Joe at the time, "Where's your girl-friend? The one with the bike."

When Petrović's sidekick had said, "I'll take care of her," had he been referring to Anna?

Petrović had seen Anna on the bike. And he'd seen Anna with Joe when he'd taken Petrović's photo coming down the steps of the yellow house. But did Petrović also know Anna from raping and burning her in Djoba?

Despite the genocidal rape and crimes against humanity in Bosnia, as far as Joe knew, Petrović hadn't committed any crime in the USA. But maybe Escalade Man had, and if so, he might have a police record.

Hai Nguyen was likely out for lunch, but Joe attached the

video and the clearest screen capture to an email, marking it *URGENT.*

He wrote, "Hai. Serbian soldier in the second row from the bottom, third in from the left. Djoba, Bosnia. I need his name." He sent the email.

Joe went to the break room for coffee, thinking about that nameless soldier raping Anna. He knew her movements here in San Francisco and had the balls to try to intimidate her. He recognized her. How could he not? Maybe he had ID'd her to Petrović.

And there was Anna, a defiant, unarmed civilian stalking a killer who just might like to put her away for good.

CHAPTER 67

ADELE ASSUMED THAT it was morning because Marko had woken her by pulling her out of the bed by her hair.

"Please. You're *hurting* me."

She didn't actually know what time it was, what day, how long she and Susan had been trapped in this gilded cage. No clocks, no outdoor light, no sense of the rhythms of the day and night. It was maddening, but it wasn't the worst of their treatment.

Despite the promise of freedom for good behavior, they had been punished repeatedly. Punched. Raped. Criticized and threatened and locked in their rooms without time or sound or hope.

Now she and Susan were in the glossy, peach-colored dressing room, pearly as the interior of a conch shell and lit with the softest of makeup lights. They sat in vanity chairs facing the large, beveled mirror.

Susan was fair, strawberry blond, tall. Adele was dark-haired, wiry, athletic. They each had been given a wardrobe and a box of cosmetics suited to their hair color and complexion.

Today they were similarly dressed in silk dressing gowns over their matching baby doll pajamas. They'd been instructed to look beautiful. But they'd never been a fraction as terrified in their lives.

The dressing room was situated between their two bedrooms. Beyond the bedroom suite was a large sitting room, thickly carpeted, luxuriously appointed with down-stuffed upholstered furniture, a marble fireplace, and a grand piano.

There were high ceilings and tall windows that were heavily draped. The room's soft lighting came from torchiere lamps and the sconces on the walls between the bookshelves. The ceilings were decorated with ornate moldings and a chandelier hanging from a gilded plaster medallion.

Adele would never forget the glittering crystal and the fancy plasterwork on the ceiling. She'd stared at it as the men had taken turns on her.

Susan was brushing her hair. She asked, "Adele? Are you all right?"

Adele said, "I can't take it. I want to kill myself. I wish I could."

Susan put down the brush and grabbed both of Adele's hands in hers.

"Del. Listen to me. You can't let them break you."

Adele pulled away from her friend and said, "Look."

She lifted the silk nightgown and showed Susan the large bruises on her breasts, the ones coloring her inner thighs.

Lifting her hair, she touched the raw place where Marko had pulled out a big clump.

Adele said, "He would kill me just for what I'm thinking. You know I'm right."

She pressed tissues against her eyes. She sobbed for a moment, then blew her nose. "How do you do it?" she asked her friend.

"I tell myself that I'm pulling off the greatest scam," Susan said softly. "I tell myself that they can hurt my body and my ego, but they can't crush me. I won't let them. Adele, can you tell this to yourself? You *must*."

Adele sighed deeply.

She said, "Sometimes I feel strong. I feel an obligation to live long enough to tell the cops what Tony did to Carly."

"Yes," said Susan. "That's right. We have to do what it takes so we can speak for Carly."

"Do you really believe we're getting out?" Adele asked. "They know we will tell. They're going to kill us no matter what we do. You know that, don't you?"

"We have to outsmart them, Adele. Wait for an opportunity."

Adele normally didn't wear makeup, but she'd watched Susan, taken tips on how to apply eyeliner, and now attempted to draw a line across her eyelid near the lashes. Her hand shook so badly, Susan took the brush away and cleaned Adele's eyes with a damp cloth.

Then she held Adele's face in her hands.

"Be still," she said. "I'll do it."

She talked to Adele about how to please the beasts in order to live another day. She suggested phrases, flattering sex talk, demonstrated moaning and gentle touching. "Use your own words," she said.

Adele saw that her friend was trying to be brave for her. She asked her, "Susan. What are you thinking? Please tell me the truth, for real."

CHAPTER 68

SUSAN PUT DOWN the eyeliner brush.

She said to Adele, "I'm trying to keep it together. But I can't stop thinking about whether we'll get out of here. Thinking that my parents are going crazy with fear. I'm wondering if people are looking for us, and how long we've been missing, and when we're going to get out of here. If."

She was thinking about that last night of freedom, when they'd left the Bridge, planning to make the short walk back to school. She pitied Carly, wept for her, but she still blamed Carly for getting them into this hell. And she blamed herself for going along with her.

Susan knew Tony, and she knew Marko. They were her drug dealers. But she'd never told her friends that. She couldn't tell them that she was hooked. She knew Carly was no squeaky-clean rich girl, but Carly didn't mess with drugs. And Adele? Susan didn't even know why she hung around with them.

But oh, God. Carly wasn't the only one to blame for getting them here.

The Monday night when they were leaving the Bridge, Tony and Marko had pulled up to them in the Escalade. Tony had leaned out of the driver-side window and asked Carly for a favor.

"Carly, darling, I was hoping to see you. A big-time restaurant reviewer is coming tomorrow for dinner at my place. Please, Carly," he said. "All of you girls. I need you to look around with women's eyes. I have questions about the paintings I bought. I am suddenly unsure of my taste in these things, but there is enough time to exchange them before dinner tomorrow."

Adele begged off. Susan also didn't want to go.

She said, "Tony, I'm sure the paintings are fine. The reviewer only cares about the food."

Tony was persuasive.

He said, "Yes, the food, but also ambiance. I know it's late, but listen, my chef has made his signature chocolate dessert for you. And the whipped cream on top is a consultant's fee. You name it. A hundred? Two hundred each. Cash for your time. One hour only. Please?"

Carly said, "Okay, Tony. Sounds like fun," and her two friends acquiesced. The three of them got into the back seat of the big blue Caddy. Marko leaned over the back seat and served the women cold champagne in crystal flutes.

Susan fell asleep, and when she woke up, she was in a strange room. It took forever to stretch out her hand, to shift her eyes. It was as if she were swimming underwater.

She noticed that the bed was so soft, it seemed to embrace her. But this room was a dark and windowless cell. Her things were gone, her clothes, her phone. She was a prisoner.

She was dressed in a transparent nightgown, and from the soreness between her legs, she realized she had been used for sex.

That first night in captivity, Susan crawled to the foot of the bed, where she could reach the doorknob, but the door was locked. She started to scream.

Tony opened the door, pushed her back onto the bed, and told her that she belonged to him now. And he laid down the rules—all of them cruel, arbitrary, cast in stone—with one promise. Follow the rules and she'd be fine. If not, they would kill her. And not quickly.

He slapped, pinched, and punched her to make his point, and then he took her with force. When he was done, he slapped her bottom, kissed her forehead, and said, "Good night, sweetheart. See you in the morning."

He left, locking the door behind him.

Susan looked at her friend now. "Adele."

Adele looked at her, reflecting her fear.

"I'm sorry. So sorry that you're here. And sorry for me."

CHAPTER 69

SUSAN SAT WITH Adele in front of the makeup mirror, thinking back on all that had happened to them, knowing in her heart that Carly had been completely taken in by Tony.

The morning after their abduction, when they were dragged from their beds and brought to the lounge, Carly went wild and fought for her life. She called Tony vile names, threw things at him, and ran to the door. Anyone could see that her attempt to escape was not only hopeless but infuriating the men.

Tony grabbed Carly by the shoulder and punched her in the belly. She crumpled and he dropped her. She gagged and threw up on the rug.

Susan tried to help her, but Tony flung her against the wall. Her head hit the plaster, and she slid down to the floor. She watched as Tony began choking Carly with his large hands, letting her breathe, then choking her again. He let up and Carly gasped and breathed out a long, terrible wheeze.

"I'm sorry," she said, looking at Susan.

Tony pulled Carly to her feet, dragged her up over his shoulder, and carried her out of the apartment.

Days later Tony showed them the pictures of Carly's lifeless body, pale and stiff, wearing one of his shirts. She looked like a wax exhibit in a house of horrors.

Tony had meant for Susan and Adele to be so terrified, they'd obey and wouldn't try to escape. But they knew more now than they had known during those first days.

Susan had played the piano for the beasts several times after the evening meal, and the music relaxed them. It gave her the idea for a fantastic plan. When the time was right, she and Adele would escape.

Sometime soon, maybe tonight while she was playing, Adele would pour the liquor and keep the glasses full. When the beasts were drowsy on food and alcohol, Adele could smuggle the fireplace pokers into the bedrooms and hide them under the mattresses while Susan played on.

Now, in the dressing room, getting ready for breakfast, Susan brushed color onto Adele's cheeks and painted her mouth with lipstick.

Then she said, "Tell me, Adele. Tell me our plan."

Adele said, "We'll get them drunk. When they're asleep in our beds, we will use the pokers to bash in their heads."

Susan kissed her friend's cheek.

"You got it."

Susan had never even killed a mouse before, but she could picture raising the poker high and bringing it down on Tony's head.

Could Adele do the same with Marko? She heard footsteps coming toward the dressing room.

The door opened.

Marko said, "Breakfast is served in the lounge, ladies. Now."

Susan said, "Give us a minute, would you, Marko? We're not quite ready."

"I said now. Tony is in the house and he wants you. Comb your hair, Adele. Move."

The door closed, and Susan said, "We'll get out. We'll find a way."

Adele was shivering, and Susan knew that she was remembering the assault last night in the lounge in front of everyone, the beating, the rape by one, two, and then a third man.

Adele said, "Susan, the only way out is to kill them or kill myself.

"Honest to God. I don't care which."

CHAPTER 70

MARKO HERDED SUSAN and Adele over to the gold tufted silk sofa in the lounge and told them to sit.

The man called Junior entered the room with a tray of food and drink: a bottle of good wine, a basket of bread, and two plates of chicken salad. He set up the meal on the coffee table and poured the wine.

Adele wasn't hungry. And this wasn't breakfast. She was no longer sure what time of day it was. Could be one of their tricks. Or it could be that she had been drugged again and had lost track of time.

She sensed a changed mood in the room that she couldn't quite identify. On the surface today was like the days before. The day shift of three nameless men guarded the front door and served the food. Marko supervised.

But today the men seemed expectant.

Marko stood in front of the two women and said, "Eat. It's good."

Adele picked up her fork, stabbed some lettuce. Marko

turned and Adele put the fork down. She heard heavy foot-steps coming down a long hallway to the lounge.

Tony.

He filled the doorway. Puffed on his cigar. Smiled like a game-show host.

"Good day, ladies. Everyone sleep okay?"

Adele and Susan murmured in unison, "Yes, Tony."

Adele remembered Tony raping her last night, pulling her hair, forcing her head back with one hand and squeezing her throat with the other.

When she'd flailed, he'd been amused at her fight and gasps for air, and before she could pass out, he'd let her go.

He had joked, "Was it good for you?"

Then he'd stood up, walked to the bathroom, and flushed the condom down the toilet. He'd stepped into his shorts and opened the door for Marko, slapped his comrade on the back. Just before Marko had crossed the threshold, Adele had heard the door open to Susan's room and Tony's voice booming, "What's new, Pussycat?"

Adele shot a glance at the fireplace pokers only thirty feet away. There were too many men to take a chance now but maybe later.

Tony dragged over an armless chair and straddled it, facing the two women over the coffee table.

He said, "I have a surprise for one of you." And then he laughed. "You both look terrified. Stop that. I'm just taking one of you out for a change of scene, maybe ice cream. And not what you call it? Funny business. I want you to have a day off."

Susan grabbed Adele's hand, and Tony held up a quarter for them to see.

Tony said, "Susan, the head or the tail."

"Heads."

The coin jumped into the air, spun, and tumbled until Tony caught it and slapped it on the back of his hand.

"Oh. Sorry, Susan. It's the tail. But you'll get your turn. Adele, there are some new clothes in your room. Get dressed," he said. "Hurry, Little A. Before it gets dark."

CHAPTER 71

ADELE SAT BESIDE Tony in the front seat of the Jaguar as he sped along a two-lane highway, going where, she did not know.

Her hands were tied uncomfortably behind her. Her new jeans were tight and binding, and the waistband painfully pressed on the bruises at her hips and stomach. Over the jeans she wore a white sweatshirt with the logo of Pacific View Prep.

Adele's arms were wrenched up behind her, and when Tony had fastened her shoulder belt, she'd pleaded with him to release the buckle.

"Tony, please no. It hurts too badly."

"Of course, Adele. I care about you. You know that, don't you?"

"Yes, I do, Tony."

He'd taken off the shoulder belt.

A blessing, but Adele was sure that the "change of scene" story was a hoax. She'd played along, even asking Tony if she could call her parents and let them know that she was okay.

Tony had said to her, "You're a funny girl, Adele. But seriously, if you ask for help or try to get away, I will have to kill you, which will really pain me."

He'd put his hand over his heart and looked at her with a fake sad expression.

Then he'd said, "Also, I will have to call Marko and he will put Susan down like a dog. I know where your parents live, Little A., and I have the names of all of your friends. So please, darling, just behave. Say, 'I understand, Tony.'"

Adele had said it.

"Say, 'I belong to you, Tony.'"

She'd choked that out, too. It was important that he trust her. "I'm going to be the perfect date. I promise."

They'd been driving for about a half hour, heading toward the setting sun. During that time Tony had been on the phone and he'd listened to music over the radio, but he hadn't spoken to her again.

Adele thought that he was distancing himself from her, and that scared her. As she'd told Susan, he would kill them both no matter what they did. Being obsequious and cooperative had bought them time. But Tony would never leave witnesses to what he'd done to them and to Carly.

Adele was alert for opportunities, hoping Tony under-estimated her. If he stopped for gas, she'd beg an attendant to call the police, or at least go to the ladies' room and leave a message on the mirror in soap. If she managed to get her hands free, she could reach over and jerk the steering wheel and run the car into a tree.

She might die, but she might kill Tony, too.

Tony gripped the steering wheel with both hands and said, "We'll be there soon, Adele darling. Don't worry. You are going to have a good time, no kidding."

"I'm glad. Thanks, Tony."

She smiled like she was his girlfriend.

"I'm getting a little bit hungry, though," she said. "And I'd like to use a restroom."

"Sure," he said. "Amenities are coming up in a few miles."

The roadway cut through woods and was bounded by scrub and trees on both sides. The waning sun painted the sky pink and cast long shadows on the road. Adele flexed her fingers to keep the blood moving, wriggled them to see if she could loosen the wire around her wrists. She pictured pulling in to a diner or even a convenience store.

He would untie her with a promise to be good.

And when she got a half a chance, she would whisper to the nearest person, "Help. My name is Adele Saran and I've been abducted. Call the police."

Tony was speaking to her.

"I have to see a man about a horse," he said, grinning. "That's the expression, isn't it?"

"Yes. So funny," Adele said.

Tony slowed and pulled the car off the road onto a gravelly verge, where he parked and turned on the emergency lights.

"Be right back," he said.

He opened his door and stepped out, walked to the front of the car and ten paces into the forest, and faced a tree.

This was it.

There were no cars, no people, and losing herself in the thick woodland was her best and maybe only chance to escape. Adele twisted in her seat, turning to face the steering wheel. While watching Tony, she felt around behind her until the door handle was in her hands.

She yanked up, and thank you, God, the door opened. Tony was still using the tree as a toilet as Adele swung her legs out of the car. She leaned against it to get her balance. Then, with the Jaguar between herself and Tony, blocking his view of her, she hunched over and ran for her life.

Tony shouted after her, "Run, Little A. Let me see you run."

CHAPTER 72

TONY WANTED HER to escape? That's what he wanted?

Well, he was going to get what he asked for.

Adele's arms were twisted up behind her back, the wind whipping her hair across her face as she crossed both lanes without incident. When she reached the far side of the paved road, she had to stop to see how she would get over the gully between the pavement and the woods beyond it.

With her arms pulled up tight behind her, she didn't have enough balance to jump across, and she was determined not to fall. If she did, Tony would seize her, and after humiliating her, he'd kill her.

She quickly sized up the width and depth of the ditch, looking for footholds, seeing where she would climb down, wade across, make it up the other side.

Watching her feet, she stepped carefully down into the ditch, then climbed up the other side, falling only once. She managed the crossing only to meet a wall of brambles between herself and the woods. The sticker bushes were everywhere, lining the woodland, and Adele did what she had to do. She leaned in, the fragile skin of her face taking the brunt of the thorns. And then she was through the barricade. She exhaled as she blended into the relative darkness of the forest.

And then, just when she had gotten free of the brambles, Tony called out to her.

"Adele. Adelll-ah, darling. You could get lost out here. You could get hurt."

The shaded woodland gave her a big advantage.

She could see where she was going, and the shadows would give her cover. Adele turned her head to see where Tony was and glimpsed his silhouette beside his car—and he saw her. But he wasn't coming after her.

He called out, "Wait there, Adele. I'll bring you back to the car."

Like hell he would.

She pushed on into the woodland, gingerly at first; but gaining balance and confidence, she steadily climbed the gently wooded slope. When the ground flattened, she ran. A hundred yards in, she stumbled over a root and pitched forward to the ground. She ignored the scrapes and bruises and used her strong core muscles to roll up into a sitting position, glad for the tens of thousands of crunches she'd done in the school gym. And thank God for the StairMaster, too; somehow she got to her feet on the incline.

Up ahead was a large tree and Adele got behind it. Tony couldn't see her as she pressed her back against the trunk, inching down until she was sitting on the leaf litter beneath the tree. Her arms hurt with unrelenting pain, but she twisted and stretched, worked her slim hips through the circle of her arms until her bound hands were in front of her.

She noticed now that the white sweatshirt stood out like neon, looking even brighter as the sun left the sky. Adele pulled the fabric over her head and bunched it around her wrists. Then she pushed up and forward, exhilarated and at the same time certain that if Tony caught her, he would wrap his hands around her throat. He would squeeze and release her airway as he did during sex, the sick bastard, and this time he wouldn't let go.

Adele was rested now.

She was moving swiftly and she wasn't alone as she ran. She gave herself affirmations, saying out loud, "Good girl. Keep going." As she tripped over logs and recovered from stumbles, she felt Susan, her parents, and even Carly flanking her path, encouraging her to run.

As she moved farther from Tony and toward who knew what, she heard the snapping of twigs.

There was a flashlight beam up ahead, swinging from left to right, and it *stopped moving* when it caught her square on. Adele shielded her eyes and saw another beam coming from her right and another farther up the hill.

Oh, my God. It's a search party.

They were looking for her.

"*Help,*" she called out. "I'm over *here*. Please help me."

CHAPTER 73

SOMEONE CALLED TO Adele from the middle distance.

"Hey, chickie. Don't stop now."

That was Marko's voice. *Marko.* What the hell was going on?

"Marko?"

"Run, Adele."

That was Tony's voice, and she could see him, silhouetted by his car's headlights, coming toward her. She saw other flashlights in the woods, flickering through the branches, seeking her out, cornering her.

She realized with a shock that she'd made an idiotic mistake. This was no rescue. These were Tony's men. And this was one of their sick games.

Tony shouted playfully, "You should run, sweetheart."

Adele's guess was that this was probably some version of hide-and-seek with a death penalty for getting caught.

She ran from the lights and the voices, and they followed her. "Adelllllllle. Are you afraid of us?"

Without stopping, Adele counted seven lights in the woods. She picked the darkest point between the lights and loped over broken ground, leapt downed branches and the scattered bones of a dead animal, and negotiated the changing grade of the land.

She accepted the numbness of her hands and arms as a handicap and focused on keeping her footing as she sprinted through the woods, frantic for the sight of a home or traffic on a road.

Adele was putting distance between herself and the men when she felt a sharp, glancing pain in her right shoulder.

A man called out, "Good one, Junior."

A second voice cheered her on, "Run, Bambi. There's a road not far. You can make it. We love you, Della."

Something shiny sliced through the air, past her face, and struck a tree, sinking an inch into the trunk. She paused a moment to see what the object was: a pointed, star-shaped piece of metal about five inches across. One like that was in the back of her shoulder, and she couldn't reach it with her tied-up hands.

Another of the things whizzed past her face, missing her by what seemed like only a fraction of an inch.

"Bad throw," said a voice closer than before. "You missed again."

"She's fast. Faster than the other one."

One of the men laughed, "Or maybe you just suck."

The flashlight beams and snapping of twigs were coming too close. She told herself, *Keep going, run faster,* and although her muscles were killing her, Adele ran up the grade to a clearing in the trees carpeted with moss and leaves. She had to stop, put her hands on her knees, catch her breath. That's when she saw it below the incline, downhill and only about a half mile from where she stood.

There *was* a road, with cars and what looked like houses close to the base of the hill.

You can make it, Del. Focus on the road.

She started down the slope, bracing against saplings when the grade was too steep. Soon she would run out in front of traffic and hold up her tied wrists, and when a car stopped, she'd tell the driver to call the police.

Adele sucked air into her burning lungs as she ran. Blood poured down her arm from the throbbing wound and the star that was still in her shoulder, but she pressed on. She was in midstride when the shock came, the blow and sharp pain between her shoulder blades that knocked her to the ground.

She thought she might have blacked out, but she was awake now, sledding on her belly over fallen leaves, toward the headlights on the road just below.

The pain was nearly unbearable, but Adele stretched her bound hands in front of her. Her descent stabilized, and as she slid slowly downhill over the dry leaves, she told herself, *I'm going to make it. I'm going to take my life back and make Tony and his goons pay for what they've done, so help me God.*

CHAPTER 74

AT 8:00 A.M. Conklin and I were in the break room with Jacobi, who was showing us the images Clapper had just sent him.

They were hard to make out across the table, so I took Jacobi's phone out of his hand and stared at the screen. I expanded the image.

"Oh, no. Is this Adele?"

Jacobi sighed and took back his phone. He said, "Claire's on her way to San Jose. Here are the coordinates. Get going. I have to get to the parents before the press does it for me."

On any other day it would have been a soul-lifting and inspirational drive alongside Crystal Springs Reservoir and the rolling hills from SF to San Jose. But this morning I felt saturated with dread.

Adele Saran had died an inconceivable death. As investigators, we would be starting over, learning what we could about the killer with the help of forensic science and our own problem-solving minds. That, combined with hope, luck, and prayer, might lead us to Susan Jones, or it might not. Based on how Adele's body was posed, her murderer was probably the same psycho who'd killed Carly Myers.

We commandeered a squad car, and Conklin took the wheel while I manned the phone and the radio, connecting with the rest of the team over the wail of our siren. We got clear of Highway 280 and Route 17, then took Camden Avenue to Hicks, a two-lane stretch of road that cut through the Sierra Azul Open Space Preserve, eighteen thousand acres of rugged wilderness.

The scenery was impressive and couldn't have been more different from the skeezy motel in the Tenderloin. Assuming the perp had killed both women, he had range. Or maybe he just liked the legendary spookiness of Hicks Road, described as Halloween any time of year. Travelers claimed to have heard banshees and seen red-eyed ghouls on Hicks. Others spoke of the blood albinos and other fanciful ghosts.

But it was morning. No wraiths or banshees made themselves known. A turn in the road opened into a forested area just up ahead, and I picked out the crime scene.

It wasn't hard.

Law enforcement vehicles flanked the road: CSI and coroner's vans, local police cruisers, and a couple of ambulances. Crime-scene tape cordoned off the road on both sides, enclosing the primary and secondary crime scenes, and an evidence tent had been set up just outside the perimeter.

Conklin pulled off the road a few yards from the tent.

I called dispatch, notifying them that we were on the scene. Conklin and I looked at each other across the front seat. Neither of us felt sunny-side up today. We'd failed Adele Saran and were heartsick about it.

I said, "Okay, Rich. Ready or not, time to go."

He badged the uniform at the tape, and as soon as we had ducked under it, Clapper appeared. We shared both shock and banalities as he walked us to the big oak tree, ten yards in from the edge of the road.

Hanging from the outspread branches was the body of a young woman, pretty, dark-haired, wearing jeans and a white sweatshirt with the words *Pacific View Prep*. She was barefoot and had been hanged by the neck with what looked like a length of white telephone-type wire.

Clapper said, "We've got our pictures, and I have two teams going through the woods looking for God knows what. She's been up there long enough. Agreed?"

I nodded okay.

Claire came up behind me and stood next to me as a van backed up to the tree. A couple of CSI techs climbed to the van's roof and very carefully, reverently, cut the wire below the knot and brought the dead twenty-seven-year-old schoolteacher down.

CHAPTER 75

JOE AND I were watching the eleven o'clock news, lying close together on the sofa, with Martha breathing deeply on the floor beside us.

I held the remote control.

I wanted to talk to Joe, but first I had to see how the media was treating the death of Adele Saran.

The headline stories on all channels, mainstream and cable, focused on the tree where Adele Saran had been found hanging. There were close-ups of the knot, the tree, the coroner's van leaving the scene, the men in white CSI coveralls bringing evidence to the tent for bagging and tagging. All of this activity was accompanied by the crackle and screech of car radios.

Press setups were dotted around the immediate area, outside the tape. Television reporters faced the camera and told their audience of the horror at the murder scene. A peppy young woman interviewed Paul Harwood, the hiker who had discovered the nightmare on Hicks Road early this morning and called the police.

Harwood told the reporter, "I didn't believe what I was seeing, that I can tell you. I thought at first it was some kind of prank. A store dummy or something like that. But I had a bad feeling, so I pulled over to make sure. And there that poor girl was, strung up like that . . ."

I muted the sound as the video switched back to the studio anchor.

Joe said to me, "So, go on with what you were telling me."

"Where was I?"

"With Claire."

"Right. Rich and I followed Clapper and Claire back from the crime scene, and we all went straight to the morgue.

"Claire sidelined everything but our victim and got right to the external postmortem. Time of death, approximately nine o'clock last night. Joe, she was alive last night!"

Joe said, "Oh, God," and then I told him what else I had learned from Claire.

"It's not for the record yet, but for the moment Claire is saying Adele's cause of death was the same as Carly's."

Joe said, "She was strangled first and then hanged. She had wounds from a throwing star?"

"Exactly," I said. "And this time it wasn't guesswork. The damned thing was still sticking out of her back. There was another deep wound in her right shoulder. Neither was fatal. She had bruises on her torso, inner thighs, around her neck below the ligature. Also, as with Carly, there was no discernible physical evidence on the body that would lead to the killer or killers. No skin cells or blood under her nails; in fact, her hands were tied tightly together."

"What about the rope she was hanged with?"

"It was coated copper wire."

"Telephone wire. You're not going to get prints off that."

I said, "Whoever hanged Adele Saran was a tidy son of a bitch. Wore gloves. Wore a condom. Clapper took blood, sexual assault kit, swabs, and clothes to the lab. Maybe the killer was sloppy and left saliva on her skin, or bled on her clothes.

"But I'm not feeling lucky."

Joe hugged me, and I burrowed in under his arm and took some deep breaths.

"Anything else?"

He always listened to everything, no matter how seemingly insignificant, and I was glad to tell. Maybe Joe would notice something I had missed.

I said, "Okay, well, here's something a little different. CSIs found three or four sets of human tracks through the woods, coming from Hicks Road, spreading out, then converging about a hundred yards in from the road.

"Adele hadn't gotten very far. The blade to her back brought her down. Judging from the disturbance on the ground, she fought a little but never got up. She was probably strangled where she fell, and carried out to the hanging tree by the road. There was nowhere for her to run, Joe. There was mostly wilderness for miles around."

Joe nodded, picturing the way it had gone down.

"So a hunt, you think," he said. "And multiple perpetrators. Not personal and yet very sadistic. What's that about? Some kind of gang—"

I had to interrupt him.

"Wait, Joe, what's this?"

CHAPTER 76

THE IMAGES EXPLODING on the TV screen had grabbed my attention. I unmuted it.

It was live footage of demonstrators surging through Civic Center Plaza and pooling at the base of City Hall. There were close-up shots of grieving students and many angry people of all ages with hand-lettered signs demanding justice for Carly and Adele.

A couple of cruisers entered the frame with sirens bleating. When they stopped, cops opened the rear doors, and I recognized Adele Saran's parents being led by a cop and an organizer to a podium. I started to boost the volume, but Joe took the clicker away from me and turned off the TV.

"That's enough, Lindsay. You're not going to get anything useful from watching more of this."

He pulled me closer, kissed my forehead. I knew he wanted me to calm down for my own good, but my mind was on fire.

We had chores to do before bed and it was way late. Joe took Martha for a walk, and I went to clean up the kitchen.

I was thinking about what Joe had said about Adele's death, and the suspicion of a gang—but tracking and killing her and posing her corpse in a *tree* was way too organized for street gangsters. The killer or killers had been careful and followed some kind of script, maybe a pattern of killings that proved the same perpetrators had killed both Carly and Adele.

As I loaded the dishwasher, I thought about the conversation I'd had with Joe last night, when we were safe in bed and I had no way of knowing that Adele Saran was running through the woods, about to be murdered.

I came back to the unplumbed coincidence of Slobodan Petrović, a terrorist military officer who was on the record for hundreds of rapes, tortures, and hangings—a man with a history of programmed military executions.

Joe had shared his frustration that he had nothing on Petrović, with two teams of agents working on it. They were watching Petrović's car, house, and restaurant, and had attached a tracker to his Jaguar, but sometimes they lost him in traffic. Or while they were watching his parked car, Petrović left the restaurant by a back door.

Discretion was critical. Petrović had made Joe as FBI—Joe's mistake—and if Petrović thought that the FBI was still surveilling him, they would never catch him in an illegal act. He'd take pains not to let that happen. They had no probable cause to get any kind of warrant.

But this emergency was about to expire without probable cause. The FBI had to catch him in an illegal screw-up if they were ever to kick him back to The Hague for his sentence to be reinstated.

"We follow him, Linds," Joe had told me. "He drives around town. Goes shopping. Gets a haircut. Goes back to his restaurant. Goes home at night. We wait and watch and follow. He's never as much as gone above the speed limit. I can't get a warrant to wiretap his phones without probable cause, and I don't have it. I can't pull him over, invade his premises, or get a warrant to search anything. He refuses to screw up."

I got into my pj's and tried to let go of the hellish images in my mind. I was running through the woods with Adele as a pack of savages threw star-shaped blades at us. I couldn't shake the feeling of how terrified that poor woman must have been.

As I got under the blankets, I was thinking that Joe and I were both good detectives. Okay, better than good. And neither of us was getting traction on our case.

I heard Joe come in through the front door with Martha. He filled her bowls, turned off the lights in the living room, then came into the bedroom and sat on the edge of the bed to take off his shoes.

He said, "Clapper's the best. If there's trace on the body or evidence in the woods, he'll find it. And this media hurricane is going to pay off, Lindsay. Someone, a witness to the abduction or the murders, is going to remember something and come forward with a bona fide lead."

If only. If there was a hot tip out there, it had to come in before we found Susan Jones.

CHAPTER 77

JOE HAD REQUISITIONED a repurposed black Toyota RAV4 with a powerful engine and high-tech bells and whistles whistles throughout.

The GPS tracking device on the underside of Petrović's car was transmitting to a monitor attached to the Toyota's dash. The blue Jaguar was still parked across the street from Petrović's yellow Victorian house.

It was a weekday morning, and Tony's Place for Steak wasn't yet open, but Joe had a team on California Street watching the front and another team on Jones with a view of the adjacent condo and garage. Petrović couldn't leave either place without being seen and followed. Period.

Joe had eyes on the target's house when the front door opened and Petrović stepped out. He locked the door behind him, then came down the front steps to the street. Joe lifted his binoculars to his eyes and watched as the hog puffed on his cigar—always managing to obscure a clear view of his face—and headed toward his car with a nice jaunty step.

Life for Slobodan Petrović was very good.

The blue Jaguar was parked within fifty yards of where Joe sat in the Toyota. He observed Petrović unlock his eighty-thousand-dollar showboat and surreptitiously look up and down the block, checking out the traffic, parked cars, neighboring homes. He seemed satisfied that there was nothing untoward around him—no danger, no tail, just another beautiful morning in the City by the Bay.

The Butcher of Djoba got into his car and started her up.

Joe switched on the little Toyota as well. He was prepared to follow Petrović to his restaurant, as he'd done every morning this week, but the Jaguar had a new flight path.

Petrović drove west on Fell, took a left turn on Masonic, crossing the Panhandle, and took another left on Oak, heading back the way he had come.

Where was Petrović going?

Joe was three cars back as the Jag took the left on Oak, a wide residential street that ran parallel to Fell. Joe followed the Jag through the awkward turn but now had to hang back so as not to be seen. And then, damn it, he caught a red light while the Jag sailed through the intersection.

Joe checked the empty one-way cross street and ran the light. Once he was clear, he called his guys at the steak house to let them know that it looked like Petrović was heading into the Civic Center area.

His team was also tracking the Jaguar on their monitors, and while one car stayed in place on California, the other tore out of a side street and headed toward the straightaway of Van Ness.

The little Toyota SUV with the hot-rod engine was the most unremarkable-looking car on the road—if you didn't know that it was loaded with a hundred thousand dollars of government electronics.

Right now the GPS was pinging the satellite and laying out the Jaguar's route on the monitor. As Joe followed Petrović's car through the crowded Civic Center area, passing Davies Symphony Hall and the War Memorial Opera House on the left, and City Hall on the right, he was concerned that Petrović was going off script.

Why? And what was his destination?

CHAPTER 78

JOE DROVE THROUGH Polk Gulch with a backup team behind him, both cars tailing the Jag, when Petrović took a right on Union where it crossed Van Ness.

Was Petrović trying to lose them? Or was this a ruse, a deliberate joke on them, taking them out of the way and then doubling back to his restaurant?

Or was this was something else entirely?

Instead of looping back, Petrović stayed on Union, climbing uphill to the high-priced neighborhood of Russian Hill.

Joe exchanged words with his teams, instructing his follow car to speed up and pass him. If Petrović had picked up the Toyota in the rearview, he would now think that he'd lost his tail.

A church was up ahead on the left, and something was happening there. A half dozen limos interspersed with media trucks were parked out front. Reporters sat on high canvas director's chairs, facing their cameras, makeup people touching up their hair. Traffic cops held up their hands to slow and detour traffic.

Just then the huge church doors swung open, and the newlyweds burst through with their wedding guests. The church emptied behind the new couple coming down the steps, waving, ducking rice, the bride pausing to turn around and toss the bouquet over her shoulder to a squealing crowd.

Joe recognized the couple, a Silicon Valley billionaire and a Hollywood movie star. He got a good look because the wedding party had produced a one-lane logjam that had slowed the flow of traffic to just under a crawl.

He was now at a dead stop. His backup team, just ahead of him, was also locked into the parking-lot variety of standstill.

Cursing to himself, Joe checked the GPS.

Petrović was zipping along Lombard within the speed limit, but at the same time was far, far away.

Joe sent the backup team to Tony's Place and checked in with the team on Fell Street who were now waiting for another team to relieve them.

Once free of traffic, Joe took the next turn that would take him back to his office. He continued to watch the Jaguar's contrail on his desktop computer, the little blip that was Petrović motoring back to the steak house.

Joe hoped that the butcher wasn't having a big laugh on him. But he couldn't dismiss the possibility.

If Petrović had anything to do with the murdered school-teachers, he was winning. And to prove it, he'd just given the Bureau a big fat middle finger.

CHAPTER 79

FIFTEEN MINUTES LATER Joe was with Steinmetz in his corner office, updating him on the day's chase.

"I have a team on Petrović's house. I have the second team watching the restaurant where Tony is now overseeing the lunchtime service."

Joe told Steinmetz about the wedding party roadblock caused by newlywed celebrities and attendant paparazzi, the frustration of seeing a renowned mass murderer drive around San Francisco with impunity.

Joe said, "How can I stop him?"

Steinmetz muttered, "We're a nation of laws."

Joe nodded his agreement, then told his supervisor what he'd learned about the murder of Adele Saran.

Steinmetz said, "I'm on top of that case. The bottom line is that there were lots of footprints in the woods, no forensic evidence, no witnesses to the crime, and no video recorders out in the middle of Sierra Azul Open Space."

"Correct," Joe said. "Lindsay is of the opinion that Petrović may be involved in the schoolteacher murders."

"Because?"

"Because Petrović liked to hang his victims."

Steinmetz cracked a smile. "That would almost be too good to be true. You had eyes on him at the time of the Saran girl's murder?"

"We had eyes on his house."

"So no. He wasn't sighted here in town. What do you know about his associates?"

"Guy who runs his restaurant, Marko Vladic, has no record. Petrović has some kitchen help that are also squeaky clean. No one wants to get caught up in an ICE sweep. The Boy Scouts have nothing on Petrović's crew."

Steinmetz said, "You're not seriously thinking of bringing him in as a suspect in the Saran murder?"

"I'm waiting for him to give me any kind of excuse," Joe said. "Littering. Jaywalking. Parking in a no-parking zone."

"You get something resembling probable cause, get back to me," said Steinmetz.

Joe said, "Will do," and feeling totally ineffectual, he walked down the hall to his office, went in, and closed the door. He checked the GPS: Petrović's car was still parked in front of the restaurant. The car staking out the back of the restaurant had been switched out for another bland-looking repurposed sedan, American brand this time. Team two was parked near the intersection of Fell and Scott in an old hippy bus, painted with swirls and flowers.

Joe checked in with the guys, got zippo, gave encouragement, and got off the phone. A moment later it rang.

Joe grabbed for the receiver. It was the security guard at the ground-floor desk saying, "She's baaaaack."

"Who?"

"Ms. Sotovina."

CHAPTER 80

JOE MET ANNA at the elevator, then walked her back to his office, hoping that she had remembered something important or that Petrović had threatened her, something that would rise to the level of probable cause to investigate him with the full force of FBI resources.

He asked Anna if she had news for him as she took a seat.

She said, "No. I don't have anything new, Joe. I thought you might have something for me."

She looked expectant and very vulnerable. The tough "don't tell me what to do" version of Anna wasn't apparent today.

"Anna, do you have any friends in town?"

"A few. Why?"

"Because I know I'd worry less if you moved in with a friend instead of living in that house where Petrović can get to you at any time. He can simply cut through a few backyards."

"You think he's going to come after me?" Anna asked him. "He couldn't care less about me, Joe. He's had me. Many times. He could have killed me, many times. Petrović isn't afraid of me. And he has no reason to fear, because if he doesn't lay a hand on me now, I can't touch him. He got a pass for all of his old crimes."

"I've told you what I think," Joe said. "He's a criminal in search of a target, and you make a pretty good one."

"It's my birthday, Joe. Forty today."

"Oh. Well. Happy birthday. Did your coworkers give you a cake?"

"Yes. And cards. And this," she said, showing him a chain with a little sparkly pendant. "It's my birthstone. But I haven't had lunch. How about taking me out for something, Joe? I haven't had steak in a long time."

"You're joking."

"Small joke. Not steak. Pasta maybe."

"Sorry, Anna. I've got work to do here at the office."

She tried to hide her disappointment, but her face colored. She picked up her handbag.

"I apologize for being…inappropriate. I'll be going now."

Joe said, "Don't worry, Anna. Really. It's okay."

He knew she was lonely. That he was a large figure in her life. He walked Anna to the elevator and told her, as he always did, that he would be in touch if he learned anything useful and she should do the same.

Later that afternoon, Joe checked in with his teams and their night shift replacements. Petrović's car was still parked in his spot in front of Tony's Place. All was quiet.

Joe turned it all over in his mind as he drove toward Lake

Street. Was Petrović up to something? Or was he on his best behavior, taking part in the American dream?

He thought about Lindsay and hoped she'd be waiting for him when he opened the front door.

He longed for a regular evening at home with Lindsay.

CHAPTER 81

IT WAS FRIDAY morning, eleven days since the school-teachers had been abducted—two of them subsequently murdered—and we were clueless in the truest sense of the word.

I stared down at the mess of papers on my desk while I was on the phone with Clapper, thanking him for getting back to me so fast on Adele Saran.

He said, "I think you mean, 'Thanks for nothing.'"

"No. I mean one door closes, another opens—if I can only find that other one."

Clapper chuckled, said, "You'll find it, Boxer. I've got faith."

I put down the receiver and threw a category-five sigh, blowing a pile of message slips across my desk onto Conklin's.

Conklin said, "Tell me. I can take it."

"Okay. Welcome back to square one, partner. The only DNA on Adele's body was hers. Nothing under her nails. No trace or prints on the wire used to bind and hang her. No prints on the throwing stars, and the only evidence in the woods was scuffled leaves from hither to thither, starting and ending at Hicks Road. Oh. On the other hand, there were *hundreds*, if not thousands, of prints on the tacomobile."

Conklin leaned back in his chair, ran both hands through his hair, and sighed, "Oh, happy day."

I went on.

"Carly's prints were on the door handles and the dashboard—corroborating what Denny Lopez told us. He drove Carly to the motel a few times. Most of the other prints were his and his girlfriend's—remember her? Three days ago seems like a year. Lucinda Drucker. But there was a match to a Barbara Fines, a prostitute, goes by the name of Daisy."

Conklin said, "Corroborating Denny's story again."

I said, "Clapper will release the taco truck to its owner, or he'll hold on to it if we want to jerk Denny around a little more."

"He's all we've got. Let's do it," said my partner. "Maybe we'll shake something loose."

I called Lopez with a burner phone so that my name didn't come up on his screen, and he picked up. He was mad about my little trick but said that he was at a bar called Bud's on Twenty-Second and Mission. I told him to hang tight, then Conklin and I were on our way in a cruiser.

Conklin pointed to Lopez, standing on the corner outside the bar. He was unkempt, with dirty hair and clothes, clearly out of work—our fault—since we'd taken the SUV away.

Lopez looked pained as we double-parked the black-and-white, and even more so as Conklin got out, opened the rear door, steered Denny into the back, then got in beside him.

"For God's sake," the pimp slurred. "You're going to get me killed, you know?"

Conklin said, "Killed, why?"

"You know why," Denny said, like he was talking to four-year-olds. "I could be seen talking to cops."

"If you help us out, Martinez could have the SUV in a few hours. You'll get your job back. Okay?"

Lopez said, "Let's talk fast. I have a lunch date with a young lady. If you get my meaning."

I slid over to the wheel, started up the car, pulled out onto Mission without tearing up the asphalt. I parked four blocks away in front of a nail salon and a donut shop, set the brake, and leaned over the seat back.

I said, "Listen to me, Denny. You were present at the scene of the crime. Prior to that, you'd seen the schoolteachers at the Bridge and had a business relationship with Carly. She's dead. Adele is dead. We could hold you as a person of interest for a lonnnng time."

"You shitting me?"

"Dig deep, Denny. There's always one forgotten thing. What haven't you told us?"

"Now that you mention it, I do remember something."

I said, "Go ahead. Blow me away."

"I actually remember a guy who came into the Bridge one time, not long ago. Sat at a table with another dude and bought drinks for those girls."

Lopez was sobering up a little bit and checking out the passersby, the customers carrying bags from Grand Mission

Donuts, the usual motley collection of jobless, homeless, hopeless, and drugged-up denizens of the Mission, along with office workers getting their morning joe.

Conklin grabbed the pimp's arm and shook him to attention.

"Denny. Tell us what the guy looked like, anything he may have said or done."

"Christ," Denny said, throwing up his hands. "He was big. I only saw him sitting, but I'm guessing he was six three. Two eighty. Carried his weight here." He put his hands on his abdomen. "He was at the Bridge and buying drinks for the girls, and Carly was shining on him. I was still hoping to get her back, so that's why I noticed."

I started up the car.

Conklin got out of the back seat, got in next to me.

"Hey. You're taking me back to Bud's, right?" Denny asked.

"Guess again," I said.

CHAPTER 82

CONKLIN SAID TO Denny, "We need you to look at some pictures at the Hall."

Lopez protested loudly.

I told him to shut up and calm down. "Two women are dead, and you knew both of them. Odds are you saw their killer."

"You arresting me?" he asked, still slurring.

"Only if you insist," I said.

He didn't speak after that. We arrived back at the Hall in fifteen minutes, left the car on Bryant, and marched Denny Lopez straight up to the fourth floor, where I stashed him in Interview 1 and told him to sit tight.

"Officer Krupky is behind the glass," I said, pointing to the mirrored window. I waved at my image. Krupky was fictitious and the observation room was empty, but Denny didn't know that. I said to him, "It's going to take us a little while," handing him a copy of the morning *Examiner*, which I'd grabbed off one of the chairs.

"You should read this."

The front-page story was about Adele Saran. There was a picture of her beautiful face and another of the hanging tree. The headline couldn't have been bolder or blacker.

TORTURE AND DEATH OF A SCHOOLTEACHER.

Denny didn't strike me as a news junkie or a reader. From the way he grabbed the paper with his shaking hands, he was learning the details of Adele Saran's murder right here and right now.

Conklin brought Denny black coffee, then he and I went to our desks and put together a photo array of big guys. One was Petrović. Jacobi and Cappy McNeil were also included, as well as three convicts doing life in maximum-security prisons.

When the glue had dried on the six-picture array, Conklin and I returned to the interview room.

I put the photo array in front of Denny Lopez, and Conklin and I took our seats, my partner telling him to give the photos a good look. "Take your time."

Lopez recognized a picture instantly, stabbed it with his right index finger. "Him. That's the guy."

"Be sure. Take another look," said Conklin.

Denny said he was sure. The camera in the corner of the ceiling duly recorded that he'd identified Lieutenant Warren Jacobi, our friend and commanding officer.

Lopez asked me, "Is that him? Did I pick the right one?"

I answered his question with a question of my own.

"The big guy who bought the women drinks at the Bridge. Did he ever get lucky? Did any of those women ever leave with him?"

"Jeez, I don't know. You think a lot of my powers of observation, Sergeant. And I'm not sure why."

It was a funny remark, but I didn't laugh.

My gut told me that Petrović was our killer, but that hunch wasn't backed by evidence of any kind.

"Let's go, Denny."

Conklin and I drove Lopez back to the vicinity of Bud's Bar and left him on the corner where we'd found him.

CHAPTER 83

ANNA WAS AT the Tesla dealership on Bush Street, off Van Ness, inside the office she shared with the copy machine.

At just before 5:00 p.m., she was finishing up the monthly books, entering last week's expenses onto the spreadsheet. The numbers were facts; sales minus dollars spent on salaries, supplies, rent, advertising, even the birthday parties, including hers.

Anna excelled in this job, but socially she was a disaster. She understood all the reasons why. But setting her own catastrophic damage aside, other people were too peculiar for her. Too not from her world.

She'd tried and failed to explain this to Dale.

Dale Winston was behind his desk in the showroom, doing some paperwork. He liked her, and she liked him, too, but not in the way he wanted. She walked across the showroom floor in time to the bouncy music coming over the sound system.

"Hiya, Dale."

He looked up. "Anna. Hey. You look good in purple. You know that?"

She thanked him, rearranged her coat and scarf, then said, "Dale, I need a favor."

"Anything. I'm all yours."

She smiled and said, "Seriously."

"What do you need?"

She told him, and he was reluctant, very, but in the end he caved, telling her to bring back the vehicle before the shop opened in the morning.

"Not a problem."

"It can't be, or we're both getting fired—or worse."

"Do not worry, Dale. You can trust me."

"I do trust you, Anna. Do you trust me? Wait. Hear me out. Maybe we could have dinner together this week. Just to celebrate your birthday."

"Uh, you know we're not allowed to fraternize, Dale. I'm sorry."

He opened the drawer and took out a key ring. He waited for her to hold out her hand, then he gave her the keys, making a point of pressing her palm with his fingers.

She clutched the keys.

"Before 9:00 a.m.," he said unnecessarily.

She nodded. "And will you call Roger? Say I'm on my way?"

Anna went back to her office, got her bag, and waved good-bye to Dale. She walked a block to the service department. Roger was behind the counter, phones ringing in the office behind him, the service bays still busy at the end of the day.

Roger looked through her without seeing her—her scar did that to people—but she was glad he didn't want to make small talk.

She just wanted to go.

"You need pointers on the car, Anna?"

Anna told him she knew the Model X and had taken a couple of test-drives with Dale. That part was a lie, but Roger seemed satisfied. He pointed to the black Tesla Model X parked outside the service center. It was a prototype with a dinged-up front fender, and while Anna usually liked things to be perfect, she only cared that this car was fast and wasn't her red Kia.

Roger said, "Have fun. But not too much."

Anna nodded and touched the door handle, and the falcon wing rose silently, majestically, revealing the car's sleek interior. *Wow. Just wow.* She took off her coat, placed it with her handbag in the passenger seat, and slipped in behind the wheel.

The car automatically adjusted the mirrors, the seat.

Anna buckled in, touched the button that started up the engine, and was rewarded by a subaudible hum and the sense that the car was alive and attuned to her.

It was *magical.*

CHAPTER 84

BECAUSE IT WAS only 5:15 p.m. and the Butcher didn't leave his house until 6:30 on weeknights, Anna decided to take the long way to Fell Street.

It wasn't every day that she got to drive a hundred-thousand-dollar car. In fact, this might be the first, last, and only.

Smiling to herself, feeling self-indulgent and rich, she set her course for the Panhandle and pulled out of the garage. The engine was surprisingly silent, accelerating and decelerating like nothing she'd ever experienced. Like the car was reading her mind.

It did everything fast, so fast.

Anna wished she'd had the Model X that first day she saw Petrović and she'd chased him on her old bike. Now she had an urge to reverse course, take Highway 101 out of the city and up the coast, burn off all her frustration and anger, and let the Tesla out for an unforgettable run.

But she couldn't do it. Couldn't avoid what seemed to be her appointment with Petrović.

Traffic parted for her as she drove through Pacific Heights to Fillmore, flying along in the perfect car, swooping downhill toward the Marina District. She gave the Tesla more pedal and felt the city blocks falling behind, becoming only faint images in her rearview mirror.

Five miles after getting behind the wheel, Anna was on Fell Street, three blocks from where she lived, and there, like a beacon, was Petrović's yellow-and-blue Victorian house.

Best of all, his Jaguar was out front, exactly where she hoped it would be. There was only one vacant parking spot, and it was at the east end of the block. She didn't get the best view of the house from there, but she would see the Jag leave, no matter what direction the Butcher took.

Anna parked the Tesla with ease and touched the image on the screen to lower her seat back a few degrees. Once she was as comfortable as she had ever been in her life, she shut down the engine and settled in to watch.

She had spied on Petrović, had followed him before through the dirty streets of the Tenderloin. But she'd always lost him, her bright-red car calling too much attention for a close pursuit. He wouldn't imagine her in this Model X.

Sitting in front of his house, she imagined trailing him, watching to see what shady activities he must be involved in here in San Francisco. She suspected drugs, human trafficking, gambling. That's who he was. A mass murderer. A monster.

Tonight she wouldn't lose him.

Anna reached for her handbag, felt around, and took out the nut-and-chocolate bar she'd stashed for a moment like this. She ate, drank water, thought about Petrović and how much she hated him—when everything went wrong. There was a violent crash from behind, and she was thrown hard into the steering wheel.

What happened?

Anna righted herself, looked behind her, and opened her door, the falcon wing creaking now, injured in the crash. Filled with fury, she got out of the car and saw him. Not Petrović. It was the man in the Escalade, he had rammed the Tesla from behind. He was backing up, putting his vehicle in gear, getting ready to ram her again.

She'd been attacked again by that vicious soldier who had raped her. He buzzed down his window.

Anna screamed at him in her native language.

"You. I see you. I know you. I know how to find you. I'm calling the police. No, the FBI."

The man with the gray beard and hair gestured *Sorry*, but Anna knew that he'd rammed her with purpose. It was a warning. She went back to her car, leaned all the way in, and got her purse from the footwell.

She would take pictures of the man and his license plate. Then she would call Joe. She was so consumed by this task, she never heard footsteps behind her.

CHAPTER 85

JOE WAS ON Tenth Avenue at California, waiting for the light to turn, when his phone buzzed.

Lindsay was texting him, saying that she was sorry. She was jammed up at work, not sure when she would be home, and he should go ahead and have dinner without her.

He texted back, *No problem. CU later.*

Joe had spent the day immersed in the Petrović files, saturated with the man's documented cruelty, as certain as Lindsay that Petrović had killed Carly Myers and Adele Saran. And also like Lindsay, he had nothing to prove it.

He checked the GPS and saw the pulsing blip representing the blue Jaguar, motionless on California near Tony's Place. He made a turn and ten minutes later Joe was parked on the corner where he had an unobstructed view of the opposite corner and the brightly lit Place for Steak.

Joe phoned Robert Diano and Bill Ennis, the team assigned to the restaurant. He told them that he was relieving them for an hour, that they should take a break.

271

Diano reported back that they would be at the pizzeria on
Bush Street.

Joe watched them head out, and he took over the surveillance of the Jag and the restaurant. A minute later, as if Joe
had materialized him, Petrović, holding a paper bag, left the
restaurant, waved at him, and crossed the street directly to
where Joe sat in the Toyota.

What the hell?

"Hey," he called out, "Joe Molinari."

Petrović shook the bag like he had a mouse in there and
he was letting his pet owl know that Daddy was home with
something tasty.

Joe ran through his options and quickly settled on his
only move. He got out of the car and spoke to Petrović over
the roof.

"Tony, right?"

Petrović said, "You hungry, Joe?"

Joe said, "How'd you know?"

He smiled, walked around the back of the car, and
stretched out his hand for a friendly shake. Petrović did the
same. Joe feinted, grabbed Petrović by the knot of his tie,
spun him, and shoved him hard against the car.

The big man expelled air and, having been thrown
off-balance, tripped over his feet, stumbled, and fell to
the pavement. He raged, "Are you crazy, attacking a
civilian?"

Joe had his gun in his hand. He pointed the muzzle at the
Butcher's head.

Petrović said, "What are you doing? I'm trying to be a nice
guy. I brought you dinner."

"I know who you are, Petrović," Joe said. "I wouldn't call you a civilian. I could shoot you now and become an overnight international hero. I've thought about it, and instead I'm going to give you a warning."

Petrović was grinning, but he wasn't pushing back.

He must have known that Joe didn't need much of an excuse, that he probably had a throw-down weapon in the car. That the dash cam was off. If he were in Petrović's place, that's what Joe would be thinking. The FBI would win this one.

Joe said, "Bike girl is under FBI protection. Hurt her, and I'm dragging you back to Bosnia myself."

"You mixed me up with someone else, Joe. She's not my type. I like them younger. And prettier."

Joe glared at Petrović for another moment, then said, "Get up."

Petrović had to use his hands and knees to leverage himself to a standing position, then he dusted himself off with his large hands. He said, "We have to do this again sometime. Did I say that right?"

"It would be my pleasure," Joe said. "Next time, dinner's on me."

Petrović smiled, turned, and limped back to the restaurant.

Joe got into his car, while keeping his eyes on Petrović. His pulse was pounding hard, as if he'd sprinted five miles. He was furious at himself, not because he'd crossed a line with Petrović, but that Petrović had made him—twice—and made sure Joe knew it.

Petrović was playing with him.

Joe had a kit in the trunk. He got out an evidence bag,

retrieved Petrović's doggy bag from where it had fallen, sealed, and tagged it.

He called Rob Diano and told him what had occurred, adding, "I have to go to the office."

"We're on our way back to your location," said the agent.

When Diano and Ennis pulled up alongside him, Joe waved, then drove to the FBI branch on Golden Gate Avenue.

He knew Petrović would be gunning for him. He hoped so. He'd like a clean shot at this piece of filth. He'd really like to put him down.

CHAPTER 86

TWENTY-FOUR HOURS after his encounter with Petrović, Joe was in his office, getting ready to head out and salvage some of his Saturday, when Agent Rob Diano called and delivered the chilling news.

"We lost Petrović. I don't know how, he—"

Joe interrupted. "When was the last time you saw him?"

"Molinari, it's complicated. Hear me out. Last night at twenty-three hundred we followed him from his steak joint to his house. The car didn't move all night. We had eyes on it throughout. Seven a.m. the car was still in front of the house when we hand him off to Carroll and Bartoff.

"Carroll turns on the GPS, and the monitor shows the car is moving. But he sees it—parked right there on Fell. Plates check out—Petrović's Jag—but the blip on the screen is moving. Obviously, the subject switched out the tracker, put it on another vehicle. So where is he? Did he leave the house on foot through the backyard overnight and someone gave him a lift? That's my guess. Sorry, Molinari. We can't cover all the bases at the same—"

Just then Carroll phoned from the Fell Street location. Without waiting for Joe to speak, he said, "Molinari. The Jag is still outside the house on Fell. I followed the signal and found the tracker on a florist's delivery truck. We're on it now. Sunshine Florist, white panel van, on Fair Oaks."

"Shit."

"I pulled them over, nice as pie, 'Would you mind? We're looking for a criminal.' No problem. They're father and son doing their store's deliveries. We checked out the van. Nobody in there. No cigar fumes. Nothing but flowers. Ran Sunshine's license, registration, plates. They're clean. Showed them a picture of Tony. They don't know him. We pulled the tracking device, so when you see the Jag moving, it's us. We're coming in to file a report."

Joe hung up, thinking that he hadn't heard from Anna in more than a day. Now that they'd lost Petrović, he felt alarmed. He called her, left a message, asked her to return his call. He texted her. No response. He called the general phone line at the Tesla dealership. After a ring he heard, "Sales, this is Dale Winston."

Joe said, "Can you put me through to Anna Sotovina?"

"And who may I say is calling?" Winston asked.

"Joe Molinari, FBI."

"Oh. Anna's not here. Actually, she didn't come in today. That's not like her. In fact, I'm worried. She's a very disciplined person, but she's forgetting things, showing up late. And now—this is the worst. I don't know why I trusted her."

Winston explained to Joe that Anna had needed to use a loaner overnight, was supposed to return it to the shop this morning by nine. She hadn't come in with the car, and he hadn't been able to reach her.

Joe took down details on the vehicle, left an urgent message for Anna with Winston, hung up, and made notes to the file.

Petrović hadn't been seen in twenty hours.

Anna hadn't come to work and hadn't returned calls.

It was premature, and highly speculative, but those facts added up.

One plus one equaled Petrović had Anna.

Where in God's name were they?

CHAPTER 87

MY ANXIETY WAS simmering as my partner and I crossed the motel's parking lot at dawn.

Dispatch had roused me an hour ago saying there'd been another murder at the Big Four Motel. Was it Susan Jones? Were we going to find her body hanging in a shower?

The motel looked subdued at sunrise. The homeless campers in the parking lot were dozing in their bags and rags, despite the sirens and flashers and squawking of car radios. Many of the motel guests had pulled on robes and jackets over their sleepwear and were grouped under the big orange awning in front of Tuohy's office.

One of the uniformed officers approached us, introduced herself as Officer Joyce Birmingham, and said that she was the first officer on the scene.

She said, "Sergeant, we got the call at five and responded. The manager asked for you. Mr. Jake Tuohy. He said you and Inspector Conklin have some history here."

Carly Myers's body was still vivid in my mind. I asked Birmingham to run the scene for us.

"The vic is a white male—"

"What's that? *Male?*"

"Yes, ma'am. Approximately thirty-five, no ID on him, but Tuohy says he knows who he is. A pimp. Denny something."

"Oh, no."

"Tuohy didn't know his last name. A guest found the body in the space between the soft drink machine and the ice maker. My partner and I taped off the vending machine area, and we're about to do the same to the parking lot. Mr. Tuohy is waiting for you in his office."

"Okay, Birmingham. Good job. You called CSI?"

"Yes, ma'am, and the ME."

I said, "We'd like to see the body now."

Officer Birmingham walked Conklin and me to the bank of vending machines on the ground floor. I couldn't believe what I was seeing. Lopez was dressed in the same clothes he was wearing when we dragged him off the street and into our house yesterday. Jeans, cotton shirt, maroon pullover, denim jacket. He was lying in the gap between two large vending machines, folded neatly into the space. I saw no blood, no signs of violence.

But there was no question. Denny was dead. I thought of him saying, "For God's sake. You're going to get me killed." Almost forty-eight hours later, it had happened.

Conklin and I looked at each other. No words were needed, but I felt responsible. It was a message. His killer was very likely the same person who'd killed the schoolteachers, or knew who did.

Conklin squeezed my shoulder. I patted his hand. And together we stared down at the dead man.

Had he been killed while loitering in the parking lot?

Or had he been murdered elsewhere? A car could have backed up to this spot to dump his body. Two men could have done it in under a minute.

I stooped to Denny's body and, using a pen, moved his collar aside. There were bruises around his neck. He'd been strangled but not hanged.

Similar MO but not identical.

And why had he been killed at all?

Conklin and I theorized over Denny's body.

Had he told the wrong barfly at Bud's that he'd been questioned about the big man buying drinks for the murdered women at the Bridge? Had the big man heard that Denny was talking and put him down?

Or was this an unrelated murder? Denny could have gotten into something in the parking lot. Then got rolled. Strangled.

Nah. Too much of a coincidence.

Normally, I didn't talk to the dead, but I heard myself say, "What happened to you, Denny?"

While Conklin notified dispatch that we were on the scene, I called Jacobi at home.

I apologized for waking him up, but hell, this couldn't wait.

"Our favorite pimp got taken out," I told Jacobi. "Denny Lopez. He gave us nothing. This was a senseless, stupid death."

"Not your fault, Boxer."

"That's not how it feels," I said.

As I signed off with Jacobi, Conklin said, "Look," and pointed to Taqueria del Lobo's delivery truck at the far end of the parking lot. He said, "That'll be back at the lab within the hour."

Conklin and I edged through the crowd, heading toward the manager's office to see Jake Tuohy and get the day rolling. I had a terrible sense of déjà vu. I pictured all the interviews that would follow, the guests who had been minding their own business, or asleep, hadn't heard a thing.

But one bright thought peeked through the clouds.

Denny's killing, compared with the others, lacked finesse. I would say it had been rushed. Maybe we were crowding our killer. Maybe we were getting under his skin.

CHAPTER 88

JOE WAS ANNOTATING the Petrović file when Diano called.

"You were right," the agent said. "The GPS had autotrack. I have the location of the car."

"Watch but don't touch it," Joe said. "Give me the coordinates."

Joe drove to the address Diano had given him in Laurel Heights, an upscale area of two- and three-story Edwardian homes, tree-lined streets, and expensive shops, everything beautifully maintained.

He easily found the Tesla with the dinged-up front fender parked in front of the Laurel Inn on Presidio. You really couldn't miss it. The back end of the car was caved in from a bad collision.

Joe touched the door handle and the falcon wing creaked open and lifted.

A purple scarf was curled up in the passenger-side footwell. Joe recognized it as Anna's, and there was a candy bar wrapper near the scarf that confirmed it.

Snickers. Anna's favorite.

Joe's backup teams joined him at the car, and they spread out. They had no picture of Anna, but her description—a woman of forty, five foot six, 130 pounds, with a scar the size and shape of a hand on the left side of her face from eye to mouth—should serve.

The five experienced federal agents went from door to door, from shop to hotel to apartment building, in a grid five blocks in all directions from the car. The wreck of the Tesla had been noticed, but no one had seen a woman matching Anna's description. The photo of Petrović also drew a negative response.

Joe phoned Steinmetz and reported what he knew: the damage to the vehicle, no indication of violence inside the car, and no sign of Anna. He suggested that Steinmetz get the SFPD involved. The Tesla had to be transported to the city's forensics lab, and they needed to file a missing person report.

Joe watched the flatbed truck take the Tesla down Presidio Avenue toward the forensics lab at Hunters Point. Once it was out of sight, he phoned Dale Winston at the dealership to ask if Anna had made contact and to tell him that the car had been seized by the FBI.

Joe returned to the office and sat down with Steinmetz, who once again stated the uncomfortable truth.

There was still nothing linking Petrović to Anna.

"But here's an idea, Molinari," Steinmetz said. "Ask Petrović for permission to search his home, car, and business. Say you just want to eliminate him as a person of interest. See what he says."

Joe thought it over and saw no serious downside. And maybe Petrović would toss them a bone, have a suggestion—or a telling misdirection.

Joe found Petrović at Tony's Place. The former military executioner said that he was "eager to help out law enforcement. No problem."

Joe, Diano, and Ennis went through the restaurant. Then Petrović led the caravan of federal agents to his house and threw open the doors.

He mocked the agents as they searched the spacious three floors.

"Maybe she's in the washing machine, Joe. Have you searched the trunk of my car? Don't forget to dust everything for fingerprints. I'll send the bill for cleanup to the FBI."

Joe was polite. But after three hours of eating shit, he was seething.

Did Petrović have Anna?

Or had she had an accident with the car and, rather than face the music, taken off to parts unknown?

Anna was strong-willed and angry at him.

If she had gone off on her own, Joe really had no clue where to look for her.

CHAPTER 89

FINALLY HOME AFTER my eighteen-hour day in the Tenderloin, I greeted Joe and Martha from the doorway. I unbuckled my gun belt, pulled off my jacket, and stepped out of my shoes, leaving it all in a heap, and made my way across the room to my husband.

I was exhausted, frustrated, and starving, but still dying to tell Joe about Lopez and kick the case around with him. He was sitting on the sofa with his laptop open on the coffee table. I dropped onto the couch next to him, put my arms around him, and hugged him to pieces.

"I'm guessing you had a bad day," he said, hugging me back.

I got right into it, telling him about Denny Lopez in snatches, knowing that Joe was an expert at making sense of random clues. Then he did the same with me.

"Anna is missing," he said. "She borrowed a car from the dealership, had an accident, and vanished."

When he'd given it all up, I saw that his case was like mine, clues everywhere, leading to nothing.

"Keep your phone charged," I said. "She could call saying she ran away from home and that she's all right."

He nodded, but from the look on his face, I knew he was deeply worried. He didn't buy my happy ending for Anna at all.

"I did find something interesting," he said, "about our pal Slobodan Petrović."

He turned the laptop so that I could see the photo on his computer screen, a slightly out-of-focus image of a group of about eight men wearing fatigues, loosely gathered in a wooded area. They looked like they were having an outing. But there was more to it than that—much more.

A female wearing only a skirt pulled up around her thighs was lying in the middle ground, encircled by several of the men. And in the background, shaded by trees, were bodies of men and women in civilian clothing hanging from branches. There had to be a dozen of them. The vignette looked unreal, like an art installation, the product of a particularly gruesome imagination. But it wasn't art. And it wasn't imaginary.

"Oh, my God," I said several times.

Then I scrutinized the pictures, looking for "our pal" Petrović.

Standing near the center of the frame was a large, wide-shouldered man with a shaved head, wearing fatigues, combat boots. There was something in his hand, small, possibly metallic, with points—like a throwing star.

Joe said, "That's him."

"Is it?" I wasn't sure.

"There's a caption. I translated it. 'Colonel Slobodan

Petrović and men after taking the Bosnian town of Djoba. Petrović is proficient in the use of *shuriken,* throwing stars.'"

I asked, "What's the source of the photo?"

"It appears to have been taken by one of the soldiers. It showed up in the trials against the Serbian Army high command. The caption was added during the trial, and it's unattributed.

"And I found this," Joe said. "A Serbian soldier testified at Petrović's trial. Here's a quote: 'Colonel Petrović and other army officers would watch the hangings. I heard but never saw this. There were rumors that they would sometimes hunt victims in the woods.'"

Joe looked at me.

"You called it, Joe. When Adele's body was discovered, you said you thought it was the work of a gang. It doesn't seem far-fetched to call Petrović the gang leader."

"I think so," he said. "Get ready for the punch line. The witness said, 'Colonel Petrović had a reputation for using a throwing star, and using it well.'"

I threw myself back on the couch. Was this proof? Was this evidence against the man who had injured Carly Myers and Adele Saran with throwing stars and then hanged them? What was the value of testimony from an unnamed witness who may have flipped on Petrović in order to get leniency from the court? Even the report of hunting in the woods was unsubstantiated.

Joe and I talked about this, concluding, naturally, that neither the SFPD nor the FBI could vet these foreign crimes attested to by unnamed witnesses. Furthermore, we still had no direct evidence that linked Petrović to throwing stars, or hanging anyone in the USA.

"It's a mile short of probable cause," I said.

"Exactly what Steinmetz said. But here's what I say. We're a step closer to landing this son of a bitch."

CHAPTER 90

THE PAIN NAGGED and pulled at Anna until she was forced to wake up and open her eyes.

She saw nothing but blackness and thought she was blind.

Panic raised a fine sweat over her whole body, and for a long moment she forgot to breathe.

What happened to me? Where am I?

The pain was excruciating. It radiated from the back of her head and seemed to spread everywhere. Her heart bucked as the pieces came together.

She was a prisoner again.

A bar of light coming from under a door showed her that she was on a bed in a small room.

How did I get here?

A feeling of flying came into her mind, then images of driving the Tesla, all speed and freedom. She'd parked outside Petrović's house. And a void opened in her memory. Something had happened.

Anna's head was killing her.

She must have taken a blow and lost consciousness. She didn't remember any of that, but she tried to recall it, clawing at the fog wrapped around her memory. And then she was dragged into the present by the ragged sound of breathing beside her.

She looked around the small room for a way out. There were no windows, just one door and the thin bar of light.

It was enough to see that her clothes had been thrown around the floor. His clothes were in a pile by the side of the bed.

Her stomach was empty but she heaved, clamped her hand over her mouth. She told herself to just lie still and breathe and think. In time she looked at the man in the bed and assessed him. How strong was he, how drunk, how much of a threat.

He wasn't big, but from what she could see, he was muscular, like the soldiers in the rape hotel in Djoba. Anna had survived the hotel because she'd focused on the future, when she would be free, and what she would do one day to her attackers.

To Petrović.

She sat up slowly, and the man shifted beside her, clacked his teeth, stopped breathing, threw his arm across her, and came awake.

He looked at her.

"What?" he said.

"Bathroom," she said.

He pointed at the door, rolled over so that he was facing the wall, and resumed his sleep.

Anna dressed in the dark. She could not find her purse,

her phone, but the door was unlocked. She stepped out into a hallway, holding her shoes. A night-light was on in the bathroom to her right, and she went in, closed the door. There was no lock.

She flipped the switch by the door and the ceiling light came on. Heart pounding, ready to spring up if the door opened, Anna used the toilet, then went to the sink.

There was a note taped to the mirror.

It was written in Bosnian in large, black block letters:

"ANNA. *STARA PRAVILA JOŠ UVIJEK PRIMJENJUJU. ZNAŠ.*"

It meant, "The old rules still apply. You know."

It was signed "SP."

CHAPTER 91

"ANNA. THE OLD rules still apply. You know. SP."

She knew Petrović's rules well.

Obey. If you don't, we will happily kill you.

SP. Slobodan Petrović had made the rules.

Images flickered, faces of women she'd known from school and the market and from neighboring homes: Dalila and her mother, Amela; her best friend, Uma; and Zuhra, her husband's younger sister. The girls who had defied the soldiers or had curled into balls and given up—they were killed.

The ones who learned fast, did as they were told, they didn't even talk to the other women about what they'd endured. What good was it to complain? They had to live another day and hope for an opportunity to get away.

By being smart, she and Dalila and a few others had survived and gotten out at the end of the war. But this was America. There was no war here. And yet here she was in a rape hotel.

Anna washed her face with hot water, and kept washing as

she remembered the hotel in Djoba. One indelible memory looped in her mind. The men berating Uma before they shot her to death. Uma hadn't cried or even put up a hand. She had wanted to die.

Anna's own hands shook as she dried off with the towel.

Then she peeled the note from the mirror and looked into her own eyes. She had gotten older since she'd last seen her face.

Her eyelids drooped, and the corners of her mouth sagged from fear and pain. She moved her hair back. The scar was livid, and there was blood behind her ear.

She released the sheaf of hair, and for a moment her younger self was reflected in the glass. Her radiant smile as she dressed for her wedding, patted powder on her unblemished skin.

Tears jumped into her eyes, and she ran the hot water again and cried into the stream, scrubbing hard, trying to wash all of this away, at the same time listening for the boot kicking in the door and the beating.

What kind of God would allow her to be taken again?

She thought about Joe's many stern warnings and the height of her arrogance.

She'd maneuvered around him, followed Petrović, refused to wait for the men with guns to do their job.

She had brought this down on herself.

Anna was so agonized by her own behavior that she couldn't stand to look at herself anymore. She opened the medicine cabinet and found a bottle of drugstore painkillers. She spilled tablets into her shaking hand, swallowed down the maximum dose, and put more pills in her pocket.

She turned off the light and quietly opened the bathroom door. There was another door at the end of the short hallway and also an opening, an entrance to another room.

Anna tiptoed on bare feet to that entranceway, and even though she didn't know what she was walking into, she stepped over the threshold.

CHAPTER 92

ANNA WAS ONLY looking for an exit, but stepping into the living room, she was taken by the size of it, the high ceilings, light coming from a large, muted TV near a fireplace.

A news show was on, an international channel, with the times in major cities displayed in the lower corner of the screen. Anna watched until it read, *San Francisco, 3:15*.

She couldn't be sure, but as best as she could remember, she'd lost herself on Friday night.

She'd been in the Tesla outside Petrović's house, prepared to follow him to whatever mysterious places he went when he wasn't at home or at the restaurant. The rear-end collision had entirely shocked her, throwing her into the steering wheel and out of the seat. She'd been furious when she'd gotten out of her smashed loaner, and then stunned to see the Serbian soldier in the blue Escalade.

Anna remembered him clearly now from the hotel in Djoba. He had beaten her with a chair leg and then…she didn't want to think about it.

He was probably here now.

Anna felt suddenly light-headed and her knees buckled. She grabbed at the wall, slipped down to the floor, and stayed until she felt she could stand.

Where was he? Was he watching her now?

She had to leave this place. She had to get out.

Anna looked around the dimly lit room, past the clumps of furniture, to the shuttered windows, back to the sofa, where she noticed the dark shape of a person sitting there with arms around tucked-up knees.

God, no. Was it him?

No. It was a woman.

Another prisoner.

Anna spoke in a whisper. "Hello?"

The woman on the couch beckoned her to come over.

"I'm Susan," she said. "Talking together is against the rules, so we have to speak softly and fast."

CHAPTER 93

ANNA SAT DOWN beside Susan, and for the next three hours they barely moved, their bodies touching from shoulder to hip to thigh. They spoke like sisters.

Susan said, "This is important, Anna. We have to play it cool."

Anna said, "I know. Buy time."

Susan told her about the routine, the names of the men who watched, cooked, used her, and Anna asked about Petrović—did he live here and how often did he come to this place?

"Petrović? I don't know that name. Tony is the boss. Antonije Branko."

"That's *him*. Tony. It's a fake name. Susan, he's a war criminal. I know him from Bosnia. Do you know if he was with me last night?"

Susan said, "No, it was my turn. He went to your room, but you were out cold. He said he likes it better when the girl has a little fight. You got Junior. He doesn't care if you're already dead."

Tears rolled down Anna's face, but she talked through them. She told Susan that she had known Tony as Colonel Slobodan Petrović and that he had decimated her town in Bosnia.

Susan grabbed her hand as Anna spoke of her losses and the months she had lived at a rape hotel. "Like this, only with shootings and bombs. I've seen a man who works with Petrović at the steak house. He has a short gray beard. He…"Anna stopped to get control of her tears. Then, "He knows me from Djoba."

"Marko," Susan said. "He's a sadist. Well. They all are."

Susan told Anna about the night two weeks ago when Tony and Marko had abducted her and her friends, how Carly had gone crazy and Tony had killed her.

"An 'object lesson,' Tony called it. Oh, it got through to us, all right," Susan said. "Then Tony said he was letting one of us go on an outing. He flipped a coin and Adele won. I wanted desperately to go, but I couldn't be mad at Adele.

"Tony brought her new clothes and then, presto, drove her away. They let her leave."

Anna asked, "Do you mean Adele Saran?"

"How did you know?"

"I'm sorry, Susan. Be glad you didn't go."

Anna told Susan what she'd seen on the news, that Adele had been killed and hanged from a tree. Susan clapped her hands over her mouth and cried. Anna put her arms around her new friend, and they clung to each other, grieving without making a sound.

When she could speak again, Susan said, "I don't know why I believed Tony. I thought if I was sweet to him...I was so stupid."

"You had hope," Anna said. "They hadn't destroyed it."

Anna wondered if it was safe to have hope now.

In the dark, while the men slept, Susan and Anna discussed what they had to do to escape. Nothing was off-limits—violence, tricks, charm.

Together they checked the front door, as Susan had done before. Maybe this time the bastards had forgotten to lock it. No such luck. The shuttered windows were also locked. Their search in the foyer for cell phones in jacket pockets turned up nothing. Knives were locked in drawers.

At six in the morning Susan and Anna went to their bedrooms and got into bed with their captors.

CHAPTER 94

AT JUST BEFORE noon, Conklin and I paid a call on Taqueria del Lobo to let Mr. Martinez know that the lab had impounded his vehicle again.

Conklin opened the door and we walked into a shit-storm in progress.

Martinez was yelling at Lucinda Drucker in the front room, which was packed with customers.

"I told you, Lucy. I warned you. And now you gave my car to that asshole boyfriend of yours and the damned thing is still missing and now you're fired. I'm calling the police—oh. *Hola*, Officers. Here they are."

I handed him the warrant and told him the bad news.

"Mr. Martinez, your vehicle was found at the scene of a crime."

"Another one? Son of a bitch. You see what I'm saying, Lucy? You are such a dummy."

Lucinda Drucker was crying now. "Mr. Martinez, please, I need my job."

Conklin interrupted the shouting and crying to say, "Ah, Ms. Drucker, I have to speak with you for a moment. Outside."

He led the sobbing woman out of the restaurant, and I took Martinez behind the counter to the kitchen doorway. As I gave the same news to Martinez that Conklin was delivering to Lucy, I was watching the late Denny Lopez's girlfriend through the plate glass.

I saw Conklin talking to her, saw her jerk away from him, a look of horror on her face. She threw up her hands, like *Get away from me.* My partner reached out to her, and she pushed him off and backed away. Then she turned and lunged off the sidewalk, directly into the stream of traffic.

I shouted "Nooooo" from where I stood behind the counter. She couldn't hear me, but Conklin was also shouting and moving fast. But Lucy was faster. I ran through the doorway and out onto the sidewalk just as the event unfolded.

Horns blared. Someone screamed, "Watch out!"

Its brakes squealing, a northbound car hit the young woman in stride, flinging her high and onto the hood of a car parked across the street. The sound of the impact was horrifying. But it wasn't over. Cars were out of control and crashing, piling up.

I ran out to our cruiser, got my hands on the radio, and shouted the address to dispatch.

"I need paramedics now at my location. And send backup."

By then Conklin had reached Lucy, and as I tried to cross the street to join him, I heard him saying her name, comforting her. I was relieved when I saw her try to sit up.

But the chaos continued. The driver of the car that hit Lucy was frantic, and her children were screaming.

The bus arrived and paramedics climbed out. Cruisers rolled up and blocked off the street. I filled in the patrol officers on the three-car collision, then retrieved Lucy's handbag from Martinez and handed it to one of the paramedics.

Conklin and I were standing together in front of the taqueria when Lucy's stretcher was loaded into the ambulance.

"You know what she told me?" said Conklin.

"No idea."

"'I know Denny. He was a good man and he took care of me. Living without him isn't worth it.'"

CHAPTER 95

JAKE TUOHY WAS in Interview 2 under protest.

We'd brought him in so he could give us a statement as to what he knew about the death of Dennis L. Lopez and the discovery of his body. He let us know that he'd pretty much had enough of all of us, civic duty be damned.

"We're not going to extract your fingernails, Jake. We just need a statement for the record," Conklin told him. "Tell us what you saw, did, and said. You're being recorded. This is as good as being under oath."

"I wasn't planning on lying to you, Officer Con Job."

"Inspector," said Conklin, "not Officer." He smiled. Unruffled as always.

Tuohy ran his fingers through his horseshoe-shaped fringe of hair and stared up at the ceiling.

"I'm asleep in the recliner in my office," he said. "The bell rings. I say, 'Aww, shit.' I say it to myself, for the record. I was alone."

"Then what?" I asked.

303

Tuohy had a way of making everything around him feel dirty. Even this plain, no-frills little interview room that got scrubbed every night felt greasy and covered in germs.

"Then," he said, "because no one said, 'Go back to sleep. I'll get it,' I got up and went out to the office. This whore was outside ringing the bell. I've seen her around with Denny. She goes by the name of Daisy Cakes or something. I don't ask women of her persuasion for ID."

"Go on," Conklin said. "The bell rings. Daisy's at the door."

"She looks worse than usual," Tuohy said. "She's been crying. She tells me that Denny is dead. She insists I come with her to see, and I go and there's his body.

"I figure, if she killed him, she's not bringing me to see the evidence, okay? So I tell her I'm calling the police and go wait in my office. She says okay. I go look at the loser pimp's body and call 911 and tell the operator to call you. Officer Boxer. And don't bother to ask me did I kill the guy. I had no reason to, and besides, I was asleep."

"Did Daisy offer any explanation for what happened to Lopez?" I asked him.

"Just what I already told 911 and what I told you. She was finished with her date. She calls Denny's cell. He's supposed to be waiting for her in the taco truck. He doesn't answer. She gets dressed, waits near the van. Then she calls him again and hears his phone ringing. Goes to the vending area, finds his body. She runs to the office and there's your full circle. She tells me all of that. I call and ask for you. And now here I am."

Conklin said, "Any idea who might have wanted to kill Lopez?"

"No."

"Did you see anyone suspicious-looking hanging around?"

"All of them. Everyone in or around the place. But nobody's going to have Jake Tuohy to kick around anymore. I quit my job. I'm moving to Ireland. I got people there. Letting you know *officially*, so you don't get bent out of shape. I can't stand this job, never liked it, but it's getting to be too many bodies and trips to this place."

Conklin asked for Tuohy's forwarding address.

"Somewhere in Dublin. I'll send you an email." With that, he stood up from the aluminum chair, said "Good-bye and good luck," and made for the door.

Conklin said, "Just one thing, Tuohy. And this is important. You're not going to Ireland. Not until we say so."

"Oh, I'm a suspect now? Is that what you're saying?"

"I'm saying don't quit your day job. Night job, either."

Tuohy snorted and walked out.

I said, "Good one, Richie. Love to hear you explain that to his lawyer. Or anyone."

My partner laughed. "I liked the way it sounded."

I liked it, too.

CHAPTER 96

WHEN CONKLIN AND I returned to the squad room, Jacobi was waiting for us with a woman he introduced as Susan Jones's sister Ronnie Hooks.

"Ms. Hooks," he said, "Sergeant Boxer's the primary investigator on this case. She's the best."

I shook the woman's hand, then introduced Conklin, and the three of us walked back to Interview 2.

Ronnie Hooks looked to be in her early forties. She was perfectly manicured and coiffed and smartly dressed in a crisp red suit, with some bling around her neck and a wedding ring.

Conklin pulled out a chair for her, and when we were all seated, he asked her how she was doing.

"No good," she said. "No good at all."

"Talk to us," I said.

She said, "Susan and I are like twins. I'm ten years older. She's my little sister. But we talk every day. Except last week—Marty and I just got back from Peru. It was

306

a long trip, two weeks, in a remote area. Normally, I talk to Susie every day. I got back to an area with Wi-Fi, and I find out the worst news imaginable. How could she be missing?"

Her crazy eyes were switching from me to Conklin to the mirrored window to her folded hands on the table. I had a thought that she might be on the verge of some kind of breakdown.

I also had a good idea why she'd come in on her own and where this was going. She was going to ask why we hadn't found Susan. She'd want to know if Susan was dead or if she should post a reward. She might get mad and threaten to go to the media with a heartbreaking story about her sister and SFPD's incompetence.

Instead, Ms. Hooks threw us a curve ball.

"Susan was a good teacher, but she didn't make enough money to pay her rent and own a car and have enough left over to get herself a decent haircut."

I said only, "Uh-huh."

"She did some freelance work," said Hooks.

"Like tutoring and such?" Conklin asked her. "She's a piano teacher, right?"

Hooks looked down at the table and spoke to her folded hands. "She's also an exotic dancer."

My jaw actually dropped. Susan Jones was a stripper? But Hooks wasn't looking at me. She was inside her story and she kept going.

"Susan worked once in a while out of a club," she said. "Never told me where, and I never asked for details because I didn't approve. I was afraid for her, but she was strong-willed and it's not for me to judge her. And she said this club was a decent place. Pfft." Ronnie laughed with no joy. "The customers were businessmen, she said."

Customers wearing jackets and ties wouldn't have eased my mind if *my* sister were dancing, but Ronnie Hooks wasn't done.

"The part that worried me," she said, "was the owner of the club was some kind of drug dealer posing as a father figure. Or the way Susan put it, 'He helps out girls who are trying to make new lives in America. Or girls like me, who need the money.' Some of those girls danced in the shows with Susan. But some of them…"

She flipped a hand. I interpreted that to mean she didn't want to say that they were prostitutes.

I said, "Ronnie, I want to be sure I understand. You're saying you think Susan was dancing as a second job?"

I saw *yes* in her very frightened eyes.

"The big boss advanced her some money, and she was supposed to work it off. That's what she told me. But now I think…he controlled them."

"Ronnie, this is important. Did Susan ever describe him, or anyone at the club?"

"I think he's from the Balkans or something. She just called him 'the big boss,' sometimes the nickname Mr. Big. But I heard her use the name Marko once, on the phone.

I said, "Might the boss's name be Petrović? Did Susan ever say that?"

She shook her head no.

"Susan was afraid of him, and she said she wanted to keep me out of it. But she really couldn't. She swore she wasn't having sex with him or anyone, and so I gave Susan money to pay off this criminal before it came to that. I guess it wasn't enough."

I told Ms. Hooks that the department had assigned every available resource to finding Susan and that I would call her myself as soon as we had any information.

It wasn't what Susan Jones's sister wanted to hear. She grimaced as she grabbed her bag. Conklin opened the door for her. She was halfway down the hall when she turned and came back to the doorway with tears streaming down her cheeks.

Hooks looked straight at me and said, "Look. I don't want to say this, because Susan warned me when I saw her last. She said, 'Don't go to the police.' But she'd heard a rumor that really scared her. She heard that Mr. Big had killed a couple of girls who didn't pay up, or who couldn't perform—drugs, I assumed. Susan heard him joking about it.

"I think..." Hooks said, "I think Susan's friends were murdered."

Susan's sister bolted from the room. I heard the elevator bell ding. And she was gone.

CHAPTER 97

CONKLIN AND I were filling out our reports when Jacobi stopped by our desks and rolled up a chair.

"How's it going?" he asked.

I said, "We need another couple of teams, Jacobi. We're nowhere on Myers and Saran. We're nowhere on Lopez. I'm afraid Susan Jones is either dead or about to be. We did just get some very interesting background on Jones from her sister, and maybe a fuller picture of what Petrović is up to, how he's making money, how these women fell into his trap. But still, we've got nothing but ghost sightings of Petrović."

"It's gotten too hot for him," Conklin said. "He's dodging us, playing a shell game with his car. He's not at his usual haunts, and we don't have enough eyes on the ground. And if we see him and pull him in for questioning, we don't have any leverage. Unless we can follow some crumbs on what Susan's sister told us, which could be something. Or it could be the TV-fueled theory of a desperate sister."

"So," I said, putting a lid on it, "that's how it's going."

"It's only been what, a week and a half since Myers?"

"More like two, Jacobi. Eleven days since Myers. Four days since Saran. Twenty-four hours, more or less, since Lopez. We cannot look under every rock, even with McNeil and Chi backing us up. Please. Get us some help."

"I've turned out all my pockets, Boxer. But I'm here. Walk me through it. How do you see Lopez's death linked to Tony's Place?"

I said, "Guessing here. Lopez was some kind of witness. He may have seen Petrović buying drinks for the schoolteachers. He may have been seen talking to us."

"So Lopez was put down before he could give up Petrović."

I said, "Or maybe he was just a victim of circumstance. Drug addict needs some cash, strangles Denny for his wallet. Seems like a stretch, but that could have happened."

Conklin added, "Either way, we still can't put Petrović at any of the murders. Everything we think we know is pure speculation."

Jacobi said, "I'm meeting with the chief tomorrow first thing. I'll get on my knees and beg for more help on this case. And as you well know, the press isn't giving us a break. But look. Two of you go get dinner and put it on my tab."

I said, "That's not necessary."

"It'll make *me* feel better, okay, Boxer?"

CHAPTER 98

CONKLIN AND I walked our hunger pangs across the street to MacBain's. We were putting down burgers and curly fries at a table near the jukebox.

Sydney refreshed our drinks and told us, "Take your time."

Conklin said, "Mr. Big is Petrović. But try to pin a murder on him. It's like harpooning a whale with a plastic fork."

I nodded, opened my bun, and applied more ketchup.

Conklin and I had been partners for so long, a couple of words took the place of speeches.

I said, "Lopez. Petrović. Schoolteachers doing double duty as naughty girls."

"You believed Tuohy?" Conklin said.

"He's got an ugly personality, but I don't think he's stupid. Not stupid enough to leave bodies at his place of employment. What do you think?"

Conklin said, "I think Jacobi would want us to have beer."

He raised his hand, and Sydney said, "Draft? Coming right up."

Conklin said, "I haven't seen Cindy in three days. It feels longer."

"Me too with Joe."

Conklin said, "Unless forensics ties Petrović to any one of our victims…"

He didn't have to finish the sentence. I said, "Let's turn it over again, look at it from a different angle."

He said, "Okay. So here's our new angle. Susan tells her sister that there's a rumor. A foreigner with a no-name name killed a couple of women. We've got two hanged women and a pimp who was connected to one of the victims, turns up strangled."

I had to lay down the details I'd been keeping back out of respect for Joe. It was time. I said, "Joe's got pictures of Petrović in Bosnia. In one of them there's hanged bodies of captives in Djoba. And apparently, he was good with throwing stars."

Conklin stopped his burger just short of his mouth. I hadn't told him about the photo of Petrović with his troops and the bodies hanging from trees in the background. It was Joe's case. FBI intel. I hadn't told my partner about Anna.

"Throwing stars? Okay, you've hooked me now," said my partner. "Keep talking."

"It wasn't mine to tell," I said. "But you need to know."

"Speak," Conklin said.

"A Bosnian war survivor, Anna Sotovina, came to the FBI because she saw Petrović in San Francisco."

"She can tie him to the victims?"

"No, but she's convinced he recognized her. Joe thought so, too. Now Anna has been missing for two days. Joe has the case. He's looking for her and Petrović. As for us, we can wait for Mr. Big to make a mistake, or we can partner up with the FBI."

Conklin said, "We've done it before. They take over and we buy them coffee."

"Who cares? Let's nail the Butcher before we find another body hanging from a tree."

Conklin grabbed his phone and called Jacobi.

I grabbed mine and called Joe.

CHAPTER 99

JACOBI HAD WORKED a small miracle.

This morning he and FBI field office supervisor Craig Steinmetz had shredded the red tape, and a joint task force had been born. Conklin and I, along with Joe and his team, were working together to locate Petrović and bring him in for questioning. Anna's disappearance was the probable cause we needed.

Petrović wasn't in his house on Fell. Likewise, the maître d' at his restaurant said that Tony wouldn't be in today, that's all he knew.

At 5:00 p.m., after a fruitless day of hide-and-seek, traffic cameras flagged Petrović's Jaguar coming across the Bay Bridge. A team of agents tailed him to the Laurel Heights neighborhood and then lost him.

Then a patrol car located Petrović's car parked on Pine Street in front of a men's clothier. An undercover went into the shop, looked around, and didn't see Petrović. When he showed the salespeople a photo, they all said they had not seen him. The cop and his partner canvassed the rest of the block before calling it quits.

It seemed that Petrović had gone underground once more, to our immense and vocal frustration.

It was now twenty past midnight.

Conklin and I waited inside a plain black Honda sedan parked on a pleasant residential block with a good view of the Jaguar. Rich was behind the wheel, and I manned the coms, which were crackling, connecting us to dispatch and to team members stationed at various places in this neighborhood.

Joe's team was inside a surveillance van stationed on Geary, four blocks away. I'd seen the van. It had a dinged-up chassis, ladders on top, a decal on the side reading KELLY'S HOME REPAIR. Inside, it was like a spaceship equipped with cutting-edge tech: listening devices, a satellite hookup, a periscope, and four agents dressed in workmen's clothes so that they could easily leave the van without bringing attention to it or themselves.

We had eyes, ears, and boots on the street, but there was nothing to report.

Shops were closed. Traffic was slight. Houses were dark. Six FBI agents, a SWAT team, and Conklin and I were on alert for one man.

It had been a long night.

At that moment Conklin was on the phone with Cindy.

"It can't be helped, Cin. And no, I can't tell you about it on the record. I just can't . . . I realize that . . . I understand. Do you understand me? Hold on."

He said to me, "Will you talk to her?"

I said, "Really?"

I reached for the phone and said, "Cindy, there's nothing to tell. We're on a stakeout."

My attention was drawn to an SUV with a broken headlight that cruised past us, slowed down, and stopped up the block, keeping the motor on.

I grabbed my binoculars and took a good look at the vehicle, a Cadillac Escalade. All I could get off the plate were the last three numbers, and even those numbers were approximate.

Rich took back his phone, saying, "Cindy, we've gotta go. Love you."

He clicked off, and together we watched as the SUV's passenger-side door opened and a large man got out. Then the car moved off, north on Presidio Avenue.

I turned my eyes back to the large man approaching a white-trimmed gray house across the street and up the block a hundred yards from where we were parked. There was a garage on the street level, and behind some shrubbery a staircase rose from the ground level to the front door on the main floor.

I sharpened my focus on the man with the thick salt-and-pepper hair and a military bearing. He was smoking a cigar.

I recognized him from his pictures. Finally, a break. Slobodan Petrović was in our crosshairs.

I called Joe.

CHAPTER 100

JOE'S VOICE WAS in my ear.

"What've you got, Lindsay?"

I told him, "Petrović was just dropped off by a dark-colored Escalade with a broken headlight at a house on Pine, middle of the block. I got three numbers off the plate. Petrović's going through the front door now."

I texted Joe a photo of the man and the house, up until now a mystery location to all of us.

Joe told all units to stand by. He assigned three teams to surrounding intersections and ordered SWAT to come in.

I used our car's computer to look up the owner of the house Petrović had just entered. The title search came up with a name: Marko Vladic, formerly a citizen of Serbia, now a naturalized American. He'd lived in San Francisco for nearly five years and owned a blue Escalade.

I checked the criminal databases, holding my breath as I wondered if Vladic had a police record. If so, Petrović was associating with a known criminal.

I ran Vladic's name through the FBI database for good measure before saying to Conklin, "He has no record. At least not under the name Marko Vladic."

Conklin said, "Try an image search."

As Joe gave orders to the teams and discussed perimeters, potential stumbling blocks, backup plans, I looked for *Vladic, Marko* in any public record I could think of.

And I found him.

I told Rich, "Active liquor license for a strip club in the Tenderloin called Skin. It's at 816 Larkin. Is that Petrović's club? Or do we have this wrong? Is Vladic Mr. Big? Is he the one who had Susan under his thumb?"

"I can't wait to ask him."

I looked up to see the SWAT truck stop at the top of the block, positioned to roll up to 3045 Pine. I wanted to look up Skin, their licenses, any violations.

But I didn't get a chance.

Moments after speaking with him, I saw Joe's van pull up to the curb a few cars ahead of us.

When Joe and his partner were standing in front of the gray house, Conklin and I got out of our Honda. I zipped my Windbreaker identifying me as SFPD over my Kevlar vest and pulled my nine. Once Conklin and I were in sync, we crossed the street and ran up the exterior stairs behind Joe and Diano.

The front door of 3045 Pine was painted charcoal gray, with a peephole and a brass knocker shaped like a fist. Joe was team leader, but I was the primary because it was under SFPD jurisdiction.

Joe said to me, "After you knock, stand aside."

When I knocked, were bullets going to come through the door? Was this my last moment on Earth? If not, what about Joe or Conklin? How would I ever bear that?

But there were other lives at stake. If Susan Jones and Anna Sotovina were here, it wasn't their choice.

I knew the drill.

I stepped up to the door and lifted the knocker.

CHAPTER 101

I KNOCKED AND announced, "SFPD. Open up."

Conklin and I took positions on opposite sides of the door. I listened for the sounds of footsteps, a voice calling out, "Keep your pants on. I'm coming," or the real possibility of shots punching through the wooden door.

There was no response.

I lifted the knocker again and put some muscle behind it as I banged it against the strike plate and shouted, "Police! Open the door or we're coming in."

Still no answer.

Joe called down to SWAT. Six guys in tactical gear got out of their armored vehicle and ran up the stairs. Before they reached the front door, there was the sound of breaking glass and an unintelligible, masculine scream. Glass sprayed out from a window on the main floor.

I saw the muzzle of a gun poking out of the window, followed by three quick bursts of gunfire.

Joe shouted "*Go!*" to the SWAT guys, who had a battering

ram. They caved in the locks, kicked in the door, tossed a flashbang into the house, and closed the door as much as possible.

The grenade discharged, shaking the windows. After a moment Joe and Diano shouldered the door in and entered the house, yelling, "FBI. Put your hands in the air."

Conklin and I followed the Feds into a dark and smoky foyer lit by our flashlights and faint streetlights. To our right was what looked to be a large living room with a broken window, dimly lit by a TV.

Straight ahead, a carpeted staircase led upward to the top floor. To our left was the down staircase to the garage. Joe signed with his hands, directing me and Conklin upstairs, while he and his team took the living room and main floor.

SWAT split up, half taking the stairs down, the others staying inside the centrally located foyer.

I heard Joe yelling, "Hands on top of your heads. Face the wall!"

Joe was okay, thank God, so Conklin and I kept going. The top floor had to be bedrooms. I was thinking ahead to Susan and Anna, with a strong feeling that we were about to find them behind locked doors, alive. My partner was right behind me when we reached the top-floor landing. I was expecting an empty hallway, a row of doors, but there was a hulking and shadowy presence right in front of me.

I swung my light into his face.

"Stop right there," he barked.

His arm was outstretched and there was a gun in his hand.

We were face-to-face with the monster, only ten feet away. If anyone fired, someone would die.

CHAPTER 102

PETROVIĆ WAS IMMENSE.

Much bigger in real life than I had imagined him. Six five? Six six? I still remember my heart beating in the red-line zone, but thank God, my training kicked in and overrode my near-paralytic shock.

I yelled, "Police! Drop the gun."

Petrović didn't move.

Conklin said reasonably, "Don't make a mistake now, Tony. The house is full of cops. You'll never leave here alive."

Petrović paused to take that in; the flashbang, the shots, and the yelling downstairs. He said, "Okay, okay, look."

He stooped, put his gun carefully on the carpet, held up his hands, saying, "I've done nothing wrong."

Conklin kicked the gun away as Petrović said, "I have a license for this. I thought you were robbers."

My heart was still banging. I could feel it beating in my chest, my throat, behind my eyes.

Conklin said, "Turn around and grab the wall."

I kept my gun on Petrović, and after Rich had cuffed him, I found the light switch. A hundred watts in the ceiling fixture blazed, and my blood pressure dropped to almost normal.

I told Slobodan Petrović that we were bringing him in as a material witness in the murder of Carly Myers.

He said, "Who?"

I ignored the question. A material witness charge would hold him long enough for us to get a search warrant for his house on Fell, the house on Pine, and the strip club, Skin. I also wanted his DNA and a bite impression while we were at it.

"You're out of your minds," he said. "I've done nothing wrong. Nothing. I own a restaurant. I live a clean life. This is a setup."

So he'd done nothing wrong. A line of crap I'd heard a few hundred times from guilty people since I first pinned on my badge.

I asked, "Where are Susan Jones and Anna Sotovina?"

"I don't know who you're talking about."

Where were they? I needed to see them, talk to them, know that they were all right.

I repeated my question and he repeated his no-answer answer.

Petrović wasn't talking.

I said, "I'll give you a choice, Mr. Branko. You can talk to us or to the FBI. It's up to you."

He made his choice.

I radioed for backup and while Conklin kept his gun on Petrović, I checked out the layout of the top floor. There were five bedrooms, three bathrooms, and I searched all of them.

The rooms were messy and unoccupied. The closets held working men's clothing, waiters' uniforms, and shoes, but there was no sign of our missing persons.

If they weren't here, where the hell were they?

Maybe Petrović would tell us.

Yeah. Right.

CHAPTER 103

PATROL OFFICERS FOLDED Petrović into the back of a police transport van and took off.

I returned to the house and found Joe in the living room, standing over two men lying facedown on the carpet with their hands cuffed behind them.

He brought me up to date on what I'd missed. The two men on the floor worked for Petrović at Tony's Place for Steak. Free rent was part of their salary, so they both bunked here.

To me, that made them probable witnesses to what had gone on in this house. I was grateful for that.

Joe left the room to check out the garage. I studied the guys on the floor.

The younger one, tattooed and pierced, looked to be in his twenties. That was Carson Wells, who was called Junior. The man lying next to him was ten years older and heavy. Randy LaPierre.

They were still stunned from the flash grenade, but Junior

lifted his chin off the floor and said to me, "Like I just said, I thought someone was breaking in. I fired. I didn't hit anyone. You've got no right to arrest us."

I stooped to their level, literally.

I said, "First one to tell me where I can find Susan Jones and Anna Sotovina makes a friend in the police department. I will work hard to get you a break from the law."

Randy said, "I don't understand. We live here. I don't know them. I swear on my mother."

"What about you, Junior? Want to be my friend?"

"What Randy said. I never heard of them."

I said, "You can tell your mothers you'll be in jail at 850 Bryant. Seventh floor."

I called to the two cops standing in the doorway, and they hauled the men to their feet.

Randy said, "Do what you want, lady. You've got shit on us."

Uniforms were taking out the trash when Joe and his partner came up from the garage level, rejoining Conklin and me in the living room.

"No one is in the house," Joe said. "Anna's not here. Susan's not here."

"Come onnnn. Don't say that."

He said, "There are three bedrooms on this floor. We found some women's clothing in closets. Street clothes and lingerie. There were boxes of makeup in a dressing room. We'll send it out for testing. If any of the women used the lipstick, we'll get a DNA match."

"So they *were* here."

"What I'm thinking is we may have just missed them," Joe said. "The garage door to the street was closed, but the rear door to the back garden was wide open. And if a car was waiting for them on Bush?"

He threw up his hands, looking more demoralized than I'd ever seen him.

Crap. Team Petrović had seen us, and maybe we'd been breathing down their necks enough that they had to make a move. So they used their exit strategy.

CHAPTER 104

Out on the street, flashers lit up the predawn morning.

Cops had strung crime-scene tape in front of the house to keep passersby out of our scene. Some people had been roused from their beds at 2:00 a.m. and were clumped together on the sidewalks to find out what had happened. We weren't talking.

Joe's ride was waiting.

He said, "Put Petrović on ice. Diano and I want to stop off at the office and file a report, but I'll see you at the Hall in an hour. I'm feeling good about this."

I was optimistic, too. The women were gone, so maybe alive. And Petrović was ours—for as long as we could hold him. How long would that be? Days? Weeks? We needed evidence if we were going to charge him.

And if we couldn't do that, we'd have to let him go.

I flashed back to Petrović pointing a gun at my face. I was still shaken by that sight and knowing that he could have pulled the trigger. We'd talked him down.

But the thought came to me. What if he got another chance at me? And I thought about Susan and Anna. Totally powerless. I'd never met them, but I felt as though I knew them. And I had a sense of the terror they'd felt, the brutality they'd been subjected to.

I looked up at Joe. I'm pretty sure he could read my face and see how close I was to tears. He reached for me. I went into his arms, and we kissed in front of cops and Feds and God and everyone. He said, "It's okay, Linds. We did great."

The Honda pulled up. Conklin honked the horn. I released Joe and squeezed his hand.

Then I got into the car and buckled up.

We passed Petrović's Jaguar, still parked in front of the men's clothing shop.

"Richie, back up."

I got out of the car and copied down the Jaguar's tag number.

Then I called the lab.

CHAPTER 105

SAME NIGHT—OR more accurately, that morning—
Jacobi stood up from his desk, opened the drawer in his
credenza, and pulled out a bag from Sam's Deli.

"Sit. Sit down," he told us.

He congratulated us on bringing in Petrović, then passed
the bag over his desk, saying, "Here's what I've got. Two
BLTs, a bag of chips, two Kind bars and some information,
for what it's worth."

Conklin tore open the deli bag, handed a foil-wrapped
sandwich to me, and said, "Hang on a minute."

He got up, headed for the break room, and returned with
the coffeepot, mugs, and fixings. He filled mugs for all of us,
then said, "Go for it, Licu."

Jacobi began, "Marko Vladic is Petrović's number two
guy. He pays his taxes. Keeps his nose clean. In public,
anyway."

Conklin said, "We checked him out. He works as day manager
at Tony's. At night he manages a strip club called Skin."

Jacobi said, "That's right. Skin is a small girly joint above a liquor store. Small equals exclusive. Club chairs. Nice little stage. The liquor is expensive. Lap dances are, too. I'm guessing it's profitable."

"That fits with what Susan's sister told us," I said. "That Susan was dancing to pay off a debt to Mr. Big. Make me happy, boss. Who owns the club?"

"Goes by the name Antonije Branko."

I said, "Oh, my God," and fell back in my chair. "Here comes the balloon drop from the ceiling."

Jacobi laughed.

I stood, threw up my hand, and gave him a high five, a low five, and a hip bump for good measure.

Richie's turn to laugh.

I sat back down, gulped some coffee, and told Jacobi that Petrović's Jaguar was on a flatbed truck, speeding out to our forensics lab at Hunters Point.

"CSI is going to hoover the hell out of it."

"Let me know if they find anything good. In the meantime, I'll stay to watch your Petrović interview," said Jacobi.

Conklin looked at his watch.

"It's almost three. Has Tony stewed in his cell long enough?"

"I'd do it soon," Jacobi said. "His lawyer won't be picking up his phone."

I said, "Joe's got a dog in this fight."

"Get him on the line."

I used Jacobi's phone, called Joe, and then gave the jail upstairs a blast, requesting that Petrović be escorted down to Interview 1 in a half hour.

I went to the ladies' room, washed my face, finger-combed my hair, and rehearsed possible interview scenarios. I reminded myself that *whatever* I had to say to get Susan and Anna home was allowed. Cops are allowed to lie.

There was a clean shirt in my locker. After I changed and felt somewhat fresh, I walked down the hall to the interview rooms. Before going into number one, I looked through the glass.

Petrović was sitting at the small gray table across from the two most important men in my life.

I flipped on the audio and listened for a minute. Joe and Rich were warming him up—talking to a psychotic mass murderer about baseball and the price of gasoline.

CHAPTER 106

WHEN I ENTERED the interrogation room, Joe stood up and gave me his chair across from Petrović.

"Forgive me if I don't stand," said Petrović.

"Relax," I said. "It's been a long night for everyone."

"Sergeant, right? Sergeant, you're wasting your time with me."

"Mr. Petrović—"

"Call me Tony."

Petrović looked comfortable in his street clothes and jail slippers. The handcuffs had been removed. His belt had been confiscated. His gun was at the lab. And although he'd told us that he had a license to carry, that was a lie.

If we needed illegal possession of a firearm to hold him, we'd do it, and we'd get him on brandishing a weapon, too. Maybe we could keep Petrović for thirty days on those charges with a sympathetic judge, but they were the smallest of beans.

We needed Petrović to tell us where to find Susan Jones

and Anna Sotovina, and failing that—there was no failing that. We had to find those women.

Meanwhile, it was very early on a Tuesday morning. Judges were sleeping. We didn't have search or arrest warrants, and it would take until Monday at the earliest to get them.

I said, "Tony, you're familiar with police procedure, so I'm going to skip the small talk. You help us, we help you."

"What do you want? What do you give?"

"We want Susan Jones and Anna Sotovina."

Joe leaned in. "Before you say you don't know them, we know that you do. Susan worked at your club. You and Anna have history in Djoba."

"I don't have these women."

Liar.

I said, "Well, we have a few things of yours. For one, we have your car."

"Where's the warrant?" he asked me in a tone as smooth as the single malt my father used to hoard for private celebrations.

I said, "We don't need a warrant if you leave it in a public space. Which you did. Now it's at our lab. We're liable for any damage, but don't worry. We're treating your car with latex gloves. You could say we're going to detail it."

Petrović cracked a smile.

He said, "How do you say it? Knock yourself out."

I smiled back.

"Oh, we will. You left a water bottle in your car's cup holder. We'll collect your DNA from that, and if we find as much as a hair belonging to Carly Myers or Adele Saran, we're going to charge you with murder."

The killer yawned. It didn't seem fake. Slobodan Petrović had beat life imprisonment before. But he might be over-confident now.

He said, "I've heard the part where I help you. Where's the part where you help me?"

I said, "We'll get there. First I want to set the table. Joe. You have that photo? The one taken in Djoba."

"As a matter of fact, I do."

Joe produced his phone, tapped an app, swiped some photos, then showed the screen to Petrović.

Petrović said, "What am I looking at?"

Joe showed Petrović the photo of him in the forest, people strung up in the woodland behind him, a throwing star in his hand. Joe read the caption—in Bosnian. I remembered the gist of the translation.

Colonel Slobodan Petrović and men after taking the Bosnian town of Djoba. Petrović is proficient in the use of shuriken, *throwing stars.*

Petrović said, "I hate to tell you, but that's not me. Slobodan is my cousin from my mother's side. Even so, this is such an old story. My cousin was exonerated, you know."

Conklin said, "Carly had wounds from a weapon like this. Adele had a throwing star in her *back*. I'm still new at this, but I think that's enough probable cause for an indictment."

"Ah, you are amateurs, you know. You've got nothing on me."

What he was saying was just true enough.

We had nothing on him in San Francisco, USA. Nothing. I pushed past the faint but creeping doubt and said, "There *is* evidence against you. You can count on it."

"*You* can count on *this*," Petrović said. He looked puffed up and happy as he sat back in his chair.

"I'm working with your federal government. I have immunity."

CHAPTER 107

I DIDN'T BELIEVE Petrović's claim that he had made a deal with the Feds.

I said, "Yeah. Right."

And that's when Jacobi pushed the door open and came into the room with a man I didn't know. But I knew the type. He was fortysomething, tailored, hair combed back, looking like he'd told his driver to wait.

Jacobi was holding a piece of paper with a government letterhead, and he looked disgusted. He said, "Petrović, your lawyer is here."

The lawyer introduced himself as Richard Constable. He said to Petrović, "Tony, I'm here to take you home. Lieutenant, please say the magic words."

Jacobi put his hands on the table, leaned down, and said to Petrović, "You're free to go." He stood up and said, "Inspector Conklin, please help Mr. Petrović check out."

When Conklin had walked Petrović and his attorney out of the room, Jacobi said to me and Joe, "Look. I'm as rocked by this as you are. Joe, a special FBI task force out of DC delivered this letter in person."

Jacobi slapped the paper down on the table so that we could read it. It was one paragraph long and stated that Slobodan Petrović, a.k.a. Tony Branko, was under protection of the FBI. It was signed by the director himself in a bold, unequivocal hand.

Jacobi said, "I'd guessed that Petrović was given protection in exchange for some deal he made with the ICC. It's clean-record dependent. His deal is good if he doesn't commit a crime.

"We know," said Jacobi, "all of us know, that we can't connect Petrović to any of those dead or missing women. We're not going to get him deported on brandishing a weapon."

"Wait a minute, Warren," Joe cut in. "We have those two dopes we picked up in Vladic's house today. They work for Tony. They have to know everything about him."

Jacobi said, "I've left a voice mail for the DA. Until we have search warrants for Petrović's house and business, and same for Vladic's house, this case is suspended.

"Go home," he said kindly. "And in case I haven't been clear, Boxer, no off-duty surveillance. Joe, Steinmetz has the same instructions for you. Stay away from this guy. We've been given our orders. Let's not screw up."

He stared at our shocked faces for a second, then said, "Good job, everyone. Sorry about this."

I was in a rage. I stood up fast, knocking over my chair, saying, "We can't just drop this like it never happened, Jacobi. Susan and Anna—"

"Trust me, Boxer, it's not over, but our hands are tied right now. Go home. Get some sleep. Tell Conklin the same."

He had to be *kidding*.

Were those two women bound and gagged inside the trunk of a car? Were *they* going to get the night off?

Jacobi shook his finger at me, emphasizing, *I mean it*. Then he walked out of the room.

CHAPTER 108

JOE AND I took Martha for a nice long walk at dawn, both of us fuming and swearing for a good half hour.

Back home, we cooled off with a pint of ice cream, followed by chilled California Pinot. After that, our clothes came off and we leaned on each other under a hot shower. The sun was fully up when we dove into bed, and speaking for myself, I slept like I was in a coma.

Sometime later Joe gently shook my arm until I woke up. He was holding my phone. "Jacobi," he said.

I grunted "Hey" into the speaker holes, and Jacobi said, "I've got news for both of you. I'm downstairs. I brought coffee cake."

Joe filled the coffeepot. I put on jeans and a T-shirt and was ready for Jacobi when the doorbell rang.

Back then, I'd known Jacobi for ten years. Some of that time I worked for him. Some of that time he worked for me. But most of those years we were partners and spent untold hours patrolling the Southern district in our squad car. We talked about everything, investigating crimes that were unforgettable and searing and educational. Working with Jacobi made me the cop I am today.

I *know* Jacobi.

And when he walked into the apartment that morning, I couldn't read his expression at all.

We went to the kitchen island, and immediately Joe said, "I'll be right back. I'll just run Martha down to the corner."

It took him longer to get back than I expected, and when he returned, Jacobi and I were well into the coffee and cake. After Joe helped himself, Jacobi gave us the reason for his visit.

He said, "After I sent you all home, Marko Vladic was picked up for that broken headlight. The patrolmen were sharp. Saw that there was a BOLO out for him, as a suspect in a kidnapping, and brought him in. First thing out of Vladic's mouth was, 'I want a deal.'"

I said, "Oh, really. What was the offer?"

"He said he knew where Anna and Susan were and he'd reveal that location in exchange for immunity. I told him, 'I want the women first, and after that, we'll talk to the DA. ASAP.' He said he didn't know if they'd live much longer."

I felt my heart seize up.

Joe said, "Jesus Christ," and put his head in his hands.

Jacobi said, "I know, I know," and then he went on.

"I told Vladic, okay, I'd give him a deal in writing. He had to give the women to us now, and I wanted evidence and testimony that Petrović killed Myers and Saran. He agreed to giving up the women. That shit told me, 'I'll give you those bitches, but I'm not going to say a word against Tony.'"

I said, "Crap. And you said?"

"I said okay."

"I don't understand," said Joe.

"I said okay, release the women to me, and I'll go to work for you. I wrote it down for him," Jacobi said. "I made it good. I swore on the authority vested in me by the state of California that I would negotiate on his behalf with the district attorney and the governor and the Federal Bureau of Investigation in exchange for his cooperation. I got Chi to type it up on my letterhead, and I signed it with a flourish. Chi witnessed it, and I had Vladic sign and date it, too.

"Then that little turd says to me, 'This doesn't seem airtight.'

"I say, 'Chi. You're a notary, right?' He starts to fumble it, says, 'I don't know where my stamp is.' As soon as he says that, he remembers. Brenda has one of those old notary public stamps she uses as a paperweight."

"I've seen it," I said. "Weighs about three pounds. You push down on the handle and it crimps the paper. Makes a seal."

"Exactly. Chi gets it from Brenda's desk, signs his name, crimps the deal sheet, and pronounces it as good as gold. It's a seal for the DMV circa 1939, but never mind. I make a copy, wave the original at Vladic, and tell him he gets the waiver when the two women are in our custody."

I said, "*Jacobi*. For God's sake. Did he give them up?"

"Yes, my friends, he did. I called fire and rescue, and those guys chopped a big hole in the stage at Skin and pulled those poor women out from the secret compartment."

Joe shouted, "We've got them? They're alive?"

"They're at Metro Hospital. Banged up and I'm going to say traumatized, but we have them. Susan and Anna are alive."

CHAPTER 109

THE LIGHTING IN the glass stalls lining the ICU was purposely dim, and the patients in their adjustable beds were completely still.

The on-duty nurse told us, "She just had surgery a few hours ago. She's doing as well as can be expected, after the internal bleeding, but she's heavily medicated and may not know that you're there. Only one of you can be in her room at a time."

Joe said, "If she speaks, we both have to be there. It's police business."

The nurse shook her head disapprovingly, then, "You've got five minutes. Do not stress her out."

She led us to one of the stalls and slid open the glass door. I said, "Joe, she knows you. You go. I'll wait here."

"Okay," he said.

I stood just outside the narrow room and looked in at Anna Sotovina. Her eyes were closed. Her head had been shaved. Innumerable tubes were going into her arms and under the blanket, and electrodes and wires transmitted to monitors that recorded her vital signs.

The scar on Anna's face highlighted what a courageous and indomitable person she was. A fighter. A survivor.

I'd been so worried that seeing her alive filled me with a wave of relief and something like love.

She'd been kicked in the gut, suffered a concussion and internal bleeding, with six broken ribs, but she was going to make it. And all of my fear and worry had been worth it.

I reached out with both hands and touched the glass.

We did it, Anna. We got you out.

Tears came up and I clapped my hands over my eyes. When the feeling subsided, I looked at Anna, her arms stuck with needles, and I thought how good it was that she was not in pain.

Joe sat down next to Anna's bed. He was speaking, but I couldn't hear his words, and it looked to me as though Anna couldn't hear him, either. He put his hand around her wrist. I thought he was preparing to say good-bye. And then her eyes opened. She turned to Joe and reached up for him with one arm.

He bent to her and hugged her very gently.

I was surprised to see this affection between them, and I have to admit to feeling a twinge of possessiveness. But I understood. She'd been through hell. He cared about her. He sat back down, all the while keeping his hand around her wrist.

Anna was speaking to Joe. She'd been speaking for more than a few minutes, slowly, deliberately, checking with her eyes to see if she'd been understood. I read her lips when she said, "I'm sorry. Thank you, Joe."

He said something to her, then turned to where I was clinging to the glass wall and pointed to me. Anna's face brightened with recognition.

She said, "Thank you, Lindsay," or at least that's how it seemed to me. Tears jumped out of my eyes then and I couldn't hold them back. This was Anna Sotovina's lucky day, and it was pretty great for me, too.

I thought I might go in and speak to her, when the nurse stepped past me and knocked on the glass door.

She said to Joe, "I'm sorry. Our patient needs to rest."

Joe stood up and said, "I'll be back tomorrow, Anna. Get some sleep."

I waved good-bye, and then I could barely wait for us to get into the elevator.

"How did she seem to you?" I asked my husband.

He took my hand, squeezed it.

"She was barely conscious, under the influence of pain meds, and probably confused. She remembers what she went through inside the house on Pine, but those memories have been fused with older memories. She mentioned the hotel in Djoba. She doesn't want to talk about any of it. Especially not Petrović."

But we need her to tell us about Petrović. We need her testimony.

Joe knew quite well what I was thinking.

"I'm not going to push her," he said. "Anna said she'll only talk to the International Criminal Court."

"But that's the court that *freed* Petrović. They made a *deal* with him."

Joe said, "Let's meet Susan. Okay?"

CHAPTER 110

IT WAS THE same hospital, on a different floor, and the mood in the room couldn't have been more different.

Susan was in her bed wearing a pretty pink robe, and her devoted sister Ronnie was beside her. Balloons floated above the footboard, a great number of flower-filled vases were lined up on the windowsill, and Conklin and Jacobi were seated at the side of her bed.

A cheer went up for me and Joe when we came through the doorway. If I'd been connected to a mood monitor, the green line would have *spiked*. It felt that good.

Conklin introduced us to Susan.

"This is my partner, Lindsay Boxer, and FBI special agent Joe Molinari."

Susan was lovely, with strawberry blond hair and pale skin and a smile that showed how glad she was to be alive.

She said, "I've heard so much about you, Lindsay. I think I would recognize you anywhere," and stretched out her arms. "Thank you so much for everything."

I hugged her, and so did Joe. We told her we had just left Anna, who was speaking and recovering.

There was relief and some laughter, and for a moment I felt giddy, as if I'd been drinking champagne. Anna and Susan were alive! I was still having aftershocks from the takedown at the house on Pine, but this was a welcome bright moment.

And finally we had to get into the hard part.

Jacobi said, "Ronnie. Would you mind if we spent about five minutes alone with Susan?"

Ronnie murmured, "Not at all," and exited gracefully.

Jacobi asked Susan to tell us how she'd come to be in that house on Pine, and to explain her connection to Petrović.

We were all gathered in chairs around her as Susan told of meeting a man at the Bridge, Tony Branko. She talked about how he'd bought her drinks, took her out to dinner twice, and then offered her a loan. Later he told her how she could pay it back. She said it was debasing, that the amount she owed escalated due to interest, but she thought she was nearly paid up. But no.

And she skipped from dancing at Skin to the night she and her friends Adele and Carly were abducted. She described the endless days and nights in the apartment, and she spared no detail; the darkness, the rules, the faceless men, what they demanded, and the punishments.

Susan skimmed over the deaths of Carly and Adele, but I felt her unspeakable pain. She was saying so much without saying it all.

When she reached the most recent part of her story, the second abduction, she said, "Anna fought Marko, but he's a soldier. He kicked her, picked up a chair, and slammed it against her head. I didn't fight. I was sure he would kill us. He tied us both up and shoved us under the stage. I tried to kick through the boards, but it was hopeless. A lot of time went by. I told Anna we were going to get out, and Anna didn't answer me anymore. Her breathing was so faint, and then I heard men's voices. 'Is anyone here?' I screamed and screamed."

Finished with her story, Susan stopped talking.

There was a silence that no one knew how to break.

So Susan did it.

She said to all of the cops grouped around her bed, "How can I help with your case against these bastards? What else do you want to know?"

I said, "The man you know as Tony Branko has a get-out-of-jail pass from government agencies here and overseas. We need evidence that he committed a crime. We need your help with that."

Susan let out a long breath, thought about it for a second, and said, "Tony is out of jail now?"

"Yes. He's free and enjoying his wonderful life."

She said, "Well, I don't know if I have *evidence*. I don't have photos or recordings or anything like that. But I can tell you that he raped all of us repeatedly. Him and Marko."

"We know him," said Conklin.

"Good. And some of the waiters at Tony's were in on it. They lived in that house and they all…did what they did. We couldn't get out, you know? They kept us locked up and they hurt us. We didn't know when we might die."

Susan's voice broke, and tears spilled down her cheeks. It was terrible to see the transformation from the happy young woman she'd seemed to be only moments ago. All smiles and flowers.

I wondered if she'd ever truly be all smiles and flowers again. Still, like Anna, Susan Jones was a fighter.

And she was alive.

"You'll testify to what they did to you?" Jacobi asked her.

"Of course I will. But I don't know how I can prove any of it."

"Leave that to us," Jacobi said.

CHAPTER 111

CLAIRE TEXTED OUR task force: *Bombshell briefing, my office @ 8am.*

By eight the next morning, all six of us were crammed into Claire's office at the morgue. Jacobi and Steinmetz had gotten there first and had taken the chairs. Jacobi tried to give me his seat, but his knees were going, so I thanked him anyway and stood against the wall with Joe, Diano, and Conklin.

Claire was behind her desk, wearing bloody blue scrubs, her hair in a cap. She stripped off her gloves, opened a folder, pulled out two items, and placed them faceup on her desk.

One was a photo enlargement of the bite mark on Carly Myers's neck that she'd taken at the autopsy. The second was the acetate tracing she'd made of the bite mark, the actual size for her records.

Claire said, "The victim stretched away from the person who was biting her. See how the marks are off center? Even if we had the subject's bite impression, unless there was an obvious dental anomaly, like severely crooked teeth, the chances are small that a mold of the attacker's mouth would match the impressions on the victim's neck."

"Therefore . . ." I said.

"Therefore, Sergeant Girlfriend, I'd write the bite off as inconclusive."

Jacobi muttered, "Bummer," but Claire wasn't done.

"And then there's this," she said. "It's either divine inspiration or maybe Carly whispering over my shoulder, 'Hey, Doc, take another look.'"

Claire ducked under her desk and reappeared holding a sealed manila envelope she'd taken from the one-cubic-foot square refrigerator she kept in her office.

"Clapper called last night," she said. "We got DNA from Petrović's water bottle. Then, when Petrović signed a release for his personal property when he was cut loose from the jail, he placed his sweaty paw down on it to sign his name. Richie, I believe it was you who secured the paper with Petrović's DNA. Inspector, please take a bow."

My partner smiled and I fist-bumped his shoulder.

Claire resumed, saying, "The DNA samples from the bottle *and* the release form are a perfect match to this."

She opened the sealed manila envelope, reached in, took out a small glassine envelope, and held it up so we could see the evidence sandwiched between two glass microscope slides.

Diano peered over Jacobi's head. "Is that what I think it is?"

Claire smiled like an angel and showed the glassine

envelope around so that we all could take a look at the sliver of evidence that just might blow the monster up.

Our esteemed medical examiner said, "I recovered this pubic hair from Carly Myers's vaginal vault. It's a 100 percent match to Slobodan Petrović and no other."

CHAPTER 112

I WAS SO proud of Claire.

We had evidence, we had probable cause. We *had* him. I beamed as we gave her a wholehearted round of applause.

She tucked the evidence back into the cooler, curtsied playfully, and said, "Thanks, everyone. I've got to go. I'm in the middle of someone."

The rest of us cleared out, and Conklin, Joe, and I went to the FBI field office with Steinmetz, where we spent the rest of that Wednesday working out the plan.

First, Steinmetz put in a call to FBI director L. Martin Roberts. He was well regarded, with movie-star looks and some kind of political future. When Roberts was on the speakerphone, Steinmetz introduced us, and Conklin and I itemized the evidence: the hanged women, their wounds from throwing stars, and the photos of Petrović in Djoba in a forested killing field, surrounded by hanged bodies and with a throwing star in his hand.

And we told Roberts about our latest findings: that we'd

rescued two bound-and-gagged victims from a subfloor inside Petrović's club.

I said, "One of the victims, a schoolteacher name of Susan Jones, made a statement that Petrović had raped her and bragged of killing Carly Myers, and she was the last person to see Adele Saran."

I finished with Claire's matching Petrović DNA evidence.

The FBI director said, "How fast can you turn all that into a memo?"

By the time the sun touched the horizon, Roberts had our memo and had reassigned the task force that had been watchdogging Petrović to a transport detail. Steinmetz contacted the CIA, which connected with the powers that be in Bosnia. Green lights all the way. Steinmetz printed out Petrović's signed deportation order.

I wanted to jump up and hug everyone, but I resisted the impulse.

Steinmetz seemed pretty pleased himself. He looked at all of us and said, "The game's in play. It's all over but the shouting."

It was an old line but a great one. Still, as we all knew, there was much to be done before anyone started shouting.

Petrović didn't know that he was breathing his last free air, and we didn't want to risk any ironic accidents, so we had to work fast.

When the meeting broke up, Cappy and Chi picked up Marko Vladic at Skin, where he was going over the damage to the stage with a contractor. Despite the fit Vladic threw about his so-called immunity, he was arrested for kidnapping, rape, and accessory to murder. He was brought to the

Hall and slow-walked through booking so that he couldn't tip off his boss.

Steinmetz, Joe, Conklin, and I blocked out plans A and B to grab Petrović. We diagrammed manpower deployment and made calls.

And then we moved out.

CHAPTER 113

AFTER LEAVING STEINMETZ, our task force plus reinforcements formed a tight surveillance detail around Tony's Place for Steak.

California Street and surrounding blocks were lined with unmarked vehicles, and two undercover teams were inside the restaurant having a leisurely meal, with mikes and eyes wide open.

Operatives outside Petrović's house on Fell gave us a heads-up, and not long afterward a taxi pulled up to Tony's Place. Petrović got out, paid the driver, and entered his restaurant through the front door.

On Joe's command, Jacobi, Conklin, and I stormed the front entrance. Joe and Diano kicked in the back door and came through the kitchen.

I took a mental snapshot. Three-quarters of the tables were full. Petrović was chatting with a customer near the front when he heard dishes crashing in the back. He turned, saw Joe, turned again toward the front door, and saw me and Conklin cutting past the maître d' and bearing down on him.

The dinner crowd reacted; a table flipped, with squealing diners hitting the floor as we advanced on Petrović with guns drawn. The four undercovers were on their feet, badges and weapons in hand.

I saw realization dawn in Petrović's eyes. He knew he didn't have a prayer of getting out of his restaurant on his terms. I ordered him to put his hands on his head and drop to his knees.

He did it, saying, "I'm not armed."

Diano frisked him from chest to ankles and nodded to let us know that in fact Petrović didn't have a weapon.

Conklin walked up behind him and slapped on the cuffs, while I said, "Mr. Petrović, you're under arrest for kidnapping, aggravated assault, rape, and murder."

I read him his rights and asked him if he understood.

He didn't reply.

"Did you hear me? Do you understand your rights?"

"I heard you."

Conklin and Diano hoisted Petrović to his feet and moved him toward the front door. He squirmed and resisted, asking, "Where are you taking me?"

I was happy to tell him.

"SFO international airport, Mr. Petrović. Your connecting flight to Sarajevo leaves at nine."

He struggled as he was marched out the front door and under the awning to the curb, wrenching his body around as he was forced into the CIA's armored SUV.

He protested, "You can't deport me. I've done *nothing*."

I answered him with my face six inches from his: "We have *nothing* but testimony from eyewitnesses and physical evidence that you raped Carly Myers."

"How many times do I have to say, I don't know this woman."

Conklin said, "You were sloppy. Or hasty, Mr. P. You left physical evidence inside your victim. We've got you by the short hair."

CHAPTER 114

WE COULDN'T JUST go home after the takedown.

The team that brought down Slobodan Petrović stood out in the darkening street, adrenaline pumping, watching the taillights dwindle as the CIA's armored Land Rover took the monster away. We were high on success but still unresolved. Until Petrović was off US soil, the shouting would have to wait.

Jacobi said, "I'm starving. Anyone else?"

He led us back into the restaurant and had waiters push three tables together at the middle of the room. The waitstaff looked freaked out, but they complied, and after all of the Feds and cops took seats, they brought menus.

One of the waiters leaned down to talk to me. He was young, in his early twenties, the name Christopher engraved on the tag on his jacket.

Christopher asked, "Is Mr. Branko coming back?"

"No. Probably not."

"Mr. Vladic didn't come in today. Is he in trouble, too?"

"I can't say," I told the waiter.

"What's going to happen to the restaurant? To us?"

I told him that I didn't know.

He said, "They're going to jail, huh? No loss. They're both scumbags."

"They are. But we're good for the bill," I told him.

"If not, what am I gonna do? Call the cops?"

He winked, added, "Don't worry about it," then attended to Jacobi, who said, "What's good here?"

We all laughed, ordered steak and wine and side dishes, and before the food came, Jacobi called the mayor. He gave him a breakdown of the events, then set the phone down in the middle of the table so we could hear the mayor in a rare happy moment.

"I'll hold a press conference tomorrow," said the mayor. "The city is grateful to every one of you."

Rich called Cindy and told her to get out to the airport and track down the next outbound flight to Sarajevo. A moment later Joe got an email from the lab.

Joe showed me his phone. Clapper had written that Vladic's Escalade had paint clinging to the broken headlight socket that matched the Tesla Anna had been driving the day she was abducted.

I said to Joe, "If Vladic is indicted for kidnapping, he'll be deported, right? I swear, if he confesses to killing Denny Lopez, I'll throw him a farewell party with champagne and a live DJ."

Joe pulled me close and we grinned at each other. He said, "Not getting ahead of ourselves, are we, Blondie?"

"I can wish, can't I?"

Meanwhile, in real time, a dozen toasts were made with Tony's wine: to Claire, to the cops who'd located the Jag and the Escalade, and to the fire and rescue workers who'd saved Anna and Susan. Glasses were raised to Joe and Diano, Conklin and me, for leading the charge and bringing it all home.

No one was left out.

Steinmetz clinked his glass with a spoon and announced that working with the SFPD had been an honor and a pleasure. Jacobi returned the favor.

Conklin's phone rang, and after he kissed it, he told us the good news.

"Cindy watched Petrović board the plane under guard. She says she kept her eyes on it until it broke the sound barrier."

Cindy was indomitable.

And after Rich made the announcement, the shouting commenced.

Petrović was *gone.*

From all that we knew about his recent past and his wartime history, it was a dead cert that Petrović's sentence would be reinstated and that he'd spend the rest of his life in a cement box of a cell inside a maximum-security prison.

We whooped and yelled and hugged people sitting next to us, even those we hadn't known before tonight. I texted Yuki and Claire, and they both arrived at Tony's in time for coffee and chocolate pie.

It was a wonderful, unforgettable finale to our hard and dangerous work.

We'd done it. Case closed.

We couldn't have known it then, but five years later, when we seldom thought about him at all, Slobodan Petrović would appeal his sentence at the International Criminal Court in The Hague.

He'd worked a deal once before.

It would be unbearable, unjust, if he did it again.

EPILOGUE

CHAPTER 115

JOE AND I stood with Anna outside the International Criminal Court in The Hague, the building's granite walls shielding us from the slashing rain.

Three years before, Anna had moved to Spokane to get away from the searing memories of her time in San Francisco. Although we'd been in touch, we hadn't seen her since.

Anna looked older now and more vulnerable. She was wearing a hooded raincoat, but the hood couldn't hide the tears in her eyes. When we hugged, I felt her shivering.

I was afraid for her. Soon she would be testifying to the tribunal, telling them about Petrović's crimes against her and her family in Djoba. She couldn't tell them about San Francisco, but I knew full well how much she'd suffered when Petrović brutalized her yet again.

I couldn't imagine how she'd gathered the courage to confront Petrović now.

Joe gripped her shoulders and said, "We're with you, Anna."

"I know. I'm glad."

The doors to the courthouse slid open, and the crowd of reporters and survivors and onlookers rushed through the entrance into the main hall like a pack of wet dogs.

Ushers directed us, sending witnesses to the main courtroom, and spectators and the press to the gallery, an elevated viewing room separated from the courtroom by a wall of bulletproof glass. When we entered the observation room, I saw rows of theater-style seats rising toward the rear of the room, giving a high-bleachers view down on the court proceedings.

Joe and I sat in the fifth tier, where we had a full view of the courtroom. It was the size of a college lecture hall, high ceilinged and austere. The judges' wood-paneled benches were centered on the wall opposite the glass barrier. Similar paneled benches, one for the defense, the other for the prosecution, were at right angles to the judges' benches.

As we watched, Anna and her attorneys entered the main chamber. Anna had shed her coat. She was wearing a subtle plaid suit with a white blouse, and her chestnut hair was cut to shoulder length again. There was no sign of the tears or the tremors I'd seen just a few minutes before. As I watched, she pulled her hair back behind her ears, plainly showing the burn scar on her face.

I clapped on my headphones and listened to the court officer's speech regarding the proceedings and the rules of decorum. He spoke in English, but his speech was translated into any of six official languages at the touch of a switch.

He called the court to order, and we were asked to rise.

A hundred people in the gallery and another fifty in the courtroom got to their feet as the judges arrived through a

James Patterson

side door. Nine men and women, wearing dark-blue robes with royal-blue trim and stiff white jabots at their throats, took their seats at the benches.

The principal judge, Alain Bouchard, took the elevated seat at the center of the back row. He had black skin and white hair and looked to be in his late fifties. I'd read about him: he was a criminal court judge in his home country of Belgium, with a background in criminal defense.

Bouchard exchanged a few whispered words with his colleagues, then spoke to the bailiff, saying, "Please bring in the prisoner."

CHAPTER 116

I THOUGHT I was prepared to see him, but when the side door opened and Slobodan Petrović was escorted by guards into the courtroom, I felt sick.

Tunnel vision, light-headedness, dropping-through-the-floor sick.

Joe gripped my arm. "You okay?"

"Uh-huh. I'm fine."

I wasn't fine. I was enraged.

When I looked at Petrović, I saw his gun pointed at my face. I had other images in my mind, ones I'd absorbed from hearing Susan's tearful rendering of rapes and beatings. I thought about meeting Anna that first time when she was semiconscious in the ICU. And I would never, ever forget the mutilated bodies of Carly Myers and Adele Saran.

Petrović had done all of that and much more. And he hadn't paid for any of it.

I'd relied on the ICC to return Petrović to his cement-block sarcophagus. My mind had rested on that image of him, a cockroach in a block of concrete.

Seeing him on his feet, well dressed, put a new picture in my head. I saw the clever, undefeated military officer who might have found another loophole. By the end of the day, he might get released for time served.

Petrović smiled at the judges as he passed the benches, before taking his place in the dock.

Joe took my hand, and together we stared at the master killer who had once been our focused obsession. Petrović looked much as he had when we'd seen him last. Yes, his hair was grayer, and he'd lost weight. But he still looked like Tony Branko in a good blue suit, a white shirt with a tie.

There was a buzz in the gallery, exclamations in many languages, muffled sobs, and his name, a sound like clearing one's throat. Petrović.

I'd researched the trials of Serbian war criminals before coming to The Hague. I knew that over the last four months this court had heard appeals from seven previously convicted former top-level officers of the wartime Serbian Army, all of whom had been betrayed by Petrović.

Six of the seven appeals had been rejected. One sentence had been reduced, owing to an error made at trial.

Today was Slobodan Petrović's turn.

I looked at him standing in the dock, his face radiant with confidence. I quickly switched my eyes across the room to Anna Sotovina. She looked resolute.

I thought that Petrović and Anna were evenly matched.

Judge Bouchard spoke, saying, "Slobodan Petrović, you were formerly a colonel in the army of Republika Srpska.

When you were tried, you were found guilty of killing, and ordering your troops to kill, over fifteen hundred civilians—men, women, and children—in Djoba, Bosnia. In addition, it was proven that prisoners were tortured and raped before execution. Afterward they were buried in mass graves."

"Your Honor—" Petrović said.

Bouchard cut him off. "I will let you know when it is your turn to speak."

Judge Bouchard summarized Petrović's testimony against his superiors, and his reward, a commuted sentence, and the terms of his release.

Bouchard's face was inexpressive when he said, "Because you violated the agreement, Mr. Petrović, your sentence was reinstated and justice was done.

"But you are appealing your sentence, requesting that the charges against you be dropped and that you be released immediately. Beyond your stated facts that you don't feel safe in prison, you did not state a reason for why you should be acquitted.

"Now, sir, if you're ready, the court would like to hear what you have to say."

CHAPTER 117

PETROVIĆ TOOK A moment to tighten the knot of his tie, secure his microphone, and sweep his gaze across the glass wall sequestering the press and interested parties.

He took a quick look at the witnesses' area, a bench similar to the judges' benches. Beside it was a bank of folding chairs, every one of them occupied by a witness.

Petrović paused for a fraction of a moment when he saw Anna among the witnesses. He may have gasped, or was that a wink? But his gaze continued past those men and women, and he turned so that he was looking directly at the judges.

He said, "Greetings, Your Honors.

"Judge Bouchard mentioned that when I was brought back to this prison, justice had been done. I find this surprising that he would make such a statement on two counts.

"First, I was arrested and thrown into an airplane to Sarajevo. I was not tried. I had no trial. I did not face my accusers. I was not presented with evidence, and I did not have a lawyer present. I was arrested, restrained, flown to prison. How is this justice?

"Justice. You speak of *justice?* Perhaps you should consider as well the absence of justice, or its selective application.

"Let me ask you, jurists. Where was the justice for Dragan Ilic? Murdered by Bosniaks, on his son's wedding day, walking in procession to the church.

"Where was the justice at Sijekovac, where eleven of our people—civilians—were fatally struck down by Croat and Bosnian units?

"There *was* no justice. No UN or ICC retribution. Were you sleeping?

"These were unprovoked crimes caused by the tragic and unlawful breakup of a country in an attempt to thwart the destiny of Greater Serbia. These were attacks on our people—*my* people—that could not remain unpunished.

"These acts, *you seekers of justice,* were acts of war."

He had the gallery and the courtroom transfixed. I was also in his grip. If I'd thought he might be slippery, manipulative, begging for his liberty, I was wrong. He was angry.

Petrović continued.

"I am a soldier. My father was a soldier. He was murdered in the Ustaša genocide, a crime against humanity perpetrated mainly against Serbs. Was I to allow the allies of those who killed my father—enemies for centuries and attackers of our beliefs and traditions—to repeat, with impunity, their crimes?

"No. You judges have been deceived if you think that any man could do that. I could not, because I am a man who believes in justice. I. Not you. I."

There was an outcry in the room—an exhalation of emotion, outrage, grief, throughout the gallery. An older woman wearing a head scarf, sitting in the row in front us, shook her head, *No, no, no,* and cried into her hands. Before us in the courtroom, one of the witnesses, a woman of about my age, got to her feet and cried out.

The judge slammed down the gavel until the sounds ceased. The witness who had gotten to her feet sat down.

Judge Bouchard said, "Mr. Petrović. You've been heard. Please step down from the dock and return to the table with your attorneys.

"Witnesses to the military operation in Djoba will give testimony about the actions of Mr. Petrović's troops on the town's people.

"Anyone, anyone at all, who cannot control their emotions will be escorted out of the courtroom.

"Mr. Petrović will have an opportunity to rebut witness testimony after all the witnesses have spoken. After which," said the translation of his words in my ear, "the court will decide if his appeal should be granted or refused. The tribunal's determination shall be final."

Bouchard turned and spoke to the bailiff.

"Mr. Weiss. Please call the first witness."

CHAPTER 118

I WAS STUNNED by Petrović's speech.

If I had not witnessed his savagery in San Francisco, I might have been moved by his story. Even so, I was rocked by his defense. He felt justified in what he'd done in Djoba, and had shown no remorse when he was brought down in San Francisco.

But he did have perspective, even if rooted in his narcissism. Innocent Serbs had died, too.

It was only ten in the morning when the courtroom's attention shifted to the witnesses against Petrović. They would be called in alphabetical order and sworn to tell the truth on the religious book of their choice, or on their honor. They were required to keep their testimony to five minutes, with a thirty-second warning from Mr. Weiss.

For the next four hours the spectators in the gallery and the participants in the courtroom heard victim accounts of murder and destruction, of loss, hope, love, and faith that could have broken even the hearts of sociopaths.

But not his.

I watched Petrović as the testimonies were given. He folded his hands on the counsel table, and sometimes he took notes.

Anna was the last witness to be called and Petrović did give her his attention.

She stepped across the polished floor to the witness area, took an oath to tell the truth, and addressed the tribunal.

"My name is Anna Sotovina, but I am speaking today for all of those who were killed in Djoba, and all of the ones who survived but who have lost everything and everyone they loved.

"When Petrović came into Djoba with military weapons, I was twenty, a housewife with a small baby. My husband told me to stay inside, and he took his rifle into the streets, where he was killed immediately. Soldiers broke down my door, took my little son from my arms, and threw me to the floorboards, where they ripped off my clothes and took turns defiling me.

"The first man to rape me was him, Petrović.

"I listened for the sound of my son and heard his cries out in the street. And they were cut short. I must have screamed for him, but Petrović told me to stop. Then he lit his lighter and did this."

Anna showed the scar on her face to the utterly silent room.

"The same day I'm telling about, the women of the town were rounded up, corralled into the school auditorium. They were stripped naked, and those who were pregnant were taken out and shot. We were told that we were to bear the children of our enemies and only when we were pregnant would we get rest.

"We were fed. We had to clean the school, and we slept on

the floors of the classrooms. We were raped repeatedly and beaten, and we did not complain or even talk to each other for fear of our lives."

Anna paused. I could see that she was keeping a tight hold on her composure. I was glad when she was able to go on.

She said, "Women with children were told that they could have more. 'You will give us little Chetniks,' the soldiers said. They put blades to the children's throats, used them as hostages to make their mothers comply. Sometimes we were gang-raped by two, four, or as many as seven revolting and cruel soldiers. He—Petrović—frequented the rape hotel.

"Sometimes a woman fought back. It was a suicide wish that was often granted by pistol or the leg of a chair. My aunts and sisters and cousins and friends were all raped and killed in the schoolrooms.

"I did become pregnant. I was brought to a doctor who said so. But before I could retire to a closet and sleep, a fight broke out and I was beaten with everyone else. I lost the baby I did not know and didn't yet love.

"Later I learned that I could not ever again bear a child.

"When the war ended, I came to the USA and found, to my horror, that he, Petrović, was living a half mile away from my door. I know that his crimes outside of Bosnia are not the purview of this court, but I say this with your permission. Petrović was not fighting his father's war or any war when he raped and beat me, and when he did the same to other women and killed them with his hands in the sunny state of California. There was no war in California. It was about him, and his love of power. His love of power over life and death.

"Please. Keep him here. Do not release him. Please."

CHAPTER 119

THERE WAS AN attenuated silence as Anna returned to her seat, and then the crying started in the observation room and the witness section. Even some of the judges put handkerchiefs to their eyes.

I sobbed into my husband's jacket and I couldn't stop. But I was forced to look up when I heard the sound of the gavel cracking through my headphones. Judge Bouchard called the court to order. He thanked the witnesses, and he adjourned the proceedings for thirty minutes.

The main hall outside the courtroom was flooded with people who couldn't stay in their seats any longer. Friends and even strangers embraced. Press spoke into phones and recorders. Lines to the washrooms were long. No one broke the tension with conversation or laughter.

Twenty-nine minutes later the gallery was full and court was in session again.

The rooms were utterly quiet, filled with expectation. Judge Bouchard's use of the gavel was pro forma.

The judge asked, "Mr. Petrović. Would you like to make a closing statement?"

Petrović got up, crossed the room with a heavy stride, and mounted the three steps to the dock. The overconfidence was gone, but his anger was fully present.

Without thanks to the court or any preamble, he said, "I am not a war criminal. You," he said, pointing a finger at the rows of witnesses, "are liars. *All* of you are liars. I am a patriot. I am a Serbian hero, and history will remember me as such. Streets and parks and sons will be named for me. So all of you can go to hell."

With that, he put his hand up to his mouth. I couldn't see what he was holding, but when he tipped his head back, I gathered that he had swallowed something.

"Joe. What was that?"

"I read that he has hypertension."

Petrović dropped something, a vial, and made an obscene gesture with his hand, waving it in a slow circle, taking in the whole room. And then he collapsed to the floor.

The bailiff moved fast. Guards left their positions at the doors. They all rushed to the dock, where Petrović slumped partially on the steps, his head on the floor.

Was this a trick?

Petrović was flung about by spasms. He writhed, grabbed at his throat, and made sounds that could only be caused by agonizing pain. I could tell from the cherry-red color of his skin, the way his open eyes bulged, that Petrović had evaded a life sentence in prison by taking cyanide—easily obtained, easily smuggled in, guaranteeing a quick but excruciating death.

Where had his self-confidence gone?

To hell. He'd known when Anna made her statement that there was no chance he'd be leaving court a free man.

Petrović's attorneys were detained by the guards. The judge cleared the courtroom, but those of us in the observation room saw the paramedics come in. It took four of them to get Petrović onto a stretcher and out the door.

They were too late.

Slobodan Petrović was finally dead. We'd never forget him.

And, for sure, Joe and I would never forget Anna Sotovina.

ACKNOWLEDGMENTS

Our thanks to these experts who shared their time and knowledge with us during the writing of this book:

Captain Richard Conklin, BSI Commander, Stamford, Connecticut, Police Department; Phil Hoffman, attorney-at-law, partner, Pryor Cashman LLC, NYC; Michael A. Cizmar, former U.S. Marine and FBI agent, SME, CCE; Steven Cerutti, Homeland Security Investigator, New York, ret.; J. M. Sereno, investigator for the U.S. Attorney's office, Connecticut; Lt. Patricia Correa, SFPD, ret.; and Lt. Lisa Frazer, SFPD, Airport Division.

We also wish to thank our fabulous researcher, Ingrid Taylar, West Coast, USA; John Duffy, passionate war historian; and Mary Jordan, who keeps the whole shebang in order and on time with some LOLs along the way.

ABOUT THE AUTHORS

JAMES PATTERSON is one of the best-known and biggest-selling writers of all time. His books have sold in excess of 385 million copies worldwide. He is the author of some of the most popular series of the past two decades – the Alex Cross, Women's Murder Club, Detective Michael Bennett and Private novels – and he has written many other number one bestsellers including romance novels and stand-alone thrillers.

James is passionate about encouraging children to read. Inspired by his own son who was a reluctant reader, he also writes a range of books for young readers including the Middle School, I Funny, Treasure Hunters, Dog Diaries and Max Einstein series. James has donated millions in grants to independent bookshops and has been the most borrowed author of adult fiction in UK libraries for the past eleven years in a row. He lives in Florida with his wife and son.

MAXINE PAEIRO has collaborated with James Patterson on the bestselling Women's Murder Club, Private, and Confessions series. She lives with her husband in New York State.

Read on for a sneak preview of the next thrilling

instalment in the Women's Murder Club series

19TH CHRISTMAS

Coming October 2019

CHAPTER 1

JULIAN LAMBERT WAS an ex-con in his mid-thirties, sweet faced, with thinning, light-colored hair, wearing a red down jacket.

As he sat on a bench in Union Square waiting for his phone call, he took in the view of the Christmas tree at the center of the square. The tree was really something: an eighty-three-foot-tall cone of green lights with a star on top, ringed by pots of pointy red flowers, surrounded by a red-painted picket fence.

That tree was *secure*. It wasn't going anywhere.

It was lunchtime, and all around him consumers hurried out of stores weighed down with shopping bags, evidence of money pissed away in an orgy of spending. Julian wondered idly how these dummies were going to pay for their commercially fabricated gifting spree. Almost catching him by surprise, Julian's phone vibrated.

He fished it out of his pocket, connected, and said his name, and Mr. Loman, the boss, said, "Hello."

Julian knew that he was meant only to listen, and that was

fine with him. He felt both excited and soothed as Loman explained just enough of the plan to allow Julian to salivate at the possibilities.

A heist.

A huge one.

The plan had many moving parts, Loman said, but if it went off as designed, by this time next year Julian would be living in the Caribbean, or Medellín, or Saint-Tropez. He was picturing a life of blue skies and sunshine, with a side of leggy young things in string bikinis, when Loman asked if he had any questions.

"I'm good to go, boss."

"Then get moving. No slipups."

"You can bank on me," said Julian, glad that Loman barked back, "Twenty-two fake dive, slot right long, on one."

Julian cracked up. He had played ball in college, a very long time ago, but he still had moves. He clicked off the call, sized up the vehicular and foot traffic, and chose his route.

It was go time.

CHAPTER 2

JULIAN SAW HIS run as a punt return.

He charged into an elderly man in a shearling coat, sending the man sprawling. He snatched up the old guy's shopping bag, saying, "Thanks very much, knucklehead."

What counted was that he had the ball.

With the bag tucked under his arm, Julian ran across Geary, dodging and weaving through the crowd, heading toward the intersection at Stockton. He waited for a break in traffic at the red light, and when it came he sprinted across the street and charged along the broad, windowed side of Neiman Marcus. Revolving glass doors split a crowd of shoppers into long lines of colorful dots filing out onto the sidewalk accompanied by Christmas music: "I played my drum for him, pa-rum-pum-pum-pum." It was all so crazy.

Julian was still running.

He yelled, "Coming through! No brakes!" He wove around the merry shoppers, sideswiped the UPS man loading his truck, and, with knees and elbows pumping, bag secured under his arm, dashed up the Geary Street straightaway and veered left to cross again.

Another crowd of shoppers spilled out of Valentino, and Julian shot his left hand out to stiff-arm a young dude, who fell against a woman in a fur coat. Bags and packages clattered to the sidewalk. Julian high-stepped around and over the obstacles, then broke back again into a sprint, turning left on Grant Avenue.

Julian chortled as oncoming pedestrians scattered. Giving the finger to someone who yelled at him, knocking slowpokes out of his way, he shouted, "Merry fucking Christmas, everybody."

God, this was fun. He couldn't see the goalposts, but he knew that he was scoring, big-time.

Julian ate up the pavement with his long strides as he listened for sirens. He glanced behind him and saw, finally, two people who looked like cops running up from behind him.

He was winded, but he didn't stop. *Show me what you've got, suckers.* He put on another surge of speed as he headed toward Dragon's Gate and the Chinatown district. He slowed only when a lady cop's authoritative voice shouted, "Freeze or I'll shoot."

CHAPTER 3

MY PARTNER, INSPECTOR Rich Conklin, was running out of time, and he needed my help.

He said desperately, "Would be nice if she told you what she wants."

"Where would be the fun in that?" I said, grinning. "You figuring it out is kind of the point."

"I guess. Make our own history."

"Sure. That's an idea."

We had slipped out of the Hall of Justice to do some lunchtime Christmas shopping in San Francisco's Union Square because of its concentration of high-end shops. Richie wanted to get something special for Cindy.

Rich had wanted to marry Cindy from pretty much the moment he met her. And she loved him fiercely. But. There's always a *but*, right?

Rich was from a big family, and while he was still in his thirties, he'd wanted kids. Lots of them. Cindy was an only child with a hot career—one that took her to murder scenes in bad places in the dead of night. And Rich wasn't the only crime fighter in the relationship; Cindy had solved more than one homicide, even shooting and being shot by a crafty female serial killer who became the subject of Cindy's best-selling true-crime book.

All this to say, Cindy was in no hurry to have a family.

It was a conflict of desires that in the past had broken up my two great friends, and it was tremendous that they were back together now. But as far as I knew, the conflict remained unsolved.

Rich pointed out an emerald pendant around the neck of a mannequin in a shop window.

"Do you like that?"

I said, "Beautiful. And very Christmasy," when I heard a scream behind us.

I turned to see a man in a red down jacket running past us, yelling, "Coming through! No brakes!" He nearly collided with a group of people coming out of Neiman's, clipped a UPS man, and just kept going.

An elderly man in a shearling coat was hobbling down the street in pursuit, with blood streaming out of his nose. He cried out, "Stop, thief! Someone stop him!"

Rich and I are homicide cops, and this was no murder. But we were there. We took off behind the man in the red down jacket who was running with all the power and determination of a pro tailback.

I yelled, "Stop! Police!" But the runner kept going.

CHAPTER 4

I DIDN'T TRUST myself to run full out. My doctor had recently benched me for two months owing to a bout of anemia. So I slowed to a walk and yelled to Rich, "You go. I'll call it in."

I got on my phone and summed up the situation for dispatch in a few words: There had been a robbery, a grab-and-dash. Conklin was pursuing the suspect on foot, running east on Geary Street turning north onto Grant Avenue.

"Suspect is wearing a red jacket, dark pants. We need backup and an ambulance," I said, and gave my location.

I trotted back to the elderly man with the bloody nose who was now on his feet, panting and leaning against a building.

He said, "You're a cop."

"Yes. Tell me what happened," I said.

He told me that he'd been minding his own business when "that guy" knocked him down and stole his shopping bag.

"What's your name, sir?"

"Maury King."

"Mr. King, an ambulance will be here in a minute."

He shook himself off. "No, no. I'm okay. Don't let that bastard get away."

"We won't. My partner is in pursuit. Stay right here," I said. "I'll be back."

The man in the red jacket had cleared a wide path for Rich, as screaming shoppers threw themselves against parked cars and buildings. I took off again, jogging in their wake.

I could see up ahead that Rich was keeping up with the runner but not gaining ground. I was following behind them on the wide, shadowed corridor of Grant Avenue, close enough to see someone pop out of a doorway right in front of the runner.

The runner stumbled and almost went down. I saw him push off the pavement with his free hand; he regained his footing but had lost his momentum.

I yelled, "Freeze or I'll shoot."

Just then, fully extending himself, Rich lunged—and tackled the runner. They both went down.

Breathless and dizzy, I caught up in time to hold my gun on the runner as Rich shouted orders and patted him down.

"He's not packing," Rich told me.

"Good."

I unhooked my cuffs and, with shaking hands, linked the runner's wrists behind his back. A cruiser pulled up to the curb.

I asked the runner for his name as I closed the cuffs.

"Julian Lambert. Still smokin' after all these years," he said, sounding far too pleased with himself.

I arrested Lambert for battery, theft, and disorderly conduct.

Conklin read him his rights and stuffed him into the back seat of the cruiser.

After my partner slapped the flank of the departing cruiser, I said to him, "Did you notice? That dude actually looked glad to see us."

CHAPTER 5

THAT DAY YUKI was in sentencing court, standing before the bar.

Across the aisle, defense counsel Allison Junker stood with her client, Sandra McDowell. McDowell was a fifty-three-year-old woman who had lost control of her car two weeks before and plowed into a gang of kids exiting a sports bar on Fillmore Street.

There had thankfully been no fatalities, but three of the boys she'd hit had been hospitalized with an assortment of injuries to heads and limbs. McDowell had been driving while intoxicated and made an illegal turn. She had pled guilty, been remanded to the court without bail, and been in jail since her arraignment. Yuki expected the sentencing hearing to be swift, smooth, and punishing.

Judge Bella Walters was on the bench, presiding over a full courtroom. It wasn't yet the end of the day, and she'd sentenced over two hundred people since breakfast. A small green pin shaped like a wreath sparkled on her collar.

The judge said, "Ms. Castellano. Talk to me."

Yuki said, "Your Honor, Mrs. McDowell drove her car into a crowd, injuring three young college students, one of whom is a rising football star. First officer on the scene gave Mrs. McDowell a Breathalyzer test. Her blood alcohol was 0.15. She was severely impaired."

The judge flipped through papers in front of her and asked, "She called the police?"

"Yes, Your Honor," said defense counsel Junker.

"And she pled guilty?"

"Yes, Your Honor."

Yuki said, "Your Honor, this is not Mrs. McDowell's first DUI. We're asking for a sentence of three to five years, time commensurate with the pain and suffering of her victims. It's too soon to tell, but some of their injuries may be permanent."

The defendant was now weeping into her hands.

The judge addressed the defendant. "Mrs. McDowell, it says here that you're a pharmacist, married, two children in college. And this prior DUI was a one-car accident?"

"Yes, Your Honor. I hit a tree."

The judge said, "Don't you just hate those jaywalking trees?"

"Your Honor," said Ms. Junker, "Mrs. McDowell is a good citizen. Her entire family is dependent on her income, including her husband, who has MS and is confined to a wheelchair. She has accepted responsibility for this accident from the time it happened and is unbelievably sorry. She intends to join AA upon her release. We urge the court to show leniency."

Judge Walters wrinkled her brow and looked up as a scuffle broke out at the back of the room. She banged her gavel and demanded silence in the court, even as Sandra McDowell continued to cry.

Yuki would be happy with a three-year sentence, she thought. It would get McDowell off the street, and during that time, she was hoping that those three boys could recover from their injuries, get PT, and return to the lives they'd had planned before McDowell ran into them with her Buick.

Judge Walters said, "Mrs. McDowell, before I impose a sentence, do you have anything to say?"

Mrs. McDowell dabbed at her face with a tissue.

"Yes, Your Honor. I'm very sorry. I'm only grateful that I didn't kill anyone, but what I did was inexcusable. Whatever sentence you think fair is okay with me."

Judge Walters said, "Mrs. McDowell, I'm revoking your driver's license and giving you a year of probation, including eight months of community service, twenty hours a week. Do not drive. If one year from now your parole officer reports to me that you've attended AA and completed your community service and automotive abstinence, this court will be done with you.

"I'm releasing you today for time served. Next time there will be no leniency, do you understand me?"

"Yes, Your Honor. Thank you very much."

"Thank my Christmas spirit. That's all. Next?"

Allison Junker smirked over her client's shoulder, and Yuki gave her a *Drop dead* look before leaving the courtroom, feeling like she'd been punched in the face by Santa Claus.

Have You Read Them All?

1ST TO DIE

Four friends come together to form the Women's Murder Club. Their job? To find a killer who is brutally slaughtering newly-wed couples on their wedding night.

2ND CHANCE
(with Andrew Gross)

The Women's Murder Club tracks a mystifying serial killer, but things get dangerous when he turns his pursuers into prey.

3RD DEGREE
(with Andrew Gross)

A wave of violence sweeps the city, and whoever is behind it is intent on killing someone every three days. Now he has targeted one of the Women's Murder Club . . .

4TH OF JULY
(with Maxine Paetro)

In a deadly shoot-out, Detective Lindsay Boxer makes a split-second decision that threatens everything she's ever worked for.

THE 5TH HORSEMAN
(with Maxine Paetro)

Recovering patients are dying inexplicably in hospital. Nobody is claiming responsibility. Could these deaths be tragic coincidences, or something more sinister?

THE 6TH TARGET
(with Maxine Paetro)

Children from rich families are being abducted off the streets – but the kidnappers aren't demanding a ransom. Can Lindsay Boxer find the children before it's too late?

7TH HEAVEN
(with Maxine Paetro)

The hunt for a deranged murderer with a taste for fire and the disappearance of the governor's son have pushed Lindsay to the limit. The trails have gone cold. But a raging fire is getting ever closer, and somebody will get burned.

8TH CONFESSION
(with Maxine Paetro)

Four celebrities are found killed and there are no clues: the perfect crime. Few people are as interested when a lowly preacher is murdered. But could he have been hiding a dark secret?

9TH JUDGEMENT
(with Maxine Paetro)

A psychopathic killer targets San Francisco's most innocent and vulnerable, while a burglary gone horribly wrong leads to a high-profile murder.

10TH ANNIVERSARY
(with Maxine Paetro)

A badly injured teenage girl is left for dead, and her newborn baby is nowhere to be found. But is the victim keeping secrets?

16TH SEDUCTION
(with Maxine Paetro)

At the trial of a bomber Lindsay and Joe worked together to capture, his defence raises damning questions about Lindsay and Joe's investigation.

17TH SUSPECT
(with Maxine Paetro)

A series of shootings brings terror to the streets of San Francisco, and Lindsay must confront a killer determined to undermine everything she has worked for.

'CLINTON'S INSIDER SECRETS AND PATTERSON'S STORYTELLING GENIUS MAKE THIS THE POLITICAL THRILLER OF THE DECADE'
LEE CHILD

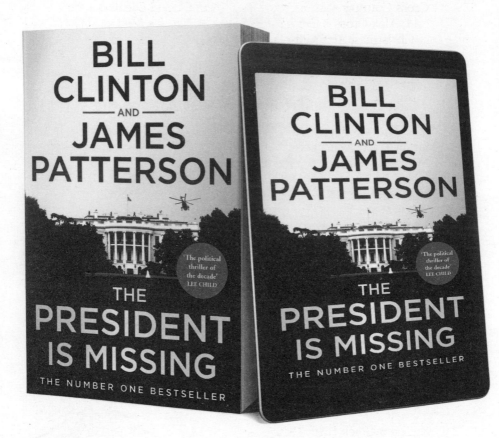

'Difficult to put down'
Daily Express

'Satisfying and surprising'
Guardian

'A quick, slick, gripping read'
The Times

'A high-octane collaboration . . . addictive'
Daily Telegraph

Also by James Patterson

ALEX CROSS NOVELS

Along Came a Spider • Kiss the Girls • Jack and Jill • Cat and Mouse • Pop Goes the Weasel • Roses are Red • Violets are Blue • Four Blind Mice • The Big Bad Wolf • London Bridges • Mary, Mary • Cross • Double Cross • Cross Country • Alex Cross's Trial (*with Richard DiLallo*) • I, Alex Cross • Cross Fire • Kill Alex Cross • Merry Christmas, Alex Cross • Alex Cross, Run • Cross My Heart • Hope to Die • Cross Justice • Cross the Line • The People vs. Alex Cross • Target: Alex Cross

STAND-ALONE THRILLERS

The Thomas Berryman Number • Hide and Seek • Black Market • The Midnight Club • Sail (*with Howard Roughan*) • Swimsuit (*with Maxine Paetro*) • Don't Blink (*with Howard Roughan*) • Postcard Killers (*with Liza Marklund*) • Toys (*with Neil McMahon*) • Now You See Her (*with Michael Ledwidge*) • Kill Me If You Can (*with Marshall Karp*) • Guilty Wives (*with David Ellis*) • Zoo (*with Michael Ledwidge*) • Second Honeymoon (*with Howard Roughan*) • Mistress (*with David Ellis*) • Invisible (*with David Ellis*) • Truth or Die (*with Howard Roughan*) • Murder House (*with David Ellis*) • Woman of God (*with Maxine Paetro*) • Humans, Bow Down (*with Emily Raymond*) • The Black Book (*with David Ellis*) • Murder Games (*with Howard Roughan*) • The Store (*with Richard DiLallo*) • Texas Ranger (*with Andrew Bourelle*) • The President is Missing (*with Bill Clinton*) • Revenge (*with Andrew Holmes*) • Juror No. 3 (*with Nancy Allen*) • The First Lady (*with Brendan DuBois*)

DETECTIVE MICHAEL BENNETT SERIES

Step on a Crack (*with Michael Ledwidge*) • Run for Your Life (*with Michael Ledwidge*) • Worst Case (*with Michael Ledwidge*) • Tick Tock (*with Michael Ledwidge*) • I, Michael Bennett (*with Michael Ledwidge*) • Gone (*with Michael Ledwidge*) • Burn (*with Michael Ledwidge*) • Alert (*with Michael Ledwidge*) • Bullseye (*with Michael Ledwidge*) • Haunted (*with James O. Born*) • Ambush (*with James O. Born*)

DETECTIVE HARRIET BLUE SERIES

Never Never (*with Candice Fox*) • Fifty Fifty (*with Candice Fox*) • Liar Liar (*with Candice Fox*)

For more information about James Patterson's novels, visit www.jamespatterson.co.uk

4